CA Ecstasy Supreme

"DON'T MAKE ANY SUDDEN MOVES, LADY, AND NO ONE WILL GET HURT."

With the gun planted firmly in her back, she felt a hand on her shoulder, gripping her and propelling her against the nearby garden wall.

A rough hand moved up and down her sides and over her back. "We don't take much to strangers showing up here," the voice said as he searched her. "Who are you, and what are you doing in Puente del Norte?"

"If you'll get your hands off me," she said through clenched teeth, "and remove the gun from my back, maybe I'll tell you."

His hand clamped down on her shoulder once more, spinning her around. "This isn't a game," he snapped, as his hands searched her breasts, and then even between her legs.

She stood rigid with shock and fury, and then finally he stood back with the gun trained on her. "Okay, lady," he said. "Answer my questions."

And for the first time in fourteen years Maddy Lambert looked up into Jake Murphy's all-seeing hazel eyes.

CANDLELIGHT ECSTASY SUPREMES

AGAINST THE WIND

Anne Stuart

A CANDLELIGHT ECSTASY SUPREME

Published by
Dell Publishing Co., Inc.
1 Dag Hammarskjold Plaza
New York, New York 10017

Dell ® TM 681510, Dell Publishing Co., Inc.

Candlelight Ecstasy Supreme is a trademark
of Dell Publishing Co., Inc.

Candlelight Ecstasy Romance®, 1,203,540, is a registered
trademark of Dell Publishing Co., Inc.

ISBN: 0-440-10051-8

Printed in the United States of America

First printing—July 1985

To Our Readers:

Candlelight Ecstasy is delighted to announce the start of a brand-new series—Ecstasy Supremes! Now you can enjoy a romance series unlike all the others—longer and more exciting, filled with more passion, adventure, and intrigue—the stories you've been waiting for.

In months to come we look forward to presenting books by many of your favorite authors and the very finest work from new authors of romantic fiction as well. As always, we are striving to present the unique, absorbing love stories that you enjoy most—the very best love has to offer.

Breathtaking and unforgettable, Ecstasy Supremes will follow in the great romantic tradition you've come to expect *only* from Candlelight Ecstasy.

Your suggestions and comments are always welcome. Please let us hear from you.

Sincerely,

The Editors
Candlelight Romances
1 Dag Hammarskjold Plaza
New York, New York 10017

CHAPTER ONE

Maddy Lambert had never been so miserably uncomfortable in her life. Sweat was pouring down her back, sticking to the split plastic of the seat of the old Toyota. The glare of the sun penetrated her dark sunglasses, giving her a pounding headache, her slow pace over the rutted road did little to discourage the flies and mosquitoes from attempting to hitchhike, and the mugginess of the humid air clung to her skin.

She would have thought the dense vegetation of the Central American jungle that surrounded the narrow track calling itself a government highway would have provided at least the comfort of shade. But the thick, lush greenery trapped the heat and kept it captive, sending it wafting forth on each soft breeze, so that Maddy was longing for the dubious improvement of a suffocating stillness. Even at twenty miles an hour the pathetic rental car couldn't avoid the blast of thermal air coming in the windows, air that would have turned grapes to raisins in a matter of minutes. Maddy had the fanciful notion that when she finally arrived in Puente del Norte she would be old and dry and wrinkled. But what the heat took away, the humidity would return. She'd be just as likely to be bloated with excess water.

And speaking of excess water, she thought with a groan as the nonexistent shock absorbers jolted her over another one of the interminable bumps on the once-paved road. She was going to have to pull off to the side of the track again, damn it all. Before setting out on this fool's errand she'd been warned to keep drinking. The tiny country of San Pablo was coming out of the rainy season into the baking heat of summer, and dehydration was only one of the dangers. Maddy had stocked up on bottled water in the war-torn capital of La Mensa, had dutifully kept swigging the lukewarm Perrier that had cost her as much as a good California Champagne, and then had dutifully stopped every slow forty miles.

How anyone could get dehydrated in such humidity was beyond her comprehension, but she didn't want to risk it. She'd have enough to contend with when she finally made it to Puente del Norte—she'd need to be at peak efficiency. Not that anyone could be efficient in such enervating heat, she thought. Even the summers in Southern California hadn't accustomed her to the rigors of a San Pablan spring.

She had to admit it was a beautiful country, those parts that weren't pitted by mortar shells, ravaged by poverty, and stripped by plundering soldiers of both the government and the resistance. For the millionth time Maddy thanked God that her father had chosen to hole up in the northern, more mountainous part of the country, where there supposedly was no fighting. There would have been no way she would have gotten to him if he'd been in the midst of the constant, hopeless battles waged between the Patronistas and the gray-shirted soldiers of President Morosa. Battles that had been waging for years now, with the enthusiastic aid of the U.S. government. And all this time her father had been in the middle.

But not for much longer. If she had to beat him over the head and drag him back, if she had to drug him and tie him up and bundle him into the back of the ramshackle Toyota, if she had to pull a gun on him (though heaven knows where she'd come across such a thing) and force him, he was coming with her. And no one was going to stop her, not after she'd come so far.

Damn it, it couldn't be much farther. The valiant little car had been climbing steadily the last two days, up north from the capital of La Mensa into the mountains where the air was thinner, if not any cooler. She was already a day later than she'd expected, and the odometer, the only instrument working on the shattered glass dashboard, suggested that she had traveled far enough to make it halfway into Mexico instead of merely the northern reaches of San Pablo. Sooner or later, sometime that afternoon, she'd make it. The next scraggly little mountain town, or the one after that, would be Puente del Norte. And there she'd find her father. And there she'd find John Thomas Murphy.

She ran a slender, long-fingered hand through her cropped brown hair, lifting it off her narrow neck. Fourteen years, she thought. Fourteen years since her father had taken off with all his high ideals intact, leaving his family behind as he sought his destiny as a saint, and Jake Murphy had gone as his willing disciple. Fourteen years without a word, only the news reports filtering back. She'd seen her father on television occasionally in the years since. For the first few years she'd turned him off, unable to look at that lean, ascetic face, that holy gleam in the pale blue eyes so unlike her own, that devotion to causes and humanity that hadn't filtered down to devotion to his own daughter.

But eventually the anger and the pain had lessened, faded into a vaguely curious apathy, so that she had taken to watching her father age before her eyes and the television camera. El Patrón, the Saint of San Pablo, he was called by the media, dispensing medical aid and education and food and his holier-than-thou support to the starving people of that oppressed country. Tolerated by the rigidly right-wing government as a harmless eccentric, worshipped by the Patronistas, the rag-tag rebel army who'd claimed him as their own, Samuel Eddison Lambert was in his element. And Maddy had watched him with mingled longing and wry acceptance. Until last week.

"He's dying, you know," her mother had said abruptly.

Maddy had finally returned her mother's constant phone calls, mentally thanking God again that she lived in Southern California and her overwhelming mother was three thousand miles to the east, in the heart of upper-class Virginia.

"Who?" Maddy replied, ignoring the sudden clutching that told her she knew perfectly well who.

"Your father, of course," Helen Currier Lambert Henderson snapped back in her brittle, perfectly modulated voice, and Maddy could see her as clearly as if all those miles didn't separate them. The narrow, delicately painted lips, the brown eyes that somehow managed to look ice cold, the perfect white skin, magnificent cheekbones, and sweep of excellently tinted dark brown hair. Her long nails would be tapping the base of the telephone as she talked to her unsatisfactory daughter, and her

12

calm, cool face would have an expression of fastidious irritation. "Who else would I be talking about?" she continued after she had waited long enough to have her displeasure known.

Maddy shrugged on the other end, a useless, unseen gesture, trying to give herself time to answer. "I don't know. Maybe Uncle Max?"

"Your stepfather is in the best of health, thank you," Helen snapped. "He takes care of himself."

"I know he does," Maddy said with just a tiny trace of malice. Maxfield Henderson's devotion to his fifty-seven-year-old body was just short of obsession, an obsession Helen shared. "What do you mean, my father's dying?" she hurried on before Helen could respond. "I saw him on Dan Rather just last week and he looked fine."

"Don't be naive, Maddy! That was file footage. Any fool could tell that was filmed during the summer months —everything was all dried out. San Pablo is just coming out of the rainy season—you won't find a patch of brown anywhere right now."

"How did you become such an expert on Central America, Mother? I thought you hated it down there."

"Of course I hate it. There was no way I was going to follow your father into his self-imposed exile—"

"Even though you deserved it more than he did," Maddy interrupted.

There was a long silence on the other end of the line, with only the long-distance crackle between them, and for a moment Maddy wondered if she'd gone too far. If her father really was ill, her mother wouldn't be beyond using it to make her recalcitrant daughter obedient. She could hang up and refuse to tell her any more until Maddy groveled, and in this case she might have no choice.

"Mother?" she said.

The silence continued. "I should hang up on you," her mother's voice came back finally.

Maddy tapped her own pale, unpainted fingernails against the scarred oak desk that was littered with papers, swallowing her own anger and irritation. "What's wrong with my father?"

"Cancer. And don't ask me how I found out what Dan Rather doesn't even know—Max has impeccable sources. Your father's been sick for quite some time now, and of course he's refused to leave San Pablo."

"Why are you telling me all this? Do you want me to send him a get-well card?" Maddy drawled. "I don't think he'd answer it. He never answered any of the letters I wrote him since he left us—I doubt that cancer's going to change matters."

"You're a cold child, aren't you?" Helen snapped.

"Like mother, like daughter," she said softly.

Once again silence reigned, and Maddy looked at her paperwork with exasperation. Her mother's phone calls were always a frustrating waste of time, and this one looked to be an award winner. "Look, Mother, I'm busy. What do you expect me to do about him? You've got a hell of a lot more connections than I do. Why don't you send a doctor down to him if you've got a belated case of the guilties?"

"I have nothing to feel guilty about. I thought you might be interested to hear that your father's dying."

"Says who? I've never found your information to be a model of accuracy before. I suppose they found some tiny benign tumor and you decided this would be a good way to get Maddy to dance to your tune," she said with a weary sigh. "Well, spit it out, Mother. What do you want from me? You've told me Samuel's dying, now tell me what you want me to do about it."

"Go down to San Pablo and bring him back."

The Toyota bounced over another crater in the roadway, pulling Maddy out of her uncomfortable memories. The jungle was less dense now. Maddy had learned enough of the San Pablan geography in the last few days to know that she was within a mile or two of another town. Maybe Puente del Norte. In a matter of perhaps minutes she'd be seeing her father for the first time in fourteen years. And the irritation that had been pushing her the thousand miles or so into the war-torn jungles of San Pablo faded into sudden nervous concern.

Not that there'd be anything wrong with him, she assured herself, avoiding the potholes in the Grand Pablan Highway that more closely resembled swimming pools. Her mother had taken some minor indisposition and blown it out of proportion, using it to bring Maddy to heel once more. It wasn't often she could manipulate the thirty-year-old daughter who'd moved out of her sphere of influence more than ten years ago. Maddy still didn't know what Helen had to gain from sending her off on what would doubtless turn out to be a wild goose chase. But after countless long-distance arguments she had finally agreed to do what she'd intended to do all along. She decided to go after her father.

For once she could be thankful that Helen Currier Lambert Henderson, daughter of a political kingmaker who would have put Tammany Hall to shame, had married someone up to her weight. Visas to San Pablo were hard to come by. Max had gotten Maddy's in a matter of hours, greasing the political wheels with his usual expertise that had always left Maddy amused and uneasy.

15

When it came right down to it, she got along with her stepfather better than with her rigidly self-contained mother. At least Max Henderson had a sense of humor. Not much of one, admittedly, but more than Helen possessed.

The Greater Hollywood Help Network had seen their grants administrator leave with something akin to panic. It took all of Maddy's considerable administrative skills to keep the small social service agency going, and all her creativity and perseverance to keep the grant money flowing in and right back out again. The money would continue moving while she was gone, but only in one direction—into the hungry bellies of the street people of Hollywood, the Armenian immigrants, and the hordes of San Pablan refugees who made their way into the country under cover of the night. And if Maddy didn't retrieve her father, bring him back to the country he'd abandoned years ago and return to the interminable grants writing, those hungry bellies would get even hungrier.

A week, she'd figured she'd be gone, ten days tops. She had clear directions on how to get to the mountain stronghold of the Saint of San Pablo, and even with her knowledge of Spanish limited to a couple of years at boarding school and a slick tourist phrase book, she had little doubt as to her ability to get the job done. She'd always had great pride in her own efficiency.

But that efficiency hadn't come face to face with a revolution until today. The almost empty plane she'd taken had been twelve hours late arriving in the capital city of La Mensa. It had detoured first to Honduras, then back to Mexico City, and then had finally been allowed to land in San Pablo after they'd cleared the debris of a bombed-out helicopter from the pitted runway. That hair-raising landing, bouncing and jouncing past the

16

twisted wreckage of untold flying machines, had started the demoralization of Maddy Lambert. The government committee that greeted her helped it on its way.

"We are very concerned for your father, Miss Lambert," General Ortega had assured her. He was very smooth, the general, and very very handsome, with that Latin condescension that was almost reassuring. He was telling her with those dark eyes of his that she was not to worry, he would take care of her, as his small, strong hand held her slim, tanned one. And Maddy had smiled blandly, every nerve alert. General Anastasio Ortega was Minister of Agriculture. Why an agriculture minister would need to be a general in the Gray Shirts was one question, why an agriculture minister would be concerned with the Saint of San Pablo's daughter was another. Maddy had little doubt he was chosen for his looks and his charm with the ladies, and she was unimpressed.

"We are a very tolerant government, Miss Lambert," he'd continued smoothly. "As is evident in our allowing your father to continue to enjoy his life in San Pablo, despite his very vocal complaints about our democracy. For many years now we have worried about his involvement with the murdering Patronistas, and we would be much relieved if you did prevail upon him to return to his own country."

Maddy murmured something noncommittal in response, and the good general continued with his speech, his liquid eyes caressing her tall, narrow body that was on a level with his, his tanned hand with the wide gold wedding band toying idly with the gun that went so well with his gray uniform.

"Any way we may assist you, you have only to let us know. My government will of course provide a limousine and driver and an armed guard. For tonight, however, the president himself graciously requests the pleasure of your company at a state dinner. And tomorrow I have been given the honor of conducting you on a tour of our improvements in La Mensa, so that when you return to the United States you may assure your government that our commitment to progress and human rights is unassailable."

Maddy smiled sweetly. "Thank President Morosa for me, General, but tell him I must regretfully decline."

"But—"

"And thank him for the offer of the car and the escort," she sailed onward, "but I have made other arrangements. Much as I long to see the improvements in La Mensa, I'm afraid that I cannot afford to wait. I'm already twelve hours behind schedule, and I planned to leave for Puente del Norte by noon today."

"Miss Lambert, I cannot allow—"

"Allow, General?" She looked at him with an innocent question in her large brown eyes. "I thought my government had made all the arrangements. I have permission to travel on my own to the northern part of the country, to retrieve my father and bring him back to the United States. Is there some way that interferes with the agricultural concerns of San Pablo?"

General Ortega opened his mouth, shut it again, and Maddy could hear the gentle grinding of teeth. "Of course not, Miss Lambert. We only wished to make things easier for you. The Grand Pablan Highway is not at all what you're used to, and while we have made great strides in law and order, the rebels have been draining our manpower in the north. I cannot guarantee your safety if you insist on going by yourself."

Maddy smiled. "I don't expect you to guarantee my safety, General. I consider that to be my responsibility."

18

"You are very headstrong, Miss Lambert. I only hope you will not regret your decision. At least wait until tomorrow to leave, and think about our very generous offer."

"I'm sorry, General. I'm leaving as soon as I can."

It hadn't been noon, it had been closer to three o'clock, and she hadn't made it more than fifty miles when darkness had begun closing around her. For a moment she'd regretted her impulsive action. She'd lied to the so-helpful General Ortega—no arrangements had been made for a vehicle or supplies. Her directions to the tiny mountain town of Puente del Norte were the only thing she relied on. But she had the very strong suspicion that if she showed up at a rebel stronghold in a government limousine with an armed guard she wouldn't be welcomed with open arms. Her father had been more than vocal about his disapproval of *el presidente*'s repressive regime, he'd been strident. Maddy didn't owe him much, but he didn't deserve to have his daughter show up surrounded by his sworn enemies.

Hertz, Avis, and their ilk had long ago abandoned San Pablo. The rusty, venerable Toyota she'd finally located had recently transported chickens and perhaps goats, and the odor, combined with the humid heat, almost sent her back to General Ortega. It would have been simple enough to find him—one of his Gray Shirts had been doing a not very effective job of following her since she'd managed to shake Ortega at the airport.

But the Toyota ran smoothly, if bumpily, enough, and the animal smell of it dissipated as the day wore on.

The road was getting worse, far worse, signaling the proximity of a semblance of civilization. Maddy slowed the Toyota to a crawl, edging along the narrow trail, straddling the ruts. Suddenly she jammed the tiny car into a quick, jolting stop that rocked the poor tin creature on its frame. A huge branch lay across the narrow road.

Maddy swore under her breath. The car had stalled, and she switched off the ignition, turning to the door handle. And found herself looking directly into the barrel of a very large, very nasty gun.

CHAPTER TWO

She swallowed, her mouth suddenly very dry, as she stared into the narrow, deadly little barrel. Slowly, carefully she raised her eyes, past a sweat-stained shirt, open to reveal a hairy chest, past a thick neck, stubbled chin, hooked nose, directly into the eyes of a very fierce young man. Those eyes were a cold, merciless brown; like a lizard's, they stared at her unwinking. Maddy could see the shadow of others behind him, but she didn't dare move her gaze from his, certain that if she did that lethal-looking gun would explode in her face. She swallowed again, wetting her lips, and tried to summon the distant trace of a smile. She could imagine the ghastly parody that issued forth.

A string of rapid, incomprehensibly idiomatic Spanish issued forth from that grim mouth, directed at Maddy, and there was little doubt that the speech contained both questions and orders.

"No comprendo," Maddy managed, which wasn't strictly true. You couldn't live in Southern California, couldn't spend the last five years working there without picking up a small amount of Spanish. She'd managed to

understand about every fifth word Lizard Eyes had directed at her. Unfortunately they were mostly pronouns.

The man grimaced and spat, the gun never wavering in its attention on her forehead. *"Gringa,"* he said slowly, furiously, and Maddy noticed with a distant amusement that his voice was high and light, almost like a girl's. "Who are you and what are you doing here? This province belongs to the Third District of the Patronistas, the Fighters Against the Oppressor—it is not the best area for *turistas.* Why are you here?"

Maddy steeled herself to ignore the gun, a difficult task considering its proximity. She could smell the hot metal, the gun oil, and she wrinkled her nose, trying to ignore the terrifying certainty that the well cared for gun saw frequent use. "My name is Madelyn Lambert. I'm Samuel Lambert's daughter, and I've come to see my father."

Lizard Eyes stared at her, unblinking, unbelieving. "A *norteamericana,"* he said finally in disgust. "I should have known." He pulled the gun away, and Maddy breathed a sigh of relief. She noticed that her hands were still clenching the steering wheel, and slowly, deliberately she relaxed her deathgrip.

"The Patronistas have no wish to antagonize the United States or any of its citizens who are foolish enough to enter a war zone without protection."

"I thought the fighting was in the south."

Lizard Eyes shrugged. "The fighting is all over San Pablo. There is no place that is untouched." Those eyes narrowed as they swept over her hot, dusty face. "You do not look like El Patrón."

"El Patrón?" Maddy echoed, mystified for a moment. "Oh, you mean Samuel. No, I'm supposed to take after my great-grandmother. She was French, and I . . ." Her voice trailed off as she recognized the inanity of the conversation. Why in the world would this guerilla warrior want to know about her French grandmother? "Anyway," she said lamely, "he *is* my father, I assure you."

Lizard Eyes shrugged. "It is of no importance. One lone *gringa* cannot cause much trouble. You are alone?" Those lizard like eyes swept back into the underbrush from whence the battered little Toyota had come. "I am surprised Ortega didn't try to stop you."

Maddy was conscious of a sudden guilty start. "Ortega?"

"Head of *el presidente*'s Secret Interrogation Squad for the Subjugation of Insurgents."

"I thought he was Minister of Agriculture," Maddy said, and then could have taken the gun out of his hand and shot herself for her stupidity.

Those lizardlike eyes narrowed and a sudden, alarmingly affable smile split his darkly tanned face. It was then that Maddy realized how very young her fierce young soldier was—probably no more than twenty-one or twenty-two. And all the more deadly because of his extreme youth. "General Ortega is a friend of yours, eh? And I suppose he's accompanied you, at a safe distance."

"He—he met me at the airport," Maddy stammered, flustered. "He offered me a car and driver but I told him no."

"Doubtless you promised to let him know once you safely arrived," Lizard Eyes offered smoothly.

"He knows how to get here on his own, I have no doubt. He doesn't need my help."

Her captor shrugged. "Who is to say? General Ortega has a reputation for making the most of his opportunities. He also has a reputation for the ladies." The sweep of those cold brown eyes was insultingly direct. "Well, *gringa*, you are not my problem. Whether El Patrón is your father or not is none of my concern. Though he has never once mentioned a family back in the United States. But it will be up to Murphy to decide what to do with you."

The name crackled along Maddy's nerve endings like static electricity, and it was all she could do to remain passive in the face of Lizard Eyes's attention. She hadn't heard his name spoken in years and had almost convinced herself that he had never existed. And suddenly, with the sound of his name, he was alive, and the past fourteen years might never have passed.

"Murphy?" She managed a creditable question in her voice.

"El Patrón's protector." Lizard Eyes shot a stream of rapid Spanish over his shoulder to one of his compatriots and was answered with a coarse laugh. "And it is to be wondered what Soledad will think of you."

"Soledad?"

"Your stepmother. I somehow doubt she will welcome you with open arms." Lizard Eyes laughed again, unpleasantly, and the gun slowly withdrew several inches and waved her onward. *"Vamanos, gringa.* We will no doubt meet again."

She sat there, unmoving, her eyes never wavering as he slowly moved back, the gun at a seemingly relaxed angle. She had no doubt it could snap back up to aim at her face once more at an instant's notice. One of the men accompanying Lizard Eyes was moving the log that had blocked the road, and he called out something to his boss. It was quite clearly something obscene, an area of the Spanish language that had so far eluded Maddy, but she could make out Murphy's name and the easily identified *gringa.*

She sat there a long time after her captors melted into

the jungle, breathing deeply. Her hands were shaking as she turned the key. The gears ground, screaming in pain, the car bucked, and she was off, down the narrow track that would lead her to her father—and to Jake Murphy.

Puente del Norte was a beaten little town, its tumbled-down mansions and overgrown parks attesting to a once more glorious lot in life. The now-familiar poverty was rampant, the fading pink and pastel adobe walls scrawled with graffiti exhorting the benumbed inhabitants to die for freedom. As Maddy limped her battered car into the village she kept her eyes alert for signs of her father's presence. She could see obvious signs of General Ortega and President Morosa's recent visits, in the bombed-out church, the shattered walls, the wary looks on the inhabitants' faces. They were all carrying weapons.

From the sturdy, black-garbed women industriously washing in the stream that ran along the side of the narrow village road, to the swaggering young men dressed in the international uniform of blue jeans and T-shirts and Nikes, they were carrying pistols and handguns and machine guns and shotguns, knives and machetes and even a sword or two. She was driving into an armed camp, and in retrospect General Ortega was looking more and more attractive. If she made it out of there, out of this miserable country alive, she would never again go any farther south than San Diego.

No one made a move toward her as she edged her way down the narrow village street, the car bouncing and lurching over the potholes. But every eye was trained on her sporadic progress, and not a word was spoken.

Maddy's hands were numb as they gripped the steering wheel. These were her father's people, she told herself staunchly, not believing a word. The people he'd devoted his life to helping. They wouldn't hurt El Patrón's daughter, they would be more likely to welcome her with parades and flowers. Wouldn't they? She was only thankful that she had no need to stop to ask for directions.

Her stepfather's sources had been very clear. Samuel Eddison Lambert was living in an abandoned villa-turned-fortress two miles past the tiny town of Puente del Norte, surrounded by a small army of followers. Max hadn't told her who led that army, and Maddy hadn't asked. Lizard Eyes had answered that unspoken question. Jake Murphy, the man who had abandoned his career in the Secret Service and his life as an American citizen to follow a crazy old dreamer, would be there, still guarding the man who'd shaped his destiny.

She'd been seventeen when she'd last seen Jake Murphy. Seventeen, and as deeply, overwhelmingly in love as any seventeen-year-old girl could be. If nothing had ever quite come close to that astonishingly powerful adolescent passion, Maddy accepted that fact with wry humor. After all, that was what being a teenager was all about. Falling in love with unsuitable older men and filling diaries about the stark tragedy of it all. She had no doubt that Murphy now possessed a notable paunch, a plump wife and four or five bambinos, and a shared affectionate remembrance of her passionate crush.

It was little wonder she'd fallen so hard. Jake Murphy was the stuff dreams were made of. Samuel Eddison Lambert had run for President that year, had even been considered a fairly good contender for the highest office in the land. And Jake Murphy was the Secret Service man assigned to protect the candidate as he had stumped around the country in search of that elusive nomination, a suavely smiling Helen by his side.

Twenty-six years old, just out of Vietnam, Jake Mur-

26

phy had seemed the epitome of romance to Maddy, who was rapidly tiring of her teenage peers. Even the stigma of being involved in that dirty little war hadn't tarnished Murphy, it had only made him more mysterious in her eyes. That he had hated it was more than clear, that there was some dark secret attached to his involvement also became clear as the months passed. It had taken an inquisitive sixteen- almost seventeen-year-old a long time to ferret it out, and by the time she had it was too late. And even that secret in all its horror wasn't enough to shatter the threads of longing that tied her to Jake.

She was almost through the tiny town, heading out toward her father's villa, and the staring faces were now watching her exhaust. Her fingers loosened slightly on the steering wheel as she thought back again to Jake, trying to dredge him up from her memory. She could remember the specifics, the close-cropped regulation haircut that she'd hated, the hazel eyes that watched constantly and never gave anything away, his tall, lean body in the dark suits that were a uniform in themselves. But she couldn't summon forth a picture of him in her mind.

Not that it mattered. She would either recognize him or not when she saw him, and they'd laugh about the past, and then he'd take her to see her father. And Samuel Eddison Lambert would smile at her out of those dreamy blue eyes of his that only saw the larger scale of things, that had never noticed when his daughter was hurting, that only concentrated on the inequities of the Third World. And reassured, Maddy would turn around and head back to L.A., secure in the knowledge that her father was safe and well.

It was a lovely fantasy, one that sustained her through the last two miles of underbrush that seemed to have more eyes than the little town of Puente del Norte. She knew as well as anyone that the chances of it bearing any resemblance to reality were tenuous indeed, but one could always hope. A hope that wavered and began to shatter when the car finally cleared the mountain forest and pulled up in front of a high-walled structure.

It had once been a villa, all right, but now it resembled nothing so much as an armed fortress. The pink walls were topped with barbed wire, scrawled with inevitable black graffiti, this time recommending long life to El Patrón. The once-neat landscaping was a tangle of encroaching jungle, the ornamental iron gates were tightly shut and guarded by a young man in jeans, Nikes, an ET T-shirt, and a machine gun. A machine gun that was pointed straight at her.

She could pride herself on being a little cooler this time in the face of danger. Her sweaty hands slipped only once as she opened the car door, and she raised them over her head with as much aplomb as possible as she moved slowly toward the young guard. Even younger than Lizard Eyes, she noticed. Where were all the men of San Pablo?

And why the hell did San Pablo Spanish have to be so far removed from Mexican Spanish? Granted there were several Central American countries in between, but you'd still think there would be more than a few similarities. The demands of the young soldier guarding El Patrón were abrupt, hostile, and nonnegotiable. Once more she summoned her best smile and her most-oft used Spanish phrase.

"No comprendo. Habla usted inglés?"

Her winning smile got her exactly nowhere, as did her tourist's Spanish. The question was repeated, and this time Maddy could begin to comprehend a few words. She took a step toward him, and the gun remained stationary.

28

She had a fair idea what she looked like to him. She was a tall woman, just over five feet nine, and her lean body with its meager curves lay hidden beneath the loose cotton shirt that now clung wetly to her back. Her long legs were encased in rumpled jeans, her own Nikes were dusty and muddy, and her close-cropped dark-brown hair swept back from a narrow, delicate face that doubtless was sweat-stained, exhausted, and scared. She hadn't bothered with makeup, having discovered that it melted off her face by noon in the damp climate, and her pale mouth and wary brown eyes that filled her face would scarcely entice the young man into any acts of conspicuous gallantry. She would have to rely on her minimal Spanish and her father's intervention. After all these years he ought to be good for something.

But after five minutes the conversation had gotten no further. Maddy's conversational Spanish made no dent on the soldier's mountain dialect, and the machine gun stayed trained on her stomach. Her arms were getting tired, but every time she tried to drop them the machine gun clicked warningly.

Once more she tried. *"Mi padre,"* she said again. *"Mi padre es El Patrón."*

The boy shook his head stubbornly, his mouth curling in contemptuous disbelief, all his responses consisting of negatives as far as Maddy could tell. At some sound beyond Maddy's hearing he turned his head, directing his attention into the compound. A moment later he turned back to her, gesturing with the gun for her to approach. As she passed him, sliding through the narrow opening in the iron gates, she tried to drop her hands. She was rewarded with the barrel of the gun jabbing her sharply in the ribs, and it was all she could do to keep from slapping the little punk. She contented herself with glaring at him

29

and continued on into the courtyard of the tumbled-down villa.

There was no one in sight. The guard had shut the iron gate after her and was now concentrating his attention on the outer world once more. Slowly she began to lower her hands, half of her expecting the bully from the front gate to shoot her in the back. But he had clearly dismissed her, and she pressed a shaking hand to her side. The blow had hurt, her rib was throbbing, but that was the least of her worries. The courtyard was a mass of fragrant flowers, a tangled jungle of scent and beauty in the midst of an armed camp. Maddy stood very still, breathing in the damp smell of the garden, every nerve tightly strung. She could feel the eyes on her, eyes that had watched her since she arrived in San Pablo, different eyes along each step of the journey to her father. And suddenly she didn't want to wait any more.

She took a decisive step toward the massive stone structure, then stopped as the short, sharp click of a gun being cocked stilled her every movement, even the beat of her heart.

She could feel him behind her, though she couldn't imagine how he could have gotten so close without her having been aware of his approach. She could feel the barrel of the gun in the middle of her back, and for a moment she felt like screaming. Three times in the last hour she had had guns pulled on her. That was three times too many for her thirty years, it was scarcely the sort of thing she was used to, and for a brief moment she struggled with the sudden urge to burst into tears of exhaustion and fright. She bit her lip, hard, and stood very still.

"That's right," a deep, scratchy voice came from directly behind her. "Don't make any sudden moves, lady, and no one will get hurt."

With the barrel of the gun still planted firmly in her back, she felt a heavy hand drop down on her shoulder, gripping her hard and propelling her against the nearby garden wall. She went up against it with a resounding thud.

"Spread your arms and legs," he drawled, and immediately she complied. A rough hand moved up and down her sides and over her back. "We don't take much to strangers showing up here," the voice said as he searched her. "Particularly friends of General Ortega's. Who the hell are you, and what are you doing in Puente del Norte?"

Maddy was getting tired of those questions, almost as tired as she was of having guns pointed at her. "If you'll get your hands off me," she said through clenched teeth, "and remove the gun from my back, maybe I'll tell you."

The gun didn't move for a moment. Then it pulled away and his large hand clamped down on her shoulder once more, spinning her around with an abruptness that made her teeth rattle. "Lady, this isn't a game," he snapped, and his hands were roughly impersonal as they searched the front of her body, her breasts, even between her legs. She stood rigid with shock and fury, and then finally his hands left her, and he stood back with the gun trained on her.

"All right, lady," he said. "Answer my questions."

And for the first time in fourteen years Maddy Lambert looked up into Jake Murphy's all-seeing hazel eyes.

CHAPTER THREE

Good Lord, he was so different! And yet so very much the same that she would have known him anywhere. Those eyes that never missed anything were looking right through her, their hazel depths flat and unreadable. When she'd last seen him he'd been twenty-six, with short hair and dark suits and a dead look in his eyes. The man standing before her looked half-savage, with the large, ugly gun in one hand and that implacable expression on his face.

It was the same face. Older, leaner, darkly tanned from years in the semitropical climate, but still the same. Lines fanned out from his piercing eyes, deep grooves were cut in the lean cheeks, bracketing a grim mouth that had forgotten how to smile. He hadn't smiled much when she'd known him before, but when he had done so it had usually been at her. He wasn't smiling now.

He had a bandanna tied around his forehead, holding back the hair that was perhaps the greatest surprise of all. It was long, dark brown streaked by the sun and by a natural graying, and it hung almost to his shoulders, adding to the look of wildness. He was wearing a rumpled, sweat-stained khaki field shirt, open to the waist, and his chest was hard and tanned and smooth. He had a knife at his belt in a worn leather holder, and the weapons were all a part of his cold, merciless savagery that terrified her more than Lizard Eyes with his pistol, or ET at the gate with his machine gun. She stood there and watched the destruction of her teenage fantasy, and it was frightening indeed.

A dead silence had fallen between them, and in the background she could hear the lazy hum of bees wandering through the profusion of flowers in this military stronghold. He was waiting for her to speak, his impatience barely held in check, and those implacable, opaque eyes of his looked right through her. It took a moment for her to realize that he didn't recognize her.

"I'm Maddy Lambert," she said in a damnably shaky voice. "Samuel's daughter."

No light filled those eyes, and the gun didn't waver. "Are you?" His voice was flat, noncommittal.

Some of the mindless panic began to leave her, to be replaced with a confused anger. She'd imagined a great many things about her arrival there, both bad and good, but nothing had come close to the simple fact that he might not know her.

"Of course I am," she snapped. "Don't you know me?"

The guard reappeared behind Jake, her pawed-through purse in his hand. He handed it to Jake, adding a military salute that only added to Maddy's uneasiness. Keeping the gun trained on her, Jake rummaged through the purse, and it took all Maddy's self-control not to protest. He pulled out her passport and Maddy breathed a sigh of relief. One that quickly changed to despair as he flipped it open and she remembered what it read.

"Allison M. Henderson," he read in that raspy voice of

his that had grown even more gravelly in the ensuing years. The sound of it had filled more than one fantasy years ago. Now it grated on her raw nerves. He looked up at her then, and his hazel eyes were cold and merciless. "No, I don't know you, Allison Henderson. I've never seen you before in my life."

"That's not my real name," she said, her voice a sudden babble of nervousness.

He raised an eyebrow beneath that sweat-stained bandanna. "Not your real name, Miss Henderson? Don't you know it's a federal crime to get a passport under a phony name? I ought to report you to the American Consulate. Unfortunately San Pablo no longer has an American Consulate. I believe it was blown up, along with half the local workers, several months ago."

"I mean, it's my legal name, but not my real name," she stammered. "My name is Allison Madelyn Lambert Henderson. My mother remarried and—"

"And being a loyal daughter you gave up your father's name," Jake supplied smoothly, still watching her out of those cold eyes, the gun never moving. "Samuel wouldn't have a daughter like that."

Maddy flinched. She wasn't about to make excuses to this hard-eyed stranger, particularly when he was holding a gun on her. Wasn't about to explain that the only way she could get a passport and visa that quickly was to take the protection of her stepfather's powerful name, the name she'd accepted through apathy when she wasn't quite eighteen and abandoned when she was twenty. "But you do admit he had a daughter?" she pressed.

There was a long silence, one that seemed to go on forever, but in actuality it was probably less than thirty seconds, as Maddy watched the man opposite her and begged him to remember her. She held her breath, waiting, praying with a fervor that she wouldn't have thought she was capable of.

Finally he spoke, the rough voice shattering a small, secret portion of her heart. "He may have had a daughter," Jake Murphy drawled. "I don't really remember. It was a long time ago."

Part of her had been expecting it, but it didn't make it any easier to take. "This is ridiculous," she said finally. "I don't have to convince you of anything. Take me to see my father. I expect his memory might be a little better."

Jake lowered the gun then, uncocking it and tucking inside the waistband of his faded khaki pants. "I'm afraid you're wrong about that."

"About what?"

"It is me you'll have to convince. Sam's in no shape to be bothered by General Ortega's latest conspiracy. I don't know what the two of you have in mind, but you're not getting within ten feet of Sam Lambert until I say so."

She stared at him, mouth agape, fury and something else warring for control. "Damn you, I want to see my father!" she demanded furiously.

For the first time Jake Murphy smiled, a cold, heartless smile that barely lifted the corners of his hard mouth. "Then I expect you'll have to go back to the States where you'll doubtless find him. That is, if you ever knew him in the first place."

It took her a moment to recognize the insult, and it set the seal of her almost incoherent fury. "Listen, Jake Murphy, if I'm not Sam's daughter, how would I know you?"

"Everyone who knows anything about El Patrón knows me," he drawled. "And I'm tired of arguing with you, lady."

Maddy had never considered herself a violent person, but she had the sudden overwhelming desire to fling herself on this hard-eyed, long-haired stranger and beat some sense into him. The gun at his waist and the knife at his hip stopped that thought, and with a great effort she drew together the shattered pieces of her calm. "All right," she said. "If you won't let me see Samuel I suppose I have no choice but to leave."

That smile again, that damnable, nasty little smile appeared as he shook his head. "You're not going anywhere."

Maddy hadn't spent years coping with the extraneous threads of the Greater Hollywood Help Network for her to quail before the likes of Jake Murphy. If she could outmaneuver General Ortega and Lizard Eyes, she could outmaneuver him. "You can't have it both ways," she said patiently. "Either you let me see my father or you let me leave. One way or the other."

He was entirely unmoved by her attempt at logic. "There's a third alternative. You stay right here until I find out what brought you here. As long as Ortega thinks his current plan is working then he won't be busy thinking up something new. Better the devil you know . . ."

"You can't keep me here!"

"Of course I can," Jake said. "For as long as I want. This is an armed camp, Allison Henderson, and I'm commander-in-chief. You'll stay right here until I decide you're harmless and let you leave." He held out his strong right hand, the one that had trained the gun on her with such unstudied aplomb. "Come along, lady. Maybe you can convince someone else of your claim. I doubt it, though, and if I were you I wouldn't even try."

She continued to watch him warily. "Why?"

"Because being Samuel Eddison Lambert's daughter

would have distinct disadvantages. We're an armed camp for a reason, lady. The Gray Shirts of your General Ortega would like nothing better than to have Lambert dead. He's an embarrassment to the government and affront to all their lip service about human rights. They would love to have him murdered by the bloodthirsty insurgents."

"But the rebels . . ."

"The rebels have been fighting an impossible war for six years now. They need a martyr. I don't think any of them would go to much trouble to stop the government from disposing of Sam. If the U.S. government got mad enough it might stop sending all that nice money to President Morosa, and the death squads might stop. It's been proven that the murder of one American citizen causes far more outcry than the slaughter of thousands of San Pablans."

"And which side are you on? The government or the rebels?"

Jake grimaced. "I'm on Sam's side. For all the good it does him." He shook his head, the long hair moving in the stifling breeze. "So you might think twice about trying to convince all and sundry that you're Sam's daughter. A young American female would make just as good a martyr as a saintly old man."

"I would think that would suit your purposes very well," Maddy snapped. "The rebels would have their American victim and I'd be out of your way. Why don't you just turn me over to them?" For the moment she trusted Lizard Eyes more than she trusted this cold, dangerous stranger.

"Don't tempt me," he ground out, that hand fastening on her elbow with a grip just short of painful. "If you

37

don't watch your step you may have no say in the matter."

"What do you mean?"

"Just that people aren't always what they seem," he murmured. "Come along and I'll introduce you to some of the others. But I wouldn't take any of them at face value, if I were you."

"Not even you?" she couldn't help asking as she was half dragged toward the looming old hacienda.

Jake Murphy glanced at her with those fathomless hazel eyes. "Especially not me," he said.

She was the last thing he needed right now, Jake thought with a barely controlled fury. It took every effort of concentration on his part not to crush that curiously vulnerable elbow he held in his grip. Damn, but he wished he were the sort of man who felt justified in beating women.

As if things weren't complicated enough, he had to have her show up, claiming to be Maddy Lambert to everyone who'd listen. Ortega and a dozen troops must be close behind, not to mention Carlos's band of merry men. Damn it all to hell!

And how was Sam going to react? Probably far better than he was. Sam had no qualms about sacrificing everything for the greater good, he wouldn't have any doubts about whether he was doing the right thing. Sam was a saint, with all the disadvantages that came with such sainthood, and Jake Murphy was just a poor, foolish mortal.

He should have told Enrique to send her away at the gate, and leave it to Ortega to deal with her. There was no way anyone could get into the fortress without his say-so and it would have simplified matters considerably.

And even once he'd made that mistake, he still could have sent her on her way. Once he'd decided he wasn't going to let her get near Sam, he should have shoved that tall, slender, rumpled body back out the gates and had Enrique send her on her way.

But he hadn't. He had given in to the impulse, inspired by those huge brown eyes that brought back feelings he'd thought long dead, by the long legs and defiant mouth and whatever lay beneath that loose cotton shirt of hers. And it was too late to do anything about it now.

He could only hope things held off for a while longer. That he could convince someone to take her and Soledad out of the country before all hell broke loose. Sam wouldn't go. They'd talked about it for years now, and his health had deteriorated to such a point that there was no longer any question of his leaving. He'd be gone soon enough, and not back to the country he'd turned his back on.

Damn, she even smelled good. Clean and fresh and feminine, not like the tropical profusion that filled the tangled courtyard of the villa, not like the overripe musk that Soledad favored. She smelled of something light and delicate and so appealing that it twisted his gut in a knot. It was no wonder Ortega was panting at her heels, no wonder Carlos had sent word once he'd accosted her on the road into Puente del Norte.

So maybe he deserved to play with fire for a change. She carried no weapons—his professional search had ascertained that, along with the fact that her breasts were small and soft and warm, that her hips were slightly bony beneath the jeans and her rear was the most delectable thing he'd seen in years. She'd have no choice but to sit and wait for him to decide what to do with her. And he'd have to damn well make sure that Ortega hadn't gotten to her first.

"Jake." The sound of her voice broke through his dangerous fantasies, and he halted under the portico that provided much-needed shade in this tropical climate, his grip sliding down her arm to capture her wrist. "Why won't you believe me?"

He looked back at her. She was just a few inches shorter than his own six feet, something he wasn't used to in this land of diminutive women. The loose cotton shirt was open at the neck, revealing a tanned column of throat, and at the base of her neck there was a faint sheen of moisture. He had the sudden, almost uncontrollable urge to lean forward and place his mouth against the dewy warmth, and his grip around her narrow wrist tightened.

"Because I have a strong sense of self-preservation," he replied shortly. "I wouldn't have made it to forty in my business if I believed every pretty lady who came up to me with some outlandish tale."

"But won't you feel like a fool when you find out I was telling the truth?" she persisted.

"I don't mind feeling like a fool," he drawled. "As long as I'm a live fool. Come along, Allison Henderson."

"Don't call me that!"

Jake could feel her pulse hammering beneath his thumb, pounding away with anger and frustration, and for a moment he wondered what it would be like to make her pulses pound from something else. And how that pounding pulse would feel beneath his mouth.

Damn, he was getting horny in his old age. He'd have to settle for keeping her furious with him. As long as she was enraged she wouldn't be able to think clearly. Strong emotion always clouded people's judgment. He looked at her. "Come on, Allison," he said again. "Only mad dogs and Englishmen go out in the noonday sun."

Maddy blinked rapidly in the sudden darkness of the cool, shadowy stillness of the hacienda, temporarily blinded by the change from bright sunlight. Jake wasn't similarly afflicted, and she had no choice but to follow along, hoping he wasn't going to lead her into a stone wall. Gradually she became accustomed to the dimness, the cracked plaster walls surrounding them as he led her down a long hallway, a flight of stairs, and around a corner. The hacienda was a tall building, consisting of at least four floors, and they must be in the basement. Jake came to an abrupt stop, and Maddy barreled into him.

The adobe walls would have had more give in them. Her lighter body jarred against his, and he absorbed the blow without flinching, without even turning. The long fingers that had been a manacle around her wrist released her, and absently she rubbed the mark his hand had made, aware that for all his manhandling, the rifle in her rib had pained her far more.

"Ladies and gentlemen, *señors y señoras,*" Jake said in his gravelly voice that might or might not have held an element of mockery, "allow me to present Miss Allison Henderson. She'll be giving us the pleasure of her company for the next few days. Come forward, Allison, and meet your fellow hostages. Though the rest of us are hostages to fortune."

There were seven of them seated around a long, rough table, clearly at the end of a rather spartan meal. Three women and four men eyed her out of wary, distrustful faces, no one saying a word.

"Who is this?" A red-faced man in his mid-fifties spoke first, his voice querulous and bearing the traces of an

41

upbringing in the southern part of the United States. He was wearing a cotton suit that had once been white, but was now dingy gray and spattered with the remnants of other, more sumptuous meals. "You know as well as I do, Murphy, that there is barely enough food to go around. What are you doing bringing in another mouth to feed? And you, young lady, what the hell are you doing in a country that's being torn apart by revolution? This is a poor choice for a vacation spot, Miss . . . Henderson, was it?"

She could tell by his voice that he was ever so slightly drunk. The smaller, darker man next to him managed a weary smile. "Doc doesn't mean to be unwelcoming, Miss Henderson," he said slowly. Another American, she realized, despite the darkness of his complexion. "But we've had a difficult time of it the last few months, and this is hardly a pleasant place to be."

Jake moved forward then, grabbing a chair and swinging it around to straddle it, his expression distant and watchful. "You may as well have a seat, Allison," he said. "You're going to be here for a while. If you behave yourself I may even see if there's a scrap of food left from lunch."

"My name isn't Allison," she shot back, ignoring the sudden shaft of longing the word food swept through her. There was plenty of stuff in the back of her car, but she'd been too nervous that morning to do more than nibble on a chocolate bar. Suddenly she was famished.

Jake only smiled faintly. "Let me introduce you to our happy family. Going clockwise around the table, we have Dr. Henry Milsom, late of North Carolina, Samuel's physician." The doctor gave her no more than a cursory nod. "Then we have Richard Feldman, late of parts unknown. The two ladies are Miss Mary Margaret Gallager and Sister Margaret Mary McDonald, relief workers who happened to be at the wrong place at the wrong time and are now seeking shelter with El Patrón." The two middle-aged women gave her shy smiles. "Then we have Ramon and Luis, two of El Patrón's guards." Two more teenagers in T-shirts and Nikes and armaments stared at her stonily. "And last but not least, Senora Soledad Alicia Maria Mercedes Lambert de Ferrara y Morales. Samuel's wife."

Maddy's full attention was caught now. The sulky beauty at the far end of the table probably wasn't as old as she was, and the look in her glittering black eyes was intense dislike. She stared at Maddy, not even sacrificing a regal incline of her intricate coiffure to welcome the interloper into the fold. The stream of Spanish she directed at Jake was rapid and rich with invective, and of all the words Maddy could make out only *gringa* and *puta,* meaning bitch or whore. Maddy had little doubt who Soledad was referring to.

Jake ignored her. "And this is Miss Allison Henderson of the United States."

"Not according to her," Richard pointed out cheerfully.

"No, according to her she is Maddy Lambert, daughter to El Patrón."

The simple words were like a bombshell. Soledad's expression darkened to one of intense rage, the two older ladies looked both pleased and doubtful, and Doc merely laughed.

"I didn't think Sam had a daughter," he said with an almost indiscernible slur. "I've been with him almost ten years and he's never mentioned one."

"There was the son, of course," Richard mused, staring at her curiously. "I remember when he died. Suicide, wasn't it?"

Maddy stood there and accepted the blows stoically enough. Stephen had been dead for seven years; surely by now it would stop hurting.

"No, it was a drug overdose," Soledad said in her charmingly accented Spanish. "And I am certain that if Samuel had a daughter he would have mentioned her at the time. You are not my husband's daughter, *señorita*. So then, who are you?"

Jake watched all this with unblinking concentration, and Maddy wondered dismally why she would have thought he'd come to her rescue. "Her passport says she's Allison Henderson. So that's who I expect she is. Carlos said she'd been seen with Ortega down in La Mensa. She must be part of one of his grandiose schemes."

"And you let her in?" Soledad shrieked. "She'll probably murder us in our beds. She's part of Ortega's gray-shirt death squad, and you welcome her with open arms. . . ."

"I wouldn't have called it open arms, would you, Allison?" he mocked. "Besides, she's unarmed. I checked."

"How thoroughly did you check?" Soledad said in a shrill voice. "She should have a body search. I, for one, do not intend—"

"Enough, *mi alma*," he drawled, the endearment an insult. "She can do no harm as long as she is watched. And I, for one, would prefer to have her within reach, rather than out in the hills meeting with her gray-shirt confederates."

"Are you certain the young lady isn't Mr. Lambert's daughter?" Mary Margaret or Margaret Mary murmured hesitantly.

44

Jake's sudden gentle politeness was a painful revelation. Maddy had seen that gentleness years ago, had been the recipient of it in another life. "Nothing is certain in this life, Mary," he replied softly. "And take comfort in the fact that Allison is a lot safer here than anywhere else in San Pablo. At least here I can protect her."

"You don't think she'll send messages to General Ortega?" one of the young soldiers demanded.

"If she's working with them I have little doubt that she'll try," Jake said. "It will be up to us to make sure that she doesn't."

Maddy was beginning to get a little tired of standing there with the bunch of them discussing her as if she wasn't in the cavernous room. She felt almost faint with hunger, and her rib was aching abominably. Without further hesitation she crossed the distance to the table and sat down in the only seat next to her elegant little stepmother on the rough bench.

Soledad pulled back with an expression of distaste, as if Maddy were a diseased bug, she thought with forced amusement.

"I do not want this woman bothering Samuel," she announced. "He is not strong, he does not need to be plagued with people like this . . . like this . . ." She supplied a Spanish word that Maddy was just as glad she didn't understand.

"Jake is giving me no choice in that matter," Maddy said sweetly. "Don't worry, *mi madrastra.*" She could feel real delight that part of her Spanish had included a translation of Cinderella, and the word for stepmother had lodged itself in her recalcitrant brain. The pale, furious expression on the woman's face was almost worth the fright and aggravation of the last few hours.

"Don't you dare call me that, *puta,*" she snarled.

45

Maddy had enough of being called a whore. *"Mamacita?"* she murmured sweetly.

She couldn't believe how fast Jake moved. One moment he was straddling the chair, seemingly at ease, in the next he was between the two of them. It took Maddy a moment to realize that his strong hand was clamped around Soledad's delicate wrist and that her hand held a very nasty-looking little knife, raised in her stepdaughter's direction. It was too small to kill without a great deal of expertise and luck, but it would have been undoubtedly painful.

A moment later the knife dropped on the table with a clatter, and Soledad's wrist was freed. With a strangled sob she pulled away from the table, rushing from the room.

Jake leaned over and scooped up the knife, his arm brushing Maddy's benumbed body. "I should warn you, lady," he said softly, "that we have all reached the limit of our endurance. Soledad is not an unreasonable woman in the best of times, but tempers are very short indeed, and I would suggest you do your best not to goad anyone. For your own sake, as well as for the others."

He moved away, and Maddy let out her pent-up breath. The others at the table were looking away, the two women studiously uninvolved, Milsom bored, Richard troubled, the two soldiers amused at the trauma. But no one was surprised that Soledad had pulled a knife on her. Maddy shivered.

"Are you hungry, Allison?" Richard said after a long, uncomfortable moment. "I could see if there's anything left."

Maddy opened her mouth, then shut it again, stubbornly.

"Allison?" Richard persisted, confused.

Jake was leaning against the wall, an amused expression on his dark face, looking for all the world as if he hadn't just stopped her from being stabbed. "I think she's not going to answer to that name. Are you?"

"My name is Maddy," she said fiercely.

"And what if only Allison gets fed?" he countered.

"Then I'll be very hungry."

It was a battle of wills. Her meager determination and pride up against a seemingly limitless force on his side. They stared at each other for a long moment, and the rest of the table was silent.

Finally he moved away from the wall, heading toward the door, a wry grin on his face that didn't quite reach his weary eyes. "See if there's any food left for Maddy," he said. "I'm going to see if Soledad is surviving. Ramon, Luis." The names were tersely shot out orders.

"Sí, Murphy?"

"Watch her." And he was gone.

CHAPTER FOUR

The room emptied swiftly. The two religious workers faded away with a reassuring smile and murmured words of confidence. "You can trust Jake, my dear. I know he seems harsh, but believe me, there's no one I'd rather place my safety with."

Maddy hadn't been able to answer with more than a noncommittal smile as she industriously scarfed down the plate of red beans and rice that had appeared before her. At this stage she wasn't about to trust anyone, even the good ladies themselves. If she had to find an ally in this armed camp, she needed one with more strength and daring than she possessed. While the ladies probably had their share of both, to be living in a war zone, they would hardly be likely to go against Jake on her say-so. Soledad was not worth considering. She'd be just as likely to turn her over to the crocodiles, and the doctor was far more interested in his bottle. That left Richard and the two teenage guards, and Richard had vanished with a guilty look on his swarthy face.

Ramon and Luis, Jake had called them. One friendly, the other not so, with their machine guns and their American T-shirts. It was a strained source of amusement to Maddy that the friendly one's T-shirt read "Kill 'em all, let God sort 'em out" and the glowering one sported Mickey Mouse. She stared at them idly over the empty plate. It would be up to the sympathetic one to get her to her father. Mickey Mouse wouldn't let him, so she would have to wait until they were alone.

With a sigh she pushed back the empty plate, ignoring the still-hungry pangs of her nervous stomach. Her two guards were looking very official, standing there by the door. She would give them some time to become accustomed to her before she made her move. The one advantage to Latino machismo was that it made men underestimate the female of the species, and Maddy needed her young guards trusting and willing.

She leaned back against the plaster wall, running a weary hand through her tangled mop of hair. The high, narrow windows let in a fitful light and no fresh air at all, and despite the coolness of the underground walls Maddy felt as if she were suffocating. Though perhaps the certain knowledge that she had unexpectedly become a prisoner added to the feelings of claustrophobia.

What had they done with her car? She was no longer so intent on rescuing her father. It seemed as if he had more than enough protectors to keep him safe from whichever side threatened him. At this point all she wanted to do was to ascertain he was safe and reasonably well and then get the hell out of Puente del Norte.

She closed her eyes for a moment. They felt dry and gritty from the trip, and oh so weary. She would have given anything for her purse and her contact lens case. Sooner or later Jake would have to take her to see her father. He couldn't put it off forever, but in the meantime she would simply have to be patient. Probably by later afternoon, or early this evening, she'd see Samuel, and by tomorrow morning she'd be driving back down that rutted trail that passed for the Grand Pablan Highway, and be back in L.A. by the weekend.

It should have been a comforting thought. She had finally laid to rest the ghosts of her childhood, and if the dissolving of almost-forgotten dreams hurt, then what was new about that? Life hurt.

But how forgotten was John Thomas Murphy? She hadn't been able to visualize his face when she was driving there, but once she had faced him there was instant recognition. And the past, fourteen long years ago, was no longer shadowy and forgotten. It was as real as if it were yesterday.

Her life had never been easy. Not being the daughter of Senator Samuel Eddison Lambert and his social, ambitious wife, Helen, who was herself the daughter of Everett Currier, one of the most powerful and least understood men in American politics. It hadn't helped that Maddy had shot up to the height of five feet seven by sixth grade, and topped five nine by fifteen, and that she was awkward and skinny and shy. Even boarding school hadn't helped. As happy as she was to get away from the rigid strictures of her parents' life in the diplomatic circles of McLean, she missed her family, her friends, her life. And most of all she missed her older brother.

For years afterward she would tell herself that everything would have been all right if only Samuel Eddison Lambert hadn't allowed himself to be talked into running for President. But everyone had wanted him to, from his wife to his father-in-law to his party to his constituents. Everyone wanted him to but his sixteen-year-old daughter.

She'd heard the results of the primaries up at her

boarding school in Massachusetts. She'd watched her father make his speeches on television and hadn't even noticed the ever-present shadow of his mandatory Secret Service protection hovering behind him. Her brother, Stephen, was in his first year at Harvard, and the two of them would meet on weekends with a pact to ignore the old man's political aspirations.

"Besides," Stephen had said, running a nervous hand through his shaggy hair, "you know this is Mother's idea more than it is Dad's. If it were left up to him he'd probably be working in the Peace Corps down in San Pablo or some god-forsaken place like that."

"Maybe he feels he can help them better as President," Maddy had offered.

"Maybe. But I know that I sure as hell don't want to end up in the White House," Stephen had said bitterly. "And I don't want to be part of this damned campaign. I'd better warn you right now, Maddy, I'm not coming home this summer to be part of this circus. If he wants to make it to the White House he'll have to do it without my help."

And all her protests couldn't move him. He'd ended up traveling cross country with a couple of his friends, out of reach of his parents' demands, and by the end of the summer their lives had changed past recognition.

Maddy could never think back to that summer without a pang of pain and longing, a longing for a life that was no more, pain for all the waste. And a wry reflection that there was nothing like being almost seventeen and in love for the first time.

She first saw him in June. She'd been home for ten days, alone in the big old house in McLean, with only the household staff to keep her company while her parents were out in California, drumming up votes. Her mother had ordered her to fly out and join them, a perfect family for the delectation of the American voting public, but Maddy had refused. The last thing she was going to do was be put on display like a great gawky overgrown schoolgirl. After miserable years of skinny flat-chested jealousy she had just begun to develop, and she was even more self-conscious than usual. She welcomed the solitude of the big old house in early summer, dreading the return of what Stephen had rightly called a circus. Complete with omnipresent reporters, Secret Service men, her mother's army of social secretaries, and the myriad of other human detritus that filled her parents' life. She could only hope she'd get lost in the shuffle.

She'd heard them come in the night before. How could she have missed it? The glare from the television camera lights on the front lawn penetrated the darkness of her third-floor bedroom, and the babble of voices filtered through the pillow over her head. She turned on her radio to drown out the noise with music, but it was the hourly news report, full of Senator Lambert's return to Washington, triumphant from his good showing in the California primary.

It was early morning when she woke up, hours before her family would awake and she'd be called upon to be The Candidate's Daughter, hours before her life was no longer her own. She climbed out of bed, pulling on her moth-eaten old one-piece bathing suit that her mother had threatened to throw out more than once. She was straining the previously flat expanse of the top of it, and she pulled on one of Stephen's outsized shirts and drew it around her. Wouldn't you know, she told herself wryly, that after years of longing for a figure it was now a source of continual embarrassment?

Not that there was even that much to be embarrassed

about. No one would have noticed, if it weren't for her mother's constant, seemingly sadistic delight in calling attention to it. Maddy leaned down and peered at her reflection in the mirror that was set too low for her height. Long, long dark brown hair, still in schoolgirl braids to keep it under control while she swam, a pale, pointed face, white teeth only recently freed from braces, large brown eyes still chained to glasses that she was too vain to wear. Not a sex symbol, certainly. And the endless arms and legs, the flat, bony body with its two embarrassing lumps didn't help matters. With a sigh she grabbed her oversized prescription sunglasses and plumped them down on her small, slightly tilted and definitely freckled nose. It was a lucky thing she wasn't going to run into anyone more threatening than the gardener at that early hour.

Even Georgia, their cook that year, wasn't up. Maddy moved through the dark, silent kitchen like a ghost, straight out into the early-morning light, pausing long enough to shed the shirt and the glasses before diving into the cool clear water of the swimming pool. The chilly chlorinated smell surrounded her, waking her up completely, and dutifully she swam her laps, breast stroke, crawl, then flipping over on her back to float peacefully, alone in the world. Sometime, she promised herself, she'd live by the ocean and be able to swim in chlorine-free water every morning.

The house was still dark and silent by the time she climbed out of the pool and began to dry herself off. It was after six by then. Georgia wouldn't make her appearance for another hour. Maddy had developed a taste for coffee during the last year, fostered by Stephen's indulgence, and it had now taken the place of her early-morning Coke. She'd have to rummage through Georgia's sacrosanct appliances and make her own, risking the cook's formidable wrath.

The smell of coffee assailed her nostrils as she reached the open french doors that led to the huge old kitchen. "Georgia, you saint!" Maddy cried as she swept into the kitchen, sans shirt and glasses, with only the too-small bathing suit clinging wetly to her body. "I was dying for some coffee. . . ." Her voice trailed off in sudden horror as she realized it wasn't Georgia standing at the sink, a cup of coffee in his large hand.

"You're not Georgia," she said lamely, standing dead still, too astounded to do more than gape. And then she rapidly did a great deal, pulling Stephen's shirt around her and plopping the dark glasses on her nose. Even through the darkness the prescription sharpened her gaze enough to get a good look at him.

"No, I'm not," he said calmly enough, his voice a deep, rasping rumble. "I'm Jake Murphy, one of your father's Secret Service men. And I presume you're Madelyn? I didn't mean to scare you."

"You didn't scare me," she said slowly. "I just wasn't expecting anyone." Not anyone like you, she added to herself. "And only my mother calls me Madelyn. I'm Maddy."

He smiled then, a strangely sweet smile in a wary, secretive face. "Good morning then, Maddy. Would you like some coffee?"

If his presence had bemused her, his smile devastated her. "I'd love some." She stood there and watched as he reached for a cup and proceeded to pour her some.

At that point most of her romantic fantasies had concerned both long-haired rock singers and Eric Thompson, her best friend's older brother. The man standing in the dawn light by her parents' kitchen sink was cut from a different stamp. He was wearing a suit, of all things, a dark, conservative suit with a white shirt and a dark tie knotted loosely at this throat. His hair was short, army-length, and his hazel eyes had a distant, wary look to them when he wasn't smiling at her. That smile had been a revelation on his dark, narrow face. When he was still the skin seemed too taut across the high cheekbones, the strong blade of a nose, the firm chin. When he wasn't looking at her he looked driven, haunted, and frighteningly romantic. When he looked back at her, smiling that gentle, reassuring smile, Maddy melted.

He was even tall. Eric Thompson was just her height, and she had once made the mistake of wearing heels when she went to visit his sister Vickie. Eric had taken one look at the tall skinny amazon towering over him and beat a hasty retreat. She wouldn't have to worry about spike heels with Jake Murphy, she thought with absent delight. His body was narrow, lean, and whipcord tough, even beneath the conservative suit. Eric was bulging with muscles, and yet Maddy had little doubt that Jake Murphy could dispose of him with one hand tied behind his back. It was a lovely, instantaneous fantasy, the two of them fighting over her. When in actuality neither of them could care less, she reminded herself dismally, pulling the enveloping white shirt tighter around her damp body.

He held out the coffee, and in her rush to get it she stubbed her toe on the kitchen table. "Sugar!" she snapped, limping the last few steps.

"Was that a curse or a request?" Jake asked, the smile still hovering over what was in repose a grim mouth.

"A curse," Maddy said, leaning against the sink and massaging her foot. "I drink my coffee black."

"Maybe if you didn't wear sunglasses in the dark you wouldn't bump into things," he offered gently.

Maddy shook her head. "If I weren't wearing these I wouldn't see anything at all. They're prescription—I left my regular ones up in my room."

"Well, there's nothing to see right now, so you may as well humor me." Before Maddy could divine his attention he'd reached out and removed the sunglasses from her nose. "That's much better. Such pretty brown eyes shouldn't be hidden."

The compliment was gentle, almost absentminded, and her immediate reaction startled even her. She struggled for something to say. "I thought Secret Service men always wore sunglasses," she said, blinking in the sudden light. He was even more overwhelming up close, without the shadow of her glasses between them.

Jake grinned. "We do. Maybe that's why I hate to see them when I'm not working."

"You're not working now?" It was an impossibly inane thing to say, she told herself mournfully, but she was desperate to keep up the conversation. If she didn't she'd have to go back up stairs, alone, away from this gloriously mysterious creature who'd turned up in her parents' kitchen.

He shook his head. "Not until your father gets up."

"Are you staying here? In the house, I mean?"

"Actually I'm staying in the pool house."

"Oh, my gosh, did I wake you?"

"I didn't know anyone still said gosh and sugar when they swore," Jake said in a wry voice. "How old are you, Maddy? I should know but I've forgotten."

"Seventeen," she lied.

His eyes narrowed for a moment. "I should tell you that I have an instinct for when someone lies. Also a good memory when it's prodded. You won't be seventeen till August."

"Close enough," she said.

"Close enough," he agreed, taking a drink of his coffee.

"How old are you?"

"A hundred years older than you," he said with a distant smile. "Twenty-six."

Maddy did a rapid calculation in her head. "That's only nine years older than me."

"Ten. You're sixteen, remember?"

"Nine and a half," she said. "Have you always been in the Secret Service?"

Wrong question. His face closed up, the light went out of his hazel eyes, and his mouth showed its full potential for grimness. "I was in Vietnam for two years."

Maddy's recoil was instinctive. Most of her father's political career had been built on opposition to that and any other war, and Maddy's revulsion was deeply ingrained. She could feel those empty hazel eyes watching her reaction, and she quickly swallowed a sip of the scalding coffee. "Good coffee," she manged in a croak.

Jake Murphy stared at her for a long, silent moment and then his mouth relaxed, his eyes warmed, and the tension left his body. "Thanks," he said, and Maddy knew he wasn't talking about the coffee.

She looked at him, less than a foot of counter space between them, and she had the sudden overwhelming longing to reach out and cradle that head against her, to kiss that bitter mouth that could smile so sweetly at her. She looked at him and fell in love, with all the passion a shy sixteen-year-old possessed. She smiled up at him dizzily. "You're welcome," she murmured.

He must have known. Those hazel eyes of John Thomas Murphy could see through any frail human emotion, and a sixteen-going-on-seventeen-year-old wasn't adept at hiding the sudden onrush of fragile passion. But he smiled back at her, a sweet, secret smile between the two of them, and Maddy told herself a bond was sealed. She had met her fate, and if he didn't quite recognize it yet, he would sooner or later. And suddenly the campaign summer seemed quite glorious to look forward to.

CHAPTER FIVE

"You wish any coffee, lady?" Was it Ramon with the soulful eyes and the killer T-shirt, or Luis? She could only guess.

"No, thank you, Ramon," she said with a shake of her head, and was rewarded with a beatific smile that revealed shattered front teeth. When the time came he might very well prove an ally. He was young and innocent enough not to like what Jake Murphy was doing to her.

His next words confirmed that impression. "Don't worry about Murphy. He is a fair man. He will take you to El Patrón when he thinks the time is right. You can trust him, *señorita.*"

Why was everyone telling her to trust him? She had little choice in the matter, but if she had it would be the last thing she would do. "Ramon, I need to see my father," she said softly, urgently.

"Don't let the *gringa* talk you into anything, *amigo,*" Luis of the Mickey Mouse T-shirt snarled from across the room. "You know what Murphy would say if you went against his orders. And she wouldn't care. All she cares about is herself." Luis spat to emphasize his point. It would make little difference on the filthy floor.

A wary look came into Ramon's deep brown eyes, and the concerned smile wavered. "All in good time, *señorita*," he said, moving away. "All in good time."

Everyone had known of Maddy's adolescent passion for her father's Secret Service man. There was no way she could hide it. When it came to a choice between being circumspect and being in Jake's mesmerizing company, she had to pick the latter, despite her mother's caustic comments.

"If I'd known Jake Murphy was all it would take to get you interested in your father's campaign, I would have done something about it long ago," Helen had drawled. Of course she had chosen a small cocktail party, with Jake in hearing range, to make that particular announcement, and Maddy had fled to her room in mortified tears.

But even that embarrassment and her mother's subsequent attempts at ridiculing humor didn't stop her starry-eyed crush. Jake's gentle forbearance only served to encourage her, so that by August every waking moment and most dreaming ones were completely absorbed in Jake. He'd always known just how to treat her—a combination of little sister, innocent young girl, his boss's daughter, and a trace of something dangerously flattering. It had done wonders for her self-esteem, and for the first time in her life that she could remember she was truly happy. Until that hideous night of her birthday, when all her dreams went crashing down and the even tenor of her life was shattered.

It was only a few days before the convention, the convention that everyone said held the keys to Samuel Eddison Lambert's presidential ambitions. He stood more than a good chance against his opponent, a conservative younger man with a good record on domestic issues, and he held up even better against the opposite party's choice of July. Sam Lambert was only a few steps away from the White House, and the tension in the house in McLean was high.

That there were other reasons for that tension, that something more than a straightforward campaign was going on, was kept from Maddy. She'd heard the arguments late at night, seen the sober emergency meetings of dark-suited men in her father's study, but none of that was terribly unusual. Her parents had always fought, and her father had always had advisors. If everyone was beginning to look a little grim around the edges, then Maddy attributed it to the greater stakes at hand.

It was the night of her seventeenth birthday party. Helen had arranged a party and dance at the local country club. She had even outdone herself and snagged Eric Thompson as an escort for her lanky daughter. Sam and Helen would make an appearance after dinner, but no one could expect them to spare much time, with the convention only a few days away. Certainly not Maddy.

The giddy thought of Eric Thompson was enough to put even Jake Murphy out of her head. She spent days looking for the perfect pair of flat sandals so that she wouldn't tower over him, her flowery summer dress floated around her narrow hips and hugged her small breasts in what could only be called an enticing manner, and her waist-length hair she left long and shining, with only a silver comb holding it back from her tanned, hopeful face. She'd have to make it through the night blind. There was no way she was going to wreck her outfit with her oversized glasses. Maybe she'd listen to her mother's constant suggestions and get contact lenses. It had only been stubbornness that had stopped her so far. Leaning forward, she peered nearsightedly at her reflection in the mirror.

"You're very pretty." His voice, like water rippling over stones, came from the door of her bedroom, and she looked up, startled, into Jake's hazel eyes.

He was leaning against the door, clad as always in that regulation suit that seemed to fit his tall body so much better than the other anonymous clones who surrounded her father. She smiled up at him, half pleased, half vulnerable. "I'm too tall," she said, grimacing.

"No, you're not."

"And I'm too skinny." She ran a disgusted hand down her narrow shape.

"No, you're not."

"And my mouth is too big."

There was a peculiar silence, as his eyes fell to her mouth, and to Maddy's fanciful mind his glance seemed to caress the trembling contours. But that may have been the fault of her nearsightedness. "No, it's not," he said finally, straightening up and starting toward her. "It's just the right size."

He's going to kiss me, she thought with sudden, dizzying panic and excitement. He's going to put that grim, unsmiling mouth on mine, pull me into his arms and . . .

He stopped a few feet short of her, and that damned, distant smile flitted over his unreadable face. "Your mother wants to see you."

The disappointment that washed over her was ludicrous, considering the panic that had preceded it at the thought of those strong, merciless hands on her body. Maddy swallowed bravely.

"What about?" Eric Thompson suddenly seemed miles away and far too young for her.

Though Jake was at a distance from her she could read the sudden disturbed look that filtered through his eyes. She could tell that he knew he shouldn't be there with her, knew that it was dangerous indeed. The thought pleased her immeasurably, and she moved closer.

"If it's something unpleasant," she added, stopping when she was within a foot of him, and she could feel the warmth emanating from his black-clad body, "then I don't want to hear it." She felt wicked, daring, and very mature. She reached out a slender hand and placed it on his arm. "Why don't you tell her you couldn't find me, Jake?" she murmured, smiling up at him provocatively. "She never has anything nice to say."

He didn't move, but she could feel the tension in him, the energy tightly held in check. "You're playing with fire, Maddy," he said finally, his voice not much more than a growl. "And you're too young to get burned."

She stood very still. The muscles in his arm were bunched beneath her fingers, and the hazel eyes that looked down into her wide brown ones were very dangerous. She had the sudden, fanciful feeling that if she didn't move fast she'd be caught.

Yet he seemed to mesmerize her, so that she was unable to move, unable to speak a word, could only stand there looking up at him, her lips parted breathlessly. And willed his head to dip closer to hers, for that mouth to capture hers.

"Madelyn!" Helen's perfectly modulated tones cut through the moment like a razor, and Maddy jumped, guilt and nervousness washing over her.

If she expected to see Jake equally confounded she was in for a surprise. His hand caught hers as she tried to jerk away, holding her tightly in a grip unseen by her eagle-eyed mother. "I was just telling Maddy you were looking for her," he said calmly, his long fingers soothing the back of her hand with a warning gesture.

"Do you spend a lot of time in my daughter's bedroom, Jake?" Helen demanded with that icy drawl she'd perfected years ago. "I hadn't realized Maddy's adolescent passion was reciprocated." Helen allowed her cool brown eyes to trail over Maddy's tall, willowy body. "You have improved, dearest. Even beyond what I imagined possible. I suppose we'll have to keep a close watch on you."

Maddy had flushed a miserable, unbecoming pink, and she opened her mouth to protest, then shut it again. Once more her cavalier came to her rescue, and she fell in love with him all over again.

"I was just telling Maddy how pretty she was," Jake said.

"I'm sure you were," Helen Currier Lambert said. "And were you telling her good-bye?"

"Good-bye?" Maddy echoed, horrified.

"Jake is leaving us, darling. Aren't you, Jake?" There was a steely look in her mother's eyes, one that Jake met with simple, utter hatred.

"That hasn't been decided yet, Mrs. Lambert." His voice was deathly cold.

Helen's smile was a deathgrin on her beautifully boned face. "Well, you'll leave us alone right now, won't you, Jake? It's time for a little mother-daughter discussion."

Maddy threw him a beseeching look, but there was nothing more he could do. Ignoring the woman at the door, he reached out and caught Maddy's hand again. "You look beautiful, Maddy," he said in a gentle voice. "Eric Thompson is very lucky."

She hadn't realized he'd even known about Eric. Before she could say anything more he'd gone, his overwhelming presence draining the frilly bedroom of energy, making it pale and sad.

Helen shut the door behind him, advancing on her daughter with a cold, determined expression on her elegant face. "There's trouble," she said abruptly. "I decided you'd better be warned."

"What sort of trouble?" Sudden panic filled her.

"With the campaign, of course. I can't go into it now. If we're lucky, if your father decides to take his head out of the clouds and face reality for once in his life, then we may muddle through. We'll know by the end of tonight."

"The campaign!" Maddy said in sudden relief, visions of her brother, long incommunicado on his cross-country trip, filling her head. "I thought it was something important."

Helen Currier Lambert reached out and slapped her daughter across the face, hard. The sound of it echoed through the bedroom, shocking both women, and through Maddy's blur of pain and astonishment she thought she saw her mother's hand shaking.

If Helen Currier Lambert ever showed weakness or regret it was only temporary. By the time Maddy had recovered from the blow Helen was once more in control. "It's time you learned a few home truths, Madelyn. About life in the big city, about politics, and about men. People don't become President without making a few deals, greasing a few palms, doing a few things that are generally unpalatable to those of your father's lofty ideals. It all boils down to 'you scratch my back, I'll scratch yours.' If your father wants to help all the waifs and homeless ones of this world, he'll have to compromise a few principles to do it."

"And Father doesn't agree with that?"

Helen shuddered delicately, moving away from her daughter to stare out the third floor window. "That remains to be seen. I expect he'll make up his mind in the next few hours—your father has never been one to be indecisive." She turned to smile brilliantly at her daughter, ignoring the imprint of her hand on Maddy's lightly tanned face. "But under the circumstances you can see that it's highly unlikely that either of us will make it to your birthday party. I hope you don't mind."

It was all so polite, with the feel on the blow still raw on her face, Maddy mused. "No, I don't mind."

"No, I didn't imagine you would. Eric Thompson will be sufficient distraction. You can't say I didn't do well by you this year. Eric Thompson is a very nice-looking young man."

"Is he my birthday present?" Maddy said coolly.

"In a manner of speaking. You've always liked him—until you developed this embarrassing crush on Murphy he was quite the center of your universe."

"Thank you, Mother." Maddy's voice was quiet and cool.

Helen roused herself from her abstraction. "And of course there's the car. Though why in the world you'd prefer a Volkswagen Beetle to a Mustang is beyond me. It doesn't do your father's campaign any good, you know. It's always wise to buy American—the voting public notices things like that."

"Screw the campaign," Maddy said.

This time she had her mother's full attention, and her smile was coolly self-contained. "You realize that if your father withdraws, as he might very well do, he'll lose his Secret Service protection?"

Maddy controlled her flinch. "Is that what you meant by Jake leaving us?"

Helen hesitated. "No, he'd be leaving us either way. I don't like the effect he has on you. I don't know what was going on when I walked in on you—"

"Absolutely nothing!"

"—but I'll have you remember that he's an adult and you're still a child. There's a word for men who like to prey on infants, and it's not a very nice one."

"You're disgusting," Maddy spat the words. "Jake and I are friends."

Helen smiled like a lizard. "Tell me, darling, do you honestly think Jake Murphy crawling into your bed is disgusting? I find that hard to believe, after watching you panting around him all summer."

Maddy held herself very still. "Why are you doing this to me?" she said finally.

Helen drew herself upright. "You're my daughter," she said. "I'm trying to protect you. I'm trying to keep you from making as big a fool of yourself as your father seems about to do."

"So if you can't attack Father you come up here and attack me?" Maddy said with surprising shrewdness. "No, thank you, Mother. I haven't got anything more to say to you. I'm sure Father will make the right decision tonight. I only hope it's not the one you want."

There was a long silence in the room. "Madelyn," Helen said, and the smoothness in her voice warned Maddy to beware. "We've never been close. I'm not the sort to seek out the company of other women, and I'm not cut out for motherhood. But it's my responsibility to warn you, however unpleasant that might be."

"I don't need any warnings. . . ."

"Oh, yes, my dear, you most certainly do. I can't

promise that Jake Murphy will be out of this house as quickly as I want him to be, but I can at least guarantee that you keep out of his way. I think in his own way he's just as fascinated with you as you are with him."

"He thinks of me as a younger sister."

"Like hell he does. I have eyes in my head, Madelyn, even if you're too busy mooning around to notice. He wants you, and I don't trust him not to do anything about it."

"And you think by telling me that it will keep me away from him?" Maddy scoffed. "Mother, I'm seventeen. That's more likely to entice me than frighten me." That was a lie, but her mother wouldn't know it.

But Helen wasn't disturbed by Maddy's bravado. "No, dear one, that's not what I'm going to warn you about. I'm going to tell you what happened to John Thomas Murphy in Vietnam, and what he did there. And then I have no doubt at all you'll keep away from him. No doubt at all."

A lazy mosquito landed on her bare arm, stalked around at a leisurely pace, and then bit. With equal abstraction Maddy swatted him, and the sound was jarring in the still room.

Ramon looked up from his position by the door and flashed her a tentative smile. "The mosquito season is almost over, *gracias a Dios.* You should be glad El Patrón decided to stay up here in the mountains, rather than along the Mosquito Coast."

"Mosquito Coast?" Maddy echoed, staring at the itching red spot where the bug had recently feasted.

"La Mosquitia. Not at all pleasant, any time of year. The bugs have almost died out up here. You can even sleep with the windows open."

"That's a relief. I would probably suffocate otherwise. Puente del Norte doesn't seem to come equipped with air conditioning," she said with a vague attempt at humor.

Luis snorted, the noise giving his opinion of elitist *gringa* pigs who have to have air conditioning to survive. Maddy surveyed him from her seat against the wall, wondering for a moment whether there was any way she could get past that angry militancy. The throbbing rib warned her that it was highly unlikely. Luis was no friendlier than Enrique, the guardian at the gate. It would take more charm than she possessed to calm their distrust.

"How long have you been here?" she questioned idly.

Ramon hesitated, then obviously decided that telling her wouldn't compromise his orders. After all, Murphy hadn't said to do anything other than watch her. If he wanted her kept in the dark he would have said so—Murphy was always direct.

"In this house, nine months. In the area, two years. It has been a long time, a long war." He sighed.

"And how long have El Patrón and . . . and La Patrona been married?"

It was Ramon's turn to snort, and even the dour Luis looked amused. "Not La Patrona," the latter said decisively. "Señora Lambert, Soledad is, but never La Patrona."

"They have been married one year," Ramon explained. "Though they have been together for longer than that."

"And why isn't she 'La Patrona?' " Maddy persisted.

Ramon grinned. "It's a title of respect, to be earned. Let us say Soledad has done nothing to earn it."

Luis seemed in the mood to talk. "She was Morosa's mistress when she was fourteen years old. He tired of her, passed her down to Ortega, but Soledad is not the kind of

69

woman to settle for second in command. She changed sides, and El Patrón is an honorable man. Not the kind of man to leave a woman helpless." The message was clear. If the Saint of San Pablo had a daughter he never would have repudiated her.

Maddy considered arguing the point, then dismissed the notion, changing the subject. "And the others? Do they have titles of respect?"

"Or otherwise. Carlos, the man you met on the road, is called the Jackal, but that is more his idea than anyone else's. Feldman is El Nabo."

"The turnip," Luis volunteered with a sour smile. "The man is useless in a fight. Don't look to him for help, *gringa.*"

Maddy gave him her best smile. "I won't. Thanks for the advice."

Luis snarled.

"The ladies are los Madres, the mothers. I don't think you would wish to hear what we call Soledad. I doubt you would even know the word, and I would not care to translate. The doctor also is called something not kind but unfortunately descriptive. And we have El Patrón, of course."

"And what about Murphy? What is he called?"

Ramon shook his head. "Murphy is called nothing but Murphy. In his case it is a title with enough respect. He needs no other."

"Do I have a name?" she questioned idly.

Ramon shook his head. "Not yet. Time will tell."

"What about La Curiosa?" Jake's gravelly voice broke through the lazy conversation. "The snoop?"

Ramon laughed his appreciation, but Maddy was suddenly stilled, that overwhelming tension filling her at his return. She had already become accustomed to the long hair, to the savage look of his worn khakis and his distant face. What she couldn't come to terms with was his reappearance in her life, when she thought he'd been gone for good.

"I am not allowed to ask questions?" she said with dignity.

Jake shrugged, his hazel eyes curiously light. "You may ask all you wish, Allison. Whether anyone chooses to answer is another matter. Come along."

Maddy sat without moving. "Are you taking me to see my father?"

"I'm taking you for a walk in the garden."

"And if I don't care to go?"

Jake's smile was scarcely reassuring. "You have no choice in the matter."

Maddy looked up at him, up into the hazel eyes that had once burned into hers, hazel eyes that had, according to her mother, watched an entire village of women and children slaughtered by his fellow soldiers in Vietnam and he hadn't been able to stop them. Had he even tried? And if he hadn't tried, would anything stop him from being equally brutal to her? He'd spent the last fourteen years on the outposts of civilization, doing penance as he protected Samuel Lambert. But just how far had he come?

He waited, seemingly patient, but the tension was thick in the room. Luis had a look of delicious anticipation on his face, obviously hoping she would refuse. Ramon looked deeply troubled, adding to Maddy's suspicion that Jake's request was only a thin excuse. But excuse for what?

Slowly she rose, throwing back her shoulders. "A walk in the garden would be very pleasant," she said slowly.

Jake's smile was less than reassuring.

71

CHAPTER SIX

He didn't touch her this time. He didn't need to. The sheer force of his presence was enough to cow her into obedience, at least temporarily. She followed him docilely enough, past the smirking Luis and the concerned Ramon, through the deserted, darkened hallways, back up the stairs. She half expected him to take her back to the front courtyard with its profusion of flowers, but instead he veered sharply to the left, past a series of empty, desolate-looking rooms, stopping outside a heavy door.

It was bolted, and it took him more than a moment to deal with the solid-looking locks. Maddy watched with silent interest, taking the moment to relive the feel and the memory of him. The hands she remembered, large and strong and tanned. The long legs, encased in khaki rather than those dark suits, also brought back lascivious teenage fantasies. The way he tilted his head, that distant, mocking glance that he cast down at her before he opened the door. How many times had he looked at Helen Currier Lambert in just that way? He'd hated her mother, and now it looked as if he might hate her.

She could only try again. "Jake, you can't have forgotten," she said in her most reasonable tone of voice as she halted by the doorway. "What about the first time we met, in my father's kitchen? You made coffee, and I'd gone swimming. It was the summer of the presidential election and you—"

"I don't remember," he said flatly.

"But you must. What about when you taught me to play poker? Or the night we stayed up late in the pool house, talking? And you remember Stephen, and how worried I was about him. You can't have forgotten all that." Her voice sounded desperate, pleading in the fragrant stillness, but Jake was clearly unmoved.

He looked down at her, and his eyes were opaque in the afternoon silence. "I don't know what you're talking about," he said wearily. He gestured to the tiny courtyard ahead of them. "After you, Allison."

Maddy could see the familiar profusion of flowers, hear the faint buzz of bees, and she was uncertain whether to believe him or not. She held her ground, glaring up at him mutinously. She had made him call her by her name once before; she could do it again. She had to reserve that small triumph in the face of a total rout.

He cocked his head to one side, and his eyes were enigmatic. "You're waiting for me to call you Maddy?"

She nodded, controlling the urge to meet his gaze. She wasn't entirely sure she was capable of keeping that beseeching look from her own expressive eyes, and she was through with pleading.

"It'll be a cold day in hell," Jake said, clamping his large hand around her elbow. A moment later she was shoved out into the garden, half dragged, half pulled, as he slammed the door behind them.

Did he know his own strength? Probably. Did he know those long, steely fingers were digging into the tender flesh of her arm, making her forget about the throbbing of her rib, giving her nothing but sheer rage to focus on? Probably. She tried to pull away, and the fingers only tightened. A tiny gasp of pain escaped her before she clamped her jaw down on it.

He pulled to a stop a few feet into the garden, and to her surprise he released her. "You don't have to make this harder on yourself," he said, but his face was remorseless.

"Why won't you believe me?" It didn't come out as she had planned. She'd hoped it would be a strong demand, instead it was wistful, showing more vulnerability than she ever wanted to show to the man in front of her. "If you'd just listen to me I can give you all the proof you need. I don't understand why you won't trust me."

She didn't really expect an answer, and when it came it surprised her. "Because I can't afford to," he said finally. "And neither can you."

"Neither can I what?" she demanded. "Trust you? Or afford to have you trust me?"

Jake shrugged. "However you choose to look at it."

"But—"

The hand clamped around her wrist this time, albeit a great deal more gently, and he began pulling her into the garden. "I didn't bring you out here to argue, Allison-Madelyn," he rasped, and Maddy allowed herself to accept the tiny sop to her defenses.

"Then why did you bring me out here?" she demanded, stumbling to keep up with him, her thin leather sandals tripping over the weed-choked path.

He grinned down at her then, the smile a lightning slash of white teeth in his dark, dangerous face. "For your peaceful company," he replied. "Oblige me by being more peaceful, or we'll continue this walk with you wearing my bandanna as a gag."

The protest that was forming on Maddy's lips was quickly swallowed. She contented herself with a glare that spoke volumes, a glare that left Jake completely unmoved.

She had no choice but to follow him, like a dutiful dog, she thought resentfully. His hand on her wrist was not ungentle, and the pace around the weed-choked garden was leisurely. Surprisingly so—through the few square of inches that their bodies touched she could feel the tension in him like a palpable thing.

She should have fought him, she berated herself. She should have thrown his words back in his face, yanked her wrist away from him, maybe even slapped him in that cool, distant, unemotional face. At least she should have told him no.

Girls say yes to boys who say no. The line came back to haunt her with sudden force, and she flinched with the memory. It was one of those smug little catch-alls of the sixties and early seventies, along with If you're not part of the solution you're part of the problem. Maddy had used the phrases often, along with her favorite paean to draft resisters, the ultimate bribe for an unsure eighteen-year-old boy: Girls say yes to boys who say no.

She had gotten very drunk at her party. Well, perhaps not very drunk. But the champagne had flowed freely, and no one had appeared to mind that half the guests at the private birthday party held at the exclusive country club were under eighteen.

Eric Thompson had been fairly dazzled by the new Maddy, with the thick straight hair hanging down to her waist, the new figure, the slight edge of desperate gaiety that clung to her. Her mother's words still ran through her head, the cold, cruel pleasure she took in recounting the court-martial that Jake Murphy had endured along with his entire unit. The court-martial that he had instigated, in the teeth of the army's attempt to cover it up, where he testified against his friends and comrades. All the champagne in the world hadn't been able to drive it from her head. Dancing barefoot, her slender body pressed up against Eric's sturdy one had only just begun to dim the edges of the awful revelations her mother had made, and the dark corner of the poolside cabana with Eric's clumsy hands on the front of her dress and his wet, hungry mouth on hers almost made it all go away. But not completely. Particularly not when it was Jake who found them there.

"Party's over," he'd said, looking down at her with unreadable hazel eyes as she sat curled up on the chaise longue, her skirt up high around her long tanned legs, her head on Eric's shoulder.

Eric had turned bright red when Jake's tall figure had appeared from out of the shadows, and he had yanked his hand away from Maddy's breast with unflattering haste. She was sitting in his lap, making no move to get up, and he could hardly dump her on the cement walkway, so he tried a little sophisticated, man-to-man banter.

"Give us just another half hour, would you, old man?" he requested, not noticing Maddy's stillness as she sat in his lap. "You understand these things."

Jake had only looked at him, his face forbidding in the moonlight. "I understand only too well. Come along, Maddy."

And she had gone, docilely enough then as now, without even a backward glance at Eric Thompson's crushed expression.

Jake had driven her new car over to the country club, and the sight of his long limbs folding into the driver's

76

seat of the shiny white VW bug had struck Maddy with inappropriate amusement. He stared up at her with great patience, waiting for her to get in the car.

When she finally did so he made no move to start it, just sat there watching her. "Where are your shoes?"

She giggled. It had been awhile since her last glass of Moet, but the giddy delight still lingered. "I have no idea."

"And your comb?"

She reached up a vague hand to push the mane of dark-brown hair away from her face. "I don't know. It's probably in the bottom of the punch bowl."

"Is that what you were drinking?" He started the car, pulling out of the crowded parking lot with practiced ease.

Maddy shook her head, the gesture making her feel slightly dizzy, and she slid lower in her seat. "Champagne," she said succinctly.

"I think we'd better go home by way of some coffee," Jake had said after a moment. "Your father doesn't need to deal with you in your current state on top of everything else."

"What's everything else?" she asked idly. Before he could answer she began humming, a little off-key, and the conversation lapsed into silence.

"Was that Eric Thompson?" he said after a long moment.

"Who?" She interrupted her humming for a moment to peer at him owlishly.

"The young man you were kissing so enthusiastically?" Jake's voice was wry.

"I don't know if I was enthusiastic. But yes, it was Eric. He might have to go to Canada," she confided.

"The war's over, Maddy."

"Well, you never know what might happen. Particularly if my father doesn't get elected."

"That's no longer even a vague possibility," Jake said under his breath as he swung into an all-night diner. "You stay here while I get you some coffee."

"He might get drafted." Maddy's mind was still clinging to Eric's dilemma.

"What were you doing, trying to comfort him?" he snapped, the first sign of emotion he'd shown since he'd found them.

Maddy smiled sweetly, recognizing the edge of anger there. "I was encouraging him to resist. Girls say yes to boys who say no."

Jake's face was very still. "Then it's a lucky thing I wasn't going to ask you, isn't it?" And he left the car.

Maddy pulled her knees up, propping her bare feet on the flat glove compartment. "It didn't work, dummy," she whispered to herself. "You didn't make him jealous, you didn't challenge him into doing anything. You just made a fool of yourself, and now he hates you." On that cheery note she pressed her flushed face against the cool cotton of her summer dress and moaned.

She didn't raise her head when she heard the car door open again, didn't look up when the light vehicle sagged beneath his weight as he got into the driver's seat. His hand reached out and caught hers, pressing a huge Styrofoam cup in it, and then she did lift her woebegone face to his.

"I'm sorry," she said in a muffled tone.

He smiled then, a wry smile, and brushed her tangled hair away from her flushed, miserable face. "Trust me, Maddy," he said in his husky voice, "it's hell to be seventeen. And it only gets worse."

She stared at him, wanting to nuzzle her face against

78

that hard, strong hand of his, still maintaining enough sobriety to keep from doing it. "It can't be that bad," she whispered.

"Not for you, I hope. Drink your coffee, Maddy. I've got to get you home."

"Why?"

"Because I have to pack."

"You're leaving?" Panic filled her voice. "Jake, you shouldn't listen to my mother. She's just a troublemaker —you know Samuel wouldn't care about your being involved in the massacre, and . . ." Her voice trailed off at the sudden bleak look in his face.

"She told you about that?"

"Y-yes."

"Then why don't you hate me? What are you doing sitting here talking to me?" He sounded so cold, so angry, so filled with hatred that could only be directed at himself.

"I could never hate you, Jake," Maddy cried with all the desperation of adolescent passion. "I love you."

The faint smile that lifted the corners of his grim mouth was self-derisive. "And I love you too, kid. Which is why I'd better get you home, fast."

It was a silent ride. Maddy sat there numbly, sipping on the too-sweet coffee that splashed her skirt and scorched her skin through the thin cotton dress. Jake flicked off the lights a moment before he turned into the driveway, and he was out of the car before she could say anything.

Slowly she followed him. The house was a blaze of lights, cars were parked all along the street, but her own third-floor windows were dark and deserted. Jake went in through the back gate, circling the pool, Maddy a silent shadow behind him. Finally he paused, long enough for her to catch up with him. She could smell the scent of freshly mown grass mixing with the acrid smell of the chlorine from the pool, hear the distant sounds of traffic and the mumble of agitated voices from the living room beyond them.

"I think you'd probably better go straight up to bed," Jake said, not even turning to look at her, keeping his attention on the house. "I don't think that coffee was enough to counteract the effects of champagne and Eric Thompson." He was making an effort at keeping his voice lightly humorous, but Maddy didn't believe him.

"What's going on, Jake?"

He did turn to look down at her then. "Your father's dropping out of the race. Some very unsavory things were done in his name, things that he can't condone. So he's withdrawing."

"And you'll be leaving?"

He nodded. "Tomorrow morning. With Sam."

Maddy stood there, absorbing the information with fatalistic calm. "And will you be back? Will I see you again?"

He hesitated, but only for a moment. "No, Maddy," he said gently.

"I see." Her voice was calm and still. "Then would you do me a favor?"

"If I can."

"Would you kiss me good-bye?"

He shook his head. "I can't, Maddy. Haven't you had enough of kissing tonight?"

She managed a smile. "Eric wasn't very exciting. I wanted some basis for comparison. Come on, Jake, it won't hurt you. No one's going to get you for statutory rape. One little kiss won't compromise your virtue."

"I thought girls only said yes to boys who say no?"

"I'm making an exception." Her voice was a little desperate. She had this strange, champagne-induced delusion that if she could just get him to kiss her he wouldn't leave her. He'd said he loved her. If he would only kiss her then he wouldn't be able to fight it.

"No, Maddy." His voice was very firm, his face set and unreadable in the midnight darkness.

She held her ground for a moment longer, and when she spoke her voice broke slightly. "All right." And then she turned and ran.

He caught her by the kitchen doorway, those strong, ungentle hands hard on her arms, spinning her around to face him, and his expression was no longer cold and distant. Before she had time to read it she was in his arms, his hard, demanding mouth on hers, kissing her with a violent desperation that both frightened and exulted her. She whimpered slightly, sliding her arms up around his neck, and the kiss gentled abruptly, his mouth teasing hers apart, his tongue slipping through to taste her. The intrusion of that tongue was a surprise, one that jolted her directly at the base of her stomach, and she shivered uncontrollably, clinging to him for dear life. One of his strong, hard hands had reached up to cradle her chin as his other arm held her close to his lean body, and she could feel the soothing stroke of his thumb beneath her jaw, the fingers stroking her fragile neck, as he continued to kiss her, caressing the soft contours of her mouth.

Slowly, shyly she reached out the tip of her tongue to touch his, and the intimacy was almost unbearable. She wanted to cry with the wonder of it, wanted to crawl inside him and hide there, wanted to feel that strong, muscled body that strangely enough trembled in her arms, wanted to feel the warmth of his skin beneath her fingers. She wanted him, all of him, under the summer moonlight, she wanted to lie beneath him and feel him around her, in her, taking her and making her the woman she longed to be, only for him.

His hand slid up her rib cage, brushing the underside of her small, soft breast, lingering there for a moment, until she thought she would explode with wanting. And then it drew away, the hand cupping her chin slowly released her, and he broke the kiss, his mouth still hovering inches above her own, and she could feel the rapid puffs of breath from that mouth that had just explored hers so thoroughly.

"Go to bed, Maddy," he said roughly.

"I don't want to," she whispered. "Please, Jake . . ."

"For heaven sake, Maddy, go to bed!" His voice was as ragged as his breathing. "If you don't go now I won't be able to let you go."

"But I don't want to. . . ."

"Please, Maddy," he said on a note of desperation. "Don't do this to me. I'll hate myself, more than I do already."

There was nothing she could say to that. The despair was clear in his eyes and face, and much as she wanted to cradle him against her, to soothe that anguish, she believed him. He would hate himself if he made love to her that night. And as much as she loved him, the only way she could show it was to leave him alone.

She stood very still, within the circle of his arms, fighting against the warmth of desire that still tingled the surface of her skin. And then she leaned forward, brushing her lips against his, softly, sweetly. "Good night, Jake," she whispered, slipping away from him like a shadow in the night.

But he wasn't going to get away so easily, she told herself as she climbed the flights to her bedroom. He wasn't going to leave tomorrow morning. She was going to be up hours before he was planning to be gone, and they'd talk then.

But her body had other ideas. Champagne and emotion took their toll, and she slept till ten the next morning. And he was gone.

Jake Murphy had left, with Samuel Eddison Lambert, and she had seen neither of them in the past fourteen years. She had almost forgotten about Jake, had him filed away in the same category as Eric Thompson—a childhood infatuation with no relationship to the future.

But as Maddy looked up at the man stalking through this overgrown tropical garden with all his tightly leashed energy, she suddenly felt seventeen again and just as bewitched.

For a tall woman she sure as hell had fragile bones. He could feel the delicacy of her wrist beneath his hard fingers, had felt her flinch when he'd been too rough with her earlier. But she hadn't said a word, she'd shut that soft, angry mouth of hers and not complained.

Another woman would have whined. Another woman would have wept. He'd seen enough of Soledad's tears to last a lifetime, heard enough of her incessant demands to have developed a healthy disregard for such things.

But the woman who paced along beside him, her huge eyes shadowed, hadn't complained for a moment. She'd railed at him, pleaded with him, but she'd kept her dignity. He could admire that, even as he cursed the events and the damnable chance that had brought her, claiming to all and sundry that she was Sam's daughter.

"What's that?" Her voice broke through his abstraction, and he halted, keeping the loose grip on her wrist, telling himself that he had to keep a hold on her, knowing he was lying to himself.

She was pointing toward the third floor of the seedy old hacienda, the outer stone stairway leading up the side of the adobe building.

He allowed himself a cynical smile. "That is where your so-called father is," he replied.

"And those steps lead up to his rooms?"

"Not very subtle, Allison. I would have thought your friend Ortega would have trained you better." He loved to watch the way she flared up when he mentioned Ortega.

"Don't call me Allison," she snapped.

"Look, lady, I don't care who the hell you say you are. I'll call you whatever I please. And those steps are so broken and crumbled by the weather that no one uses them any more. Not to mention the very real danger of sniper fire."

Her eyes widened in unfeigned nervousness. "Sniper fire?" she echoed in a hollow voice, looking around with sudden uneasiness. "What am I, target practice?"

"There's no danger now. It's more likely to happen at dusk, or after dark. I would suggest you not even consider trying to sneak up to Sam's rooms this way."

He could tell by the line of her jaw that she didn't believe him. He'd have to remember to warn Ramon to be doubly careful when he watched her. He was so damned tired. It must have been weeks since he'd had more than four hours' sleep. Why in heaven's name did he have to be saddled with this new problem, just as things were disintegrating?

Jake glanced up at the top floor, at the figure barely discernible at the shaded window. The woman at his side was looking up, curiosity and something more devious filling her thoughts. He should have distracted her, but her angle gave a good view of her face to the third-floor watchers above. He waited, patiently enough, until she turned with a cold little smile that he had seen once before in his life. It was with a start that he realized he'd seen it on Sam Lambert's first wife.

"Do you think he's had a good enough look at me by now?" she said in a silken tone.

He shouldn't have underestimated her. God willing, he wouldn't again.

"I expect so," he replied, controlling the start her words had given him. "Maybe you could just turn to the left for a few moments?"

"Go to hell."

Jake smiled faintly. "Then let's walk some more." Not that his hand on her wrist gave her much choice, he thought.

"Why? Didn't you bring me out here so that Sam could get a look at me and see whether I'm his daughter or some San Pablan Mata Hari?"

"Of course I did. We're just waiting for word from him." A displeased expression crossed his face. "And I think this is it."

Maddy lifted her head, staring at the figure coming across the tangled garden with a fine disregard for the remnants of walkways and the profusion of roses and wild gardenias beneath his booted feet. "Lizard Eyes," she said under her breath.

Jake snorted in amusement. "That's a good name for him. But he's better known as Carlos, with real or imagined connection to his idol, Carlos the Jackal."

"Charming," she muttered under her breath.

Carlos stopped before them, sweeping Maddy a mocking bow, but the look in his lizard's eyes as he met Jake's was distinctly challenging. "El Patrón has a message for you, *amigo,*" he said amiably enough.

Jake controlled the start of irritation, the very real anger that had swept over him as Carlos's leer glanced off the set face of the woman beside him. Carlos fancied himself a ladies' man, and there were few ladies who disputed him. Would the still, set face of the woman beside him hide a reluctant admiration for Carlos's swagger? At least she stood a full inch taller than he—Carlos wouldn't like that.

Carlos made no effort to deliver the message, continuing to practice his leer on his companion. Jake had the strong feeling that she didn't like it, or Carlos, but that might be only wishful thinking on his part.

"A message, Carlos?" Jake prompted dryly.

Carlos roused himself. *"Dispenseme, compadre.* He said to tell you that the *gringa* is"—he paused for dramatic effect, and Jake could feel the muscles tighten beneath his loose grip—"in no way his daughter, or any kin to him." Carlos shrugged.

The swift intake of breath beside him sounded like an animal in pain. "He was sure?" Jake persisted.

"Absolutely. The *gringa* is not his daughter. Therefore"—Carlos grinned, an essentially evil grin—"she is a spy."

CHAPTER SEVEN

Maddy had spent more comfortable evenings. Carlos's pronouncement had become the accepted fact. Even Ramon no longer looked on her with quite such deference. The churchwomen kept their distance, albeit a sympathetic one, and the good doctor kept on drinking.

Jake had taken her back to the communal room in the basement of the old hacienda, leaving her there to Enrique's reluctant attention, his glowering face at odds with the benign ET T-shirt. She could only guess that Luis had taken his place at the gates, and she couldn't decide which one was worse. At least Luis hadn't been partial to using his rifle barrel as a cattle prod.

So there she sat, in miserable, confused silence, thinking that she would have given ten years of her life to have someone to talk to. Someone who could help her deal with the fact that her father, the man who had once been the center of her universe, the man who had abandoned her when she was at her most vulnerable age, had once again denied her.

Not that she should be surprised. He'd made no effort to contact her in the ensuing years, no effort to respond to the few letters she'd sent him. Of course it was a matter of debate whether he'd received those letters. In the first few years of his self-imposed exile he'd moved around quite a bit. It wasn't until the mid-seventies that he'd finally allied himself with San Pablo and all its problems.

If only one, just one of those damned, suspicious people would believe her, would even give her the benefit of the doubt, she thought. Ramon had been inclined to at first, but not since Lizard Eyes's pronouncement, and the embarrassed, sidelong glances of the motley group were more infuriating than reassuring.

It didn't help that Carlos the Jackal sat across from her, dividing his attention between a leering regard for El Patrón's smugly flirtatious wife and a cold-eyed sneer at her stepdaughter. As Maddy caught the cold, lizardy gaze she felt a little frisson of horror run down her backbone. If the eyes were the window of the soul, then there was nobody home with Carlos the Jackal. She had the fanciful, horrifying feeling that he could kill without blinking that basilisk gaze, and that no one else would blink, either.

And for some reason it didn't help that there was no sign of Jake. Of all people, he was the one who had betrayed her, he whose memory was like a sieve and whose sense of morality was limited indeed, she thought savagely. So why in heaven's name did she wish he were there, as buffer between the ill-assorted group with their condemning expressions and her lacerated soul?

No one spoke to her through the uncomfortable meal of flour tortillas and some bland bean paste. The two churchwomen conversed quietly between themselves, Carlos and Soledad flirted, and the doctor stared into his whiskey glass and ignored his tasteless meal. Richard Feldman—El Nabo, Luis had called him—sat in the corner with Ramon and Enrique. Luis was nowhere to be seen, and that lone consolation was not enough to give Maddy any sense of comfort. One by one they drifted away, some with an apologetic glance in her direction, some with contempt, some didn't even look her way at all. Until, praise be, she was left alone with Ramon. Even Enrique was gone.

"It's a warm night," she said after a long moment.

Ramon jerked nervously, managing a wary smile. "It always is, this time of year."

Maddy pushed the sleeves of her loose cotton shirt up to her elbows, then ran a tired hand through her tangled mop of dark brown curls. "I think I would give anything for a breath of fresh air." It wouldn't do any harm to try it, she thought, gauging Ramon's reaction out of the corner of her eye.

It wasn't promising. "I'm sorry, *señorita*," he muttered. "But Murphy said you were to wait here until he came for you."

"I've been waiting here for hours," she said with an attempt at reasonableness. "It must be night already."

"It is almost ten o'clock," Ramon agreed.

Maddy sighed. "A short walk in the garden is out of the question?"

"Completely."

Maddy leaned back against the rough wall, closing her eyes. If she really were a San Pablan Mata Hari, sent to dispatch Samuel Eddison Lambert to his ancestors, would she be sitting there so meekly, with only a teenage boy guarding her? Granted, he did have a rather nasty-looking gun tucked in his ragged jeans. And granted, she had little doubt that even a boy of seventeen or eighteen had killed in this war-torn country. But killing another

89

soldier was a great deal different from shooting an unarmed female.

Not that she could count on that. If she made a run for it she might very well end up with a bullet between her shoulder blades, and her father had yet to prove that he'd be worth that sacrifice. He had yet to prove he was worthy of her crossing the street for him, much less dragging herself down to San Pablo and being put through the gauntlet of everyone's disbelief and suspicions.

If and when she got out of that mess, she promised herself grimly, if and when she ascertained that her father was in decent enough health, then she would turn her back on him and on Jake Murphy, and never again would she let the memories drift back into her consciousness. She had had enough of Sam Lambert and his ideologies.

She looked over at Ramon. His thin dark face was shadowed with exhaustion, his head dropping slightly on a narrow neck that seemed almost too frail to support it. He was sitting on the rough stone floor, leaning against the wall, his arms hanging limply by his side. Maddy watched with fascination as he struggled with a huge yawn and lost the battle. He looked up at her, smiling sheepishly.

"You're tired, Ramon," she said softly, feeling deliciously insidious.

"We all are, *señorita*. Most particularly Murphy. There are not enough of us for guard duty." He yawned again.

"When did you last get a good night's sleep?"

"I don't remember." He shrugged, then grinned up at her sleepily. "Murphy says this will all be over before long. Then I will get a chance to sleep all I want. I can only pray to God that it won't be an eternal sleep."

Sudden guilt assailed her. "Me too." She leaned forward, resting her arms on the rough wood table in front

90

of her, listening to the imperceptible sounds of the night. The distant scrape and clatter from the kitchen and the fierce-looking old woman who accepted no assistance in her kingdom. The faint echo of nightbirds out past the thick walls. No voices, no footsteps. Nothing but the unexpected, faint sound of a snore.

Slowly she turned. Ramon's head had fallen forward, his eyes were shut, and his breathing was deep and steady. "Ramon?" she said, her voice a thin thread of sound in the stillness of the room.

No answer. She tried it slightly louder, and he responded with a snort and a minor shifting of position. The gun at his hip scraped the floor, and still he slept on, oblivious.

Why the hell did she feel guilty? Maddy demanded of herself as she slowly rose from the rough wooden bench. Why did she feel like the wicked adventuress everyone believed her to be? She was doing the only thing possible to prove her innocence. Jake refused to believe her, refused to let her anywhere near her father. And Sam Lambert himself hadn't recognized her. Her only hope was to make her way through the smaller courtyard, up the crumbling steps to his bedside. After all, her father was almost seventy and in poor health, and the distance from that third-floor bedroom to the ground was substantial. It was probably just too far for him to see. Once he saw her up close he couldn't fail to recognize her. She simply hadn't changed that much in fourteen years.

Ramon didn't stir as she tiptoed out of the room, her sandaled feet silent on the long flight of stairs that seemed cut into the rock. It was dark and eerie. The electric lights were dim and intermittently placed. Maddy breathed a sigh of relief as she made it to the first floor without encountering anyone. They must be all locked away in their rooms in this bleak fortress, and she couldn't blame them. If she had her choice she wouldn't be there at all, and she sympathized with their trying to avoid each other's less than enthralling company.

The locked door to the courtyard wasn't where she remembered it. Of course she hadn't been paying proper attention at the time. All her thoughts and emotions had been tied up with the man taking her there. She was a complete washout as a spy, she thought miserably. She couldn't even remember the most essential things. She might as well go back down and wake Ramon up, may as well stop trying to convince Jake of anything he didn't want to believe.

Turning a corner, she headed back down a hall she'd already traversed twice in her search for the garden. And there, recessed into the wall where she'd passed it without seeing, was the peeling green door that led to the garden. With a padlock uniting the heavy chain that festooned it.

She let out a miserable little moan that broke the stillness of the darkened hallway, and then swallowed it as she realized that the padlock wasn't fastened. And why should it be? The only danger in their midst had a constant guard. Never mind that that guard was a teenage boy in the advanced stages of exhaustion who'd fallen asleep and let his vicious prisoner escape.

Very carefully she slid the padlock from the links of chain, letting the heavy steel swing silently to the floor. The wide wooden bar was another barrier, and she could feel the splinters dig into her palms as she shoved it upward, straining against its stubborn tightness. The two heavy bolts were rusty and hard from disuse and shrieked in the stillness. Maddy tugged at the door, but it didn't budge.

Maddy pulled at the door, hard, but it remained firm. She yanked at the door, throwing all her weight behind it, and with damnable perversity it flew open, out of her hands, banging against the wall with a crash that doubtless could be heard throughout the three floors and meandering ells of the old villa.

Maddy didn't wait for pursuit. The garden was brightly lit from the almost full moon, the outer stairway hidden in the shadows. She was through the door like a shadowy wraith herself, only vaguely aware of the figure that had raced down the stairs in her direction. Her white shirt stood out like a beacon in the moonlight as she ran through the tangled growth, the stairway beckoning her. She heard a shout behind her, calling her name, and she knew it was Jake, and that he was close behind her. With a burst of speed she leaped ahead, over a low-growing bush, suddenly desperate.

It all happened at once. She heard his voice directly behind her. A hand clamped down on her shoulder, spinning her around, a heavy body slammed into hers, knocking her to the ground and flattening her beneath it, and the sudden whine of a bullet sped past her head as she fell.

She opened her mouth to scream, but his hand clamped across it, just as his heavy weight pressed her into the dusty ground. She could hear his voice in her ear, feel the moist warmth of his breath. "If you make a noise, a sound, even a tiny movement, I'll snap your neck."

She didn't believe him. His hand was on her mouth, not her neck, the other arm holding her tightly against his body. She also wasn't about to test her theory. She looked up into his eyes in the dark, moonlit night, her own mutely pleading. "Will you do as I tell you?" His voice was no more than a thread of sound. "Blink your eyes twice if you will."

Dutifully she did so, and his hand slowly pulled away from her mouth. "That's better," he whispered. "Because they're waiting to shoot again—the slightest sound, the tiniest movement, and we'll both be Swiss cheese. And I'm not ready to die."

There was a stone beneath her shoulder blade, but she couldn't shift, even if she'd wanted to. Her rib was throbbing again, and she tried to concentrate on that pain, on the grinding beneath her back. But all she could think about was the feel of his hips weighing hers down, his long legs that lay on top of hers, of the warmth of his skin where it touched hers and the strength in his arms. And the smothering, enveloping weight of him, pinning her there.

She couldn't help the words that slipped out. The whole situation was absurdly melodramatic. "Do you know what the definition of a gentleman is?" she grated in a tone barely audible. "It's a man who takes his weight on his elbows."

He laughed then. It made no sound, but she could feel his stomach vibrate against hers, and for a brief moment his cold, merciless eyes lit up. "Sorry, lady." He bent down so that his mouth hovered directly above hers. "But I've never been a gentleman."

His breath smelled just lightly of whiskey. It was a pleasant smell, faintly erotic, mixing with the heat of the night and the overwhelming scent of the flowers. Wild gardenias and roses and something else she didn't quite recognize. Maddy lay beneath him, conscious of a thousand strange and maniacal longings. She wanted to bridge that gap, press her mouth against his, she wanted to wrap her long legs around his and pull him into her,

94

she wanted to weep in his arms. She stared up at him, saying nothing.

"We'll wait till the moon goes behind a cloud," he continued softly, "and then we'll run for it. I'm going to hold on to your wrist, so you'd better be prepared to be fast. I'll break your arm before I let go."

"I'm sure you would and probably enjoy doing it."

He smiled down at her then, a slow, lazy smile, and the weight against her seemed to heat and expand. "Don't tempt me, lady. I warned you about snipers."

"So you did. You also didn't give me any choice."

The light dimmed slightly, and he looked upward. There were fitful clouds, none that seemed large enough to do the trick. "We may be here for a while."

"Great," she muttered.

"You asked for it. You can suffer the consequences. Of course, we can always try something else. I could let you continue heading toward the staircase, and while they're busy shooting at you in your damned white shirt I can make it safely back into the villa."

He was bluffing, she knew that full well. She'd played poker herself, played it with him years ago in that cool dusty house by her father's swimming pool. "All right," she said. "Get off me."

The speed at which he began to comply took her by surprise, and she reached out to clutch his shoulders before she could think twice. He laughed, that silent, demoralizing little laugh. "Maybe next time," he suggested.

"I wouldn't want to make your life too easy," she said in dulcet tones. "I'm sure I'm an added complication, and—"

His hand covered her mouth again, and she barely controlled the strong urge to bite it. "Get ready to run," he whispered in her ear, and she could feel his muscles tense in the heavy body that still covered hers. His hand reached down and caught her wrist, just as the moon disappeared behind the clouds, plunging the garden into darkness.

They flew across the wide expanse of garden, there was no other word for it. Maddy's sandaled feet barely touched the ground as she raced after Jake's dark figure, her wrist felt like it was caught in a steel trap, and she held her breath throughout the headlong dash, her ears straining for the sound of gunfire, her body ready to feel the recoil from a thousand bullets.

But none came. Before she even realized it they were through the door, the heavy wood slammed shut behind them, and she had collapsed up against the wall, her breath coming in rapid, frightened pants, her eyes huge, her wrist still imprisoned in Jake's grip.

He dropped it without looking at her, locking the door again, setting the wooden bar in place, this time fastening the redoubtable padlock. Then he turned to her, and Maddy realized with a sudden start that the danger was far from over.

"Who was watching you?" There was no room for evasion in that rough demand, no possibility of not answering.

Fortunately she wasn't given the choice. Ramon appeared out of the shadows, his head hung in shame, guilt and despair written on his dark young face. "It was me, Murphy. I failed you."

Murphy didn't contradict him, didn't say a thing. He just stood there watching him out of dark, fathomless eyes.

"It wasn't his fault," Maddy broke in, the oppressive silence unnerving. "You should have known he'd be no match against the Mata Hari of San Pablo."

But Ramon would hear none of it. "I have no excuse, Murphy. I fell asleep. I know what the punishment is for falling asleep during guard duty."

"No," Maddy shrieked. "It wasn't his fault. He was exhausted, he hasn't had enough sleep—"

"None of us has," Murphy said, and his voice was deadly. "Ramon is right, he has no excuse."

"But you can't—"

"Be quiet." Jake's voice was low, harsh, and completely quelling. She closed her mouth, glaring up at him mutinously as he turned back to the miserable boy. "Go back to the common room. I'll be down before long."

"*Sí*, Murphy." Shoulders back, head straight, Ramon turned and disappeared back down the stairs, like a soldier marching to his doom. Maddy watched him leave with a sense of panic.

"You can't kill him," she said, her voice little more than a plea. "It wasn't his fault, I took advantage of him. . . ."

"Then it is time you learned that others might have to pay the price for your thoughtlessness," he said. "Come along."

"You can't kill him," she said again. "I won't let you."

He'd turned away, but at that stubborn note he turned back to look at her. "And how do you intend to stop me?"

It was a reasonable enough question, one for which she had no answer. She stared up at him, despair and anger fighting for control. "I don't know," she said. "But I will."

To her amazement a wry smile lit the dark corners of his face for a moment. "Very fierce from the Mata Hari of San Pablo," he murmured, his voice strangely like a caress. "Have no fear, *pequeña,* I am not going to kill

97

young Ramon. Nor do I eat children for breakfast. I'm not one of Ortega's Gray Shirts."

If he expected her to bristle at the mention of her supposed lover, he was doomed to disappointment. She returned his smile with a brilliant one of her own. So grateful was she that she didn't fight him when he took her wrist and led her up the wide staircase.

"Where are you taking me?" she questioned after her first relief had worn off, following him docilely enough around the corner and down one dark, narrow alleyway of a hall.

He didn't bother to turn back this time, and his voice was distantly amused. "To your quarters for the night," he replied. "My bedroom."

CHAPTER EIGHT

It did her no good at all to pull away from him as he dragged her down the hallway. He took no more notice of her than if she'd been a recalcitrant child. The hallway was shadowy and deserted, dust and the ominous sound of scratching, scurrying things adding to her rising sense of unease.

"I'm not going to sleep with you, Murphy," she said, her voice quietly defiant.

He didn't even bother to look back. The flimsy wooden door opened easily beneath his strong hand, and a moment later she was pulled into a small, barren room, the door slamming shut behind them. A dim light bulb illuminated the shabby confines, the narrow, sagging bed that was neatly made, the roughly made dresser with its scraps of paper and change, the small pile of books by the bed. It looked like a monk's cell.

"I don't give a damn whether you sleep or not," Jake replied, releasing her wrist. "I don't expect you will."

Somehow that seemed even more ominous. He looked tall and dark and very dangerous in the dimly lit bedroom, and it took all Maddy's determination not to let him frighten her.

She managed a cynical smile. "Are you planning to rape me?"

Jake's look would have withered a far braver woman. "No. I'm planning to ensure myself a good night's sleep. Since it appears I can't trust anyone to keep a good watch on you, I'm going to have to do it myself."

"If you're watching me how will you be able to sleep?"

His smile wasn't reassuring. "I'm going to tie you to the bed. You won't be able to unfasten the ropes without waking me."

"You wouldn't dare!"

"Spare me your dramatics. I'd dare just about anything," he said in a weary voice. "Do you need to use the bathroom?"

"No!"

"No? If I were you I wouldn't let pride and temper let you in for an even more uncomfortable night than I've already got planned. I won't take too kindly to being woken up at three in the morning to take you to the bathroom." His face and voice were implacable, and no more threat was necessary. "Do you need to go or not?"

It would have been stupid beyond belief to say no again. Her eyes felt swollen and gritty from the contact lenses, and if her bladder wasn't in immediate need she certainly wasn't going to last the night. Besides, there might be a window or another unguarded doorway to the bathroom. They were on the second floor—one flight away from her father.

"Yes." She glared at him. "And I need my purse."

"Why? You don't have any kind of weapon in there—I checked."

She'd already seen him pawing through her purse, but his offhanded announcement infuriated her anyway. "I need my contact lens case."

For a moment he paused, arrested, and those distant hazel eyes of his looked into hers. "Oh," he said, and his voice sounded strange, like a man who'd just found the answer to a puzzle. Before she could even begin to guess what was going on behind his impassive face he shrugged. "You'll have to make do with two water glasses. I don't know where your purse is any more."

"But my passport, my money . . ."

"I have your passport, Allison Henderson," he replied with that cynical grin. "I imagine Carlos has your money. For now you've got more important things to worry about."

"Such as?"

"Such as how you're going to manage to sleep with your wrists tied to the bedpost." Once more his hand clamped around her wrist like a manacle as he started for the door.

"Why don't you just use handcuffs?" she snapped, making no effort to break away this time. She'd already learned it was useless.

"I would but I don't happen to have any. I'm going to have to make do with rope," he replied in that raspy voice that had once delighted her. "Do you want me to tie you up now? It might make your time in the bathroom somewhat difficult."

"What? You aren't coming in with me?" she said in her snottiest voice. "I can't believe that you'd trust me."

"I don't." He'd stopped outside a narrow door halfway down the hall. "But considering there's no window and no other exit, I'll take the chance. Unless you want me to come in?"

She didn't dignify that with an answer. She slammed the door behind her, noting with despair the lack of a simple lock. The room was small and dark and dirty, and she went through her ablutions hurriedly, washing her face and patting it dry with the loose tail of her cotton tunic. A sharp rap on the door made her jump, and a moment later Jake's strong hand appeared through the crack with two dirty glasses.

She accepted them without a word of thanks, slamming the door shut, half hoping she'd catch his wrist in it. But he was too fast for her, and she had to content herself with the noise it made.

If she'd felt impotent and angry before, taking out her colored contact lenses made it far, far worse. She could see, but things tended to take on a blur around the edges, and the lack of sharpness to her vision tended to leave her feeling vulnerable and unarmed. Leaning over the small, dirty sink, she stared at her reflection, at the eyes that were now a chocolate brown rather than green in her narrow, exhausted face. She'd managed to wash the sweat streaks off, but beneath the golden tan the pallor of exhaustion and fright lurked. Her eyes were wide and far too expressive, and her pale mouth looked much too helpless. She gritted her teeth, hoping for a stronger look. It only made her look more frightened.

Without warning the door opened. "Come along, lady," Jake drawled. "Time for bed."

She turned to look up at him, blinking rapidly through her near-sighted eyes. "I don't suppose you could find my extra pair of glasses either?"

He shrugged. "Maybe tomorrow. You won't be needing to see anything tonight."

With a docility she hated, she followed him back down the hallway to the small room. "Are you alone on this floor?"

"We're alone," he corrected. "And only in this wing. The others are within screaming distance."

"And will they respond if I scream?" She wouldn't let him frighten her, she told herself fiercely.

He shut the door behind them, leaning back against it, and a smile played about his mouth. "I was thinking you'd be happier if it was me screaming."

"I'd like that fine."

"Well, that'll give you something to fantasize about while you're trying to sleep," he replied, unmoved. "You can daydream about getting your revenge on my unrepentant soul. In the meantime, take off your clothes."

"What?"

"You heard me. Take off your clothes. I have no intention of sleeping with someone wearing all that. Nights are hot here." He moved away from the door, and for a moment she considered running for it, then gave up the idea. He'd catch her before she was even halfway to the door. Those hazel eyes of his saw everything and more. He was rummaging through the rough-hewn dresser, and a moment later he tossed her a soft cotton shirt. "You can wear this. It should be cool enough."

"Go to hell, Murphy."

"Of course I can always undress you myself. You won't like it, but then, pleasing you is not a very high priority with me right now."

She didn't doubt him for a moment. "Could you leave the room?"

"Not without tying you up, and you'd have a hell of a time changing with your wrists bound."

She tried again, a little desperately. "Could you turn your back?"

He let out a weary, long-suffering sigh, and without a word turned his back. "Now," he ordered.

She stood very still in the center of the room, fighting against anger and fear and panic. Even with his back turned she felt vulnerable. She knew very well he would undress her if she refused; he certainly was going to tie her to the bed. The very thought was humiliating, and yet for some strange reason Murphy seemed to be trying to make it less so. His attitude was very matter-of-fact, free from sexual innuendoes or any other kind of sexual threat. She didn't know whether to be relieved or offended.

She had no choice. Slowly she began to undo the shirt, a button at a time, keeping her eyes downcast. Not that it would matter, she thought wryly. He could watch her if he wanted and there was nothing she could do about it. She'd just undress quickly and efficiently and put on the enveloping shirt he'd thrown at her, and if he was standing there peeking with a salacious grin on his face she wouldn't have to see it.

Without hesitation she pulled her shirt over her head, wincing slightly as her rib pained her. She reached for Jake's shirt, determined to remove her bra only when she was modestly covered with the new clothing, when he moved quickly, and she had to accept the fact that he'd been watching her after all.

She was unprepared, and for a moment she thought he was going back on his promise not to rape her. She shrieked, but the hands that caught her arms were gentle, not rough, and up close she could see that the expression on his dark, shuttered face was a deep, concerned anger, not unbridled lust.

"How did this happen?" His voice was low and gravelly as his long, warm fingers delicately probed her rib cage beneath the lacy bra.

She winced, looked down, and winced again. A large purple bruise had stained her ribs, spreading from where Enrique's rifle barrel had connected. The sight of his long, dark fingers moving gently against the bruise gave her an odd feeling in the pit of her stomach, one she told herself was pain.

She still hadn't answered, and he looked up. It must have been her nearsightedness that made him look like that, she thought. Surely Jake Murphy no longer cared that much for her. He didn't even know who she was.

"Who did it?" There was no way she could not answer. His voice sounded calm, matter-of-fact as he probed the bruise, and she wondered if she'd imagined that sudden, blinding rage. "Was it Carlos?"

"No. Enrique, when I came through the gate. I dropped my hands for a moment. Maybe he thought I was going for a gun or something."

"Or maybe he didn't." His hands left her, and he reached down for the shirt, tossing it to her. "I don't think it's broken. Cracked maybe. We'll see how you feel tomorrow. If you want I can tape it for you."

"What about Dr. Milsom?"

"At this hour Doc isn't much use to anyone." He turned his back then, moving toward the narrow, deepset window to look out into the darkness. He stood there, motionless, as Maddy quickly made use of the time to pull the clean shirt over her head.

It hurt her rib to snake her arm under and unclasp the bra. She dropped it on the floor, undid her jeans, and slid them down her legs. The shirt came well below her hips, affording her modesty enough, she supposed. She looked back at Jake's back, opened her mouth to tell him she was ready, then closed it again. He looked dark and removed there in the corner by the window, almost as if he'd forgotten she was there. Why couldn't she find comfort in the notion?

She picked up her discarded clothes and began folding

them, and at the sound Murphy turned back to her. There was a sudden, constrained silence. "If I promised not to leave, not to try to escape, would you not tie me?" she found herself asking in a quiet voice.

He shook his head. "I can't take that chance."

"But you could put a guard outside the door. . . ."

"There already is one. You're too persuasive, lady," he said gently, and she thought she could see real regret in those fathomless eyes of his. "Lie down."

He had a coil of thin rope in his hands, and as he advanced on her she knew a sudden moment of panic. "Don't do this, Murphy. Please, I—"

The last trace of sympathy left his impassive face. "Do you want me to have to gag you? Lie down."

Being tied was bad enough; she thought if he gagged her she'd go mad. It would do her no good to fight, it would only make it worse.

Without another word she lay down on the narrow bed, pulling the cotton shirt down toward her knees. With quick, quiet efficiency he tied her wrists to one plain bedpost, leaving the bonds loose enough not to inhibit circulation.

Her eyes met his for a long, silent moment. "I'll never forgive you for this," she said.

"No, I don't expect you will." He rose to his full height, looking down at her. "There'll be a guard at your door so I wouldn't try anything foolish if I were you."

"Where are you going?" If his presence was infuriating, his absence was terrifying.

"A question of discipline," he said in a deceptively mild voice.

Ramon, her mind shrieked. "Don't kill him."

Murphy's smile wasn't the slightest bit reassuring. "I'll try not to." And then he was gone.

She heard the low murmur of voices outside her door, assuring her that she did indeed have a guard. And if it was Luis or Carlos, the last thing she wanted was to have either of them come in and find her bound and helpless in Jake Murphy's bed.

Except that she wasn't particularly helpless or tightly bound. If she worked at it for any length of time she could unfasten the loose knots at her wrists. He hadn't tied her ankles, and she could scrunch up and around into a kneeling position and work on the ropes with her teeth and . . .

She dismissed the idea. Where would she go at this hour? Jake had taken her neatly folded clothes with him, and she didn't fancy wandering around that gloomy old fortress dressed in panties and a loose shirt. That expression on his face as he left the room hadn't augured well for Ramon. Maddy certainly didn't want to risk having anyone else's blood on her hands. What would he do to that poor, tired boy? And even if she managed to free her hands for comfort, Jake would only tie her up again.

The dim, spare light bulb had attracted a small swarm of mosquitoes, and it wouldn't take long before they found the succulent flesh awaiting them on the bed. Maneuvering with her long legs, Maddy slid under the rough-woven sheet, catching the hem with her teeth and pulling it up around her neck. She would be a mass of welts before morning. Well, if that was the worst thing she would suffer that night she'd be doing well.

Her eyes felt gritty and tired, and she closed them, listening to the cacophony of the night, the hum of insects, the chatter of the night birds, the distant sound of an occasional human voice and the soft swish of the wind through the trees. The smell of the air was damp and sultry, perfumed by the overgrown flowers from the garden below and strangely sensuous. And there she was, half dressed, lying like a trussed chicken in Jake Murphy's bed.

It was too ridiculous to worry about. Hunching up, she rested her head against her arms, closing her eyes in sudden weariness. Tomorrow everything would make sense. Tomorrow she would see her father, tomorrow Jake would apologize profusely, and tomorrow she'd be on her way, back to La Mensa and eventually L.A. Wouldn't she?

There were no guarantees, but she couldn't allow herself to panic. Despite Jake's threat she knew quite well she wouldn't see him until tomorrow. She'd have a relatively undisturbed night's sleep, if she could just ignore the uncomfortable position. The thick cotton cover was hot, but the mosquitoes would be worse. Ignoring the brightness of the dim light bulb, she willed herself to sleep.

Willing herself to sleep did her as much good as would winning the Irish sweepstakes in her current situation. An hour later she was lying there, eyes wide, staring at the bare light bulb, when she heard the hushed mumble of conversation, the quiet scrape of the door.

He didn't look like a man who'd just killed a teenage boy. But looks could be deceiving. Jake moved closer to her in the dimly lit room, his face impassive. "Still awake?"

"Did you kill him?"

He smiled, a wry, self-deprecating smile, and held out his hands. They were cut, bruised and swollen, but their significance was momentarily lost on Maddy. "No, I didn't kill him."

"What happened to your hands?" It came out sounding far too concerned, but Jake ignored it as he began unbuttoning the loose khaki field shirt.

"I thought I told you. A minor problem of discipline."

"You beat him up?" She was horrified.

"Better than killing him." Jake dropped the large, ugly-looking gun on the table beside the bed. "He deserved far worse."

"For God's sake!" she cried. "He's just a kid!"

"Old enough to know better." The knife clattered to the table beside the gun, the shirt was tossed in the corner, and he began undoing his belt.

"All he did was fall asleep. You didn't have to hurt him."

Murphy dropped the belt on the floor, then sat down on the bed to remove his boots. "I didn't hurt Ramon. I sent him to bed."

"But then . . . what happened to your hands?"

He turned to look at her, and in the dim light his eyes were cool and distant. He said only one word. "Enrique."

There was no reply she could make to that. He'd risen again, his hands on his zipper, and she let out a small shriek of protest. He ignored it, stripping his pants off, flicking off the overhead light and climbing into bed with her.

She lay very still, waiting for the assault she knew would come. There was no way she could fight him, no way she could stop him from doing what he wanted. She lay there, rigid, waiting.

She had a long time to wait. The tropical darkness closed around them like a velvet shawl, warm and soft and silent. He made no move, no sound as the minutes ticked by, until finally Maddy realized that he wasn't going to touch her, wasn't going to do anything more than fall asleep beside her.

Slowly, bit by bit, her tensed muscles began to relax. He lay very still, his breathing even, but she knew he was as wide awake as she was. His body jerked suddenly, then was still again, and the silence lengthened.

"Jake," she said softly, half convinced he was asleep.

He wasn't. "What?"

"Do you remember the night of my birthday? When you picked me up at the country club? I was with Eric Thompson, and you took me away from him and drove me home in my VW and kissed me."

There was a long silence from the man lying beside her, and she waited. "Lady," he said finally, wearily, "stop trying to convince me. Anyone could know about that night."

"But how? I never told anyone."

She could feel the shift of the mattress as he turned to look at her, and in the murky darkness she could feel his eyes on her. "But I did," he replied.

There was no answer she could make to that, none that she cared to make. Clearly the high point of her adolescence was nothing more than a locker room joke to him. He probably wouldn't even believe her when her father recognized her. He must have some deep-rooted need not to know her. The thought was little consolation in the lonely darkness of the night.

The scratching sound brought her suddenly, rudely awake, and she jerked, the rope catching her arms painfully. She could tell that the man beside her was similarly alert, waiting, listening, for that sound to come again.

They weren't disappointed. Someone was at the door, turning and twisting the knob, and Maddy realized with sudden surprise that Jake had locked it when he'd returned last night. She lay there, unmoving, waiting, as she felt Jake sit up and reach for his gun.

And then the voice came. A soft, quiet, slightly drunken voice. Definitely pleading, definitely female. "Let me in, Jake. I'm so frightened and lonely. Please, darling. I don't want to be alone. Let me in." And definitely no one but Soledad Lambert.

The moon had risen, illuminating the small bedroom and Jake's wary figure. He sat there, motionless, and then his hand left the gun, and he sank down in the bed again.

"Please, Jake, let me in. No one's ever found out about you and me, you know we'd be safe. Please, baby. I need you so much. I don't want to be alone tonight. I—I can't be alone tonight. Please, Jake. Just one last time."

Maddy turned her head then, to look directly into Jake Murphy's moon-silvered eyes. She said not a word, her contempt visible enough in her dark eyes and the curl of her lip. He met that gaze, without repentance, without apology, as the eerie, pleading voice came again.

"Please, *mi amor*. I know you're in there. Don't shut me out, baby. Let me in." Her voice was getting louder, rising drunkenly, and the soft scratching on the door was turning to a pounding.

Jake sat up again, pushing the covers aside, when another voice joined Soledad's. "Come on, Soledad," Richard Feldman's light voice said. "Come back to my room. Jake's asleep. Leave him alone."

"But I don't want to go with you," she said petulantly. "I want Jake."

"But Jake doesn't want you, Soledad," he said gently. "You know that."

"Of course he wants me. He's just afraid Sam will find out. But Sam wouldn't care. He'd want me to be taken care of." The pounding began at the door again, louder this time.

"He's asleep, Soledad. Come back with me. I have some brandy in my room, and it's very quiet there. You'll be able to sleep."

"But I don't want . . ." Her voice trailed off down the hall, as Richard Feldman obviously led her away. El Nabo he might be called, but he was good at diverting drunken women, Maddy thought with gratitude.

She turned back to Jake's still figure. "You bastard. You conscienceless, miserable basard. To sleep with his wife, while all the time he trusted you, treated you far better than he ever treated his own children, loved you . . ."

"I don't owe you any explanations," he broke in harshly. "And I'm not about to give them to you. You have no right to judge me, lady. It's none of your damned business."

"You can't even defend yourself," she said in a bitter voice. "I don't understand how you can call yourself his friend."

"I've heard enough," he said, and before she realized what he was doing his mouth stopped hers quite effectively, silencing the angry, bitter words as he kissed her. His body half covered hers, and with her arms tied she couldn't dodge or avoid him. His strong hand caught her chin, holding her head still for the driving onslaught of his kiss, his tongue dipping deep into her mouth, plunging, plundering, hurting and destroying the last tiny bit of hope she had left. And for the first time that day tears came to her eyes.

He couldn't have known. The moonlight wasn't enough to illuminate the room, and the tears that spilled silently down her cheeks didn't touch him. But suddenly

112

the kiss softened, the hands gentled on her, the lips coaxed and teased and healed. And without any more thought she was kissing him back, reaching for him with her mouth while her hands were held back, seeking him out with her tongue, calling him to her in the only way she could. And suddenly it was magic again, like nothing had been since a hot August night fourteen years ago.

And yet the magic was different. An older, more mature feeling was sweeping over her, one that held the depth and promise of eternity. This wasn't a childhood crush fondly remembered, this wasn't a nostalgic trip back to adolescence. This was real and now and overwhelming. There was only the rough cotton sheet between his naked body and hers. Her shirt had come up to her waist in her sleep, and she could feel him, hot and hard and wanting against her. And she accepted that wanting, as she accepted her own, with a sudden sense of destiny.

But destiny and Jake Murphy had different plans. A moment later she was released, and he fell back on his side of the bed, not touching her, his breath coming heavily in the silent darkness. They lay there without a word, and Maddy could feel her pulse racing through her body, feel the tight constriction of her nipples against the soft cotton shirt. And she waited.

A low, mocking laugh came from the man beside her. "You aren't going to seduce me into believing you either," he drawled.

"Me seduce you?" she cried in a soft shriek. "You rotten, miserable—"

"Watch it," he warned. "You should remember how I stopped your mouth a few minutes ago."

She shut her mouth abruptly, and he laughed again, a slightly strained sound. "That's right. Go to sleep. Your virtue is safe with me." And the bed creaked as he rolled over and away from her.

She stared at his turned back balefully for a moment. In the moonlit darkness she could see the smooth curve of his shoulder, the long brown hair dark against the whiteness of the small, lumpy pillow. He was close enough that she could reach out and bite him or reach out and kiss that smooth, tanned skin.

She lay very still. Tomorrow, she promised herself. Tomorrow she'd make him sorry. With that wistful thought she fell asleep. Leaving Jake Murphy to lie there, hollow-eyed, into the dawn.

CHAPTER NINE

He was up long before she awoke, moving silently around the shabby little room, staring out into the early-morning sunlight. It was still cool and damp, with none of the blazing humidity that would assault them later in the day. Jake leaned against the open window, barefoot, barechested, the khakis riding low on his narrow hips, as he stared unseeing at the garden beneath him.

He knew he was simply putting off the inevitable. Sooner or later he was going to have to face Sam Lambert, sooner or later he was going to have to let the woman sleeping in his bed go free. Events were crowding in on him, people and problems that could no longer be resolved were sweeping over the small fortress, and soon —today, tomorrow, or next week—it was all going to blow up in his face. And he was so damned tired of fighting.

He knew the moment she woke up. He could feel those warm brown eyes on his back, the eyes that yesterday had been uncharacteristically green. Colored contact lenses, he mused. He should have guessed. And for the twentieth time he wished things could be different. But he knew they couldn't. Once more he affixed a bland, uninformative expression on his face as he turned to greet her.

She was staring at him owlishly, the nearsighted eyes vague and surprisingly endearing. "I don't suppose you feel like finding my glasses?" she said in an admirably caustic tone of voice. She blew it by yawning in the middle of her question like a small child, and the tousled dark curls framed her sleepy face like a halo. She was sitting up, the covers pulled around her like a shawl, and the ropes dangled uselessly from the bedpost.

"I'll ask Carlos," he said, moving across the room towards her. "Did you sleep well?" The ridiculously polite question amused him, but he waited patiently for her answer.

"I did. Once I got the ropes untied."

"I figured you'd settle down once you managed it," he agreed gravely. "No ill effects from your night?"

"None. And you?" She was matching him, cool for cool, and the thought amused him even more.

"Once Soledad was distracted I slept very well," he lied, remembering the damnably disturbing feel and scent of the body that slept so soundly next to his. On an impulse he sat down on the bed next to her, catching her wrists in his larger hands. He watched her eyes skitter across his chest with an absurdly virginal shyness, her gaze coming to rest somewhere in the vicinity of his chin.

There were red marks on her wrists from the ropes, and he let out a soft curse as his thumbs gently rubbed the abrasions. There was no way he could or would apologize, but the touch of his hands on hers was a soothing repentance.

"Are you going to behave yourself today?" Stupid question, he told himself. She'd already proved that she wasn't about to let anything get in the way of what she wanted.

"I doubt it. When are you going to let me see my father?"

"Still at it? You'll see El Patrón when and if he's ready, and not before. In the meantime, I would suggest you be very demure. Neither Enrique or Ramon is too pleased with you."

"And what about your mistress?" she demanded, pulling her hands away from him.

He smiled blandly. "Which one?"

"My father's wife, of course," she snapped back. "I didn't realize there were any other wives for you to plunder, but then, I haven't been here long. Ramon's girlfriend, perhaps? Carlos's mother?"

His laughter filled the room, suddenly lighthearted. "If you had ever seen Carlos's mother you would never have such wild imaginings. No, *mi amor,* there is no one else to attack you but your supposed stepmother. Soledad won't like the fact that you spent the night in my room, but she won't do anything about it. If you'd been listening carefully to her wine-induced pleas you would have realized that anything between us is long in the past. Not that I need to explain to you, even if you were Madelyn Lambert."

"At least you finally admit such a person does exist," she said shrewdly, and Jake winced.

"I admit she existed."

"And you called me Maddy when you caught me in the garden last night," she continued, suddenly remembering.

He shrugged. "I was foolishly intent on saving your life. I didn't want you to end up with a bullet in your back because I happened to call you Allison."

117

She was sitting very still in the narrow bed, watching him out of those huge, cool eyes of hers. "If you're expecting me to thank you for saving my life you're wasting your time."

"I expect nothing of you." He was being a fool, and he knew it, sitting there on the bed with her and wasting his time trying to get her to smile. He had to get up and away from her as fast as he could.

"Ortega has trained you well," he murmured, rising, a small distant part of his brain taking note of the way she bristled furiously. "But I'm not about to spend the morning flirting with you. Someone will bring you water and fresh clothes, someone else will bring you breakfast. In the meantime I suggest you sit there and meditate on your sins and what excuse you're going to give Ortega for failing to accomplish your mission."

"Go to hell."

"So you've said." He reached down a hand and gently brushed the tangled curls away from her face. It took her a moment too long to bat his hand away. "Behave yourself."

It was an endless morning. A sullen, silent but unscathed Ramon brought her a bowl of warm water to wash in and the glasses containing her contact lenses. Her suitcase also appeared, having been thoroughly ransacked by rough hands, but she greeted its arrival with her first feelings of optimism. The sponge bath felt marvelous, despite her fear that Jake might walk in on her at any moment, and the rough white cotton dress that was nothing more than an oversized shirt was cool and flattering. She refused to consider why it would matter as she carefully inserted her lenses and stared at her reflection in the grainy mirror above his dresser.

She looked better than last night, but that wasn't saying a whole lot. Her short-cropped brown hair framed a troubled face, and even her most self-assured expression couldn't quite banish the fleeting sense of unease that lingered around the edges of her eyes.

All her books were still in the car, along with her doubtless melted candy bars and hot Perrier. Grabbing the first of the pile of books that lay beside Jake's bed, she climbed back onto the mattress, her long legs stretched out in front of her, wiggling her toes nervously. She was hungry, she was nervous, and she was lonely. Much as she hated the man Jake had become, she wished he hadn't abandoned her up there in his barren cell. She wished he were there to argue with her, to flirt with her with those cold, merciless eyes of his, to kiss her again. . . .

That set the seal on it, she thought grimly. There must be insanity in her family. First Samuel Eddison Lambert turns his back on almost limitless money and power to immure himself in a Third World revolution that was bound to kill him sooner or later, and then his idiot daughter starts having erotic fantasies about a man who was treating her worse than any man had ever treated her in her life. Sado-masochism was an ugly word, but she considered it unflinchingly and then rejected it.

It wasn't when Jake hurt her or threatened her that she got turned on. It was the memory of her adolescence and his sweetly tender charm. It was the hungry demand of his kiss, once he'd gotten past his anger. It was the hint of a look in his eyes, when he thought she wasn't watching.

Still and all, there was no room for her in Jake's life, not at this late stage. He'd gone past the last vestiges of civilization. The hacienda was a final outpost, and its leader a half-savage mercenary with little resemblance to the somber-suited Secret Service man who'd filled her childhood fantasies. And the sooner she got away from him, the sooner she'd realize it.

It was only logical she'd be fascinated with him, she reassured herself, ignoring the book that lay opened in her lap. He'd always been someone of mythic proportions, and she was alone, vulnerable, in a country where danger surrounded her on all sides. Never mind the fact that John Thomas Murphy was the greatest threat of all. From the moment she'd seen him again after fourteen long years she'd felt drawn to him, inexorably. And the only way to break that tie was to get out.

Would it be better or worse once he knew who she was? He seemed more than capable of shutting off any trace of human tenderness, concern, or emotion. Their shared history would have little effect on a man of his determination.

She was still staring toward the window that overlooked the garden, a troubled expression on her face, when the thin wooden door opened once again. She didn't bother to turn, half aware of the picture she must present, sitting on his bed with her long bare legs stretched out in front of her.

"Get up, *gringa,*" Soledad ordered. "This tray is heavy."

It said a lot for her sense of isolation, Maddy thought with a trace of humor, that she would even greet the advent of her sullen stepmother with gratitude. She was off the bed in a flash, taking the tray from Soledad's hands and setting it on the dresser.

"Thank you for bringing me something to eat," she said with a real attempt at friendliness. "I was starving."

Soledad sniffed, eyeing the bed with distaste as she moved to appropriate the only chair in the room. "If it was up to me I'd let you starve," she said sweetly. "We scarcely have enough food to go around as it is. We can't afford to feed another mouth that shows up, unwanted and unasked."

Maddy looked down at the chipped plate, the dried-up flour tortilla and the everpresent bean paste, and heaved a resigned sigh. The cup of coffee was black and covered with a thin film of oil, and it smelled more like chickory than coffee beans, but beggars can't be choosers. She tried the coffee first, swallowing it with a shudder. "I'm sorry to be a burden," she said, trying again. "Perhaps if you could talk Jake into letting me see El Patrón . . ."

"No one talks Jake Murphy into anything," Soledad said. "You'll see him when Jake wants you to, and not any sooner."

"But couldn't you talk to Sam? You're his wife. Surely he'd listen to you."

The smile that curved Soledad's pretty face did little to reassure Maddy. "I, also, see El Patrón when Jake decrees. You fail to understand, *gringa*. Samuel Lambert is sick. Is probably dying. Even if Murphy wanted to let you see him it would partially depend on Doc and what kind of day Sam is having."

"And what kind of day is he having?"

Soledad shrugged. "I don't know. I haven't seen him in over a week."

And haven't missed him a bit, Maddy thought caustically. "So I just have to sit and wait?" She put the coffee down half finished. Even for the sake of the blessed caffeine she couldn't stomach the foul brew.

"It appears you have no choice. But trust me, *gringa*, you won't have long. You may wish you did, but . . ." She let the sentence trail.

"What do you mean?"

"The government forces are getting closer. The guerrillas are determined to make a stand—Puente del Norte is as far north as they go. Sam Lambert is caught in the middle, an interfering *norteamericano* who will make a perfect martyr for the cause. When he dies, and I promise you that it will be quite soon, the Patronistas will blame the Gray Shirts, and the Gray Shirts will blame the Patronistas. And the revolution will go on."

Maddy stared at her in horrified fascination. "You talk about it as if it had no bearing on you. Don't you care?"

Once more Soledad shrugged her pretty shoulders. "I have long ago learned not to fight against what I can do nothing about. Sam won't leave, so I'll have to go without him. Plans are already being made for my escape. I expect to be a very wealthy widow before too many months pass. It will have its compensations."

Maddy gave up all pretense at friendliness. "You make me sick."

Soledad's smile was condescending. "You gringos, all so innocent, so idealistic. If you had lived with poverty, with a war that never ends, with the constant threat of death hanging over your head, you would not be so noble. You would take life's pleasures as they came to you, and accept the bad with grace."

"You seem to forget, it's my father you're talking about abandoning, my father who's going to prove the martyr for this crazy country."

"I do not forget."

"But you don't believe me," Maddy said bitterly. "I forgot this entire place seems determined to think me a liar and a spy."

"You may be a spy," Soledad murmured in a languid tone, rising from her chair with boneless grace, "but I do not think you are a liar."

122

Maddy held herself very still, scarcely daring to believe her. "Does that mean that you think I really am Sam's daughter?"

"Of course you are," Soledad said with a delicate yawn. "I've never had any doubt of that at all. But then, I've had the advantage of seeing that picture of you when you were a young girl. In a silly pink dress, all long arms and legs, great big eyes and too much hair. You still look just like that awkward girl," she said. "I recognized you the moment I saw you."

"Sam has that old picture of me?" she whispered, confusion and delight warring within her. She would never have guessed that Sam Lambert would have cared enough to keep that old photograph of her. Her brother, Stephen, had taken it during the three days he was home that summer so long ago, and it was just as Soledad described it. An innocent young girl that still looked very much like thirty-year-old Maddy Lambert.

Soledad's black eyes met hers. "Not Sam. Jake."

"What!"

"You heard me, *gringa*. It's Jake who carries your picture in his wallet like a lovesick schoolboy, and always has. Samuel isn't capable of caring for something as ordinary as a daughter. The only way you'll ever get his attention is by starting a revolution."

"I don't believe you."

Soledad smiled. "Then why don't you ask the man yourself? He's standing right behind you."

"Mi alma," Jake's rough voice broke the sudden silence, "you have a very busy mouth. It would give me great pleasure to have it silenced for you some day."

"Do not threaten me, Jake," she cooed. "I know you far too well to be frightened by empty threats. It was more than time for the little chick to know the truth. Or at least as much as you deign to tell me." She sauntered past Maddy's stunned figure. "Let me know if I can be of further service, *gringa,*" she murmured.

Slowly Maddy turned to face him. He stood there, cool, withdrawn, unrepentant. "You knew," she said. "You knew the whole time."

He didn't bother to deny it. "The moment I saw you."

"Then why . . . ?"

"Why did I lie? I tried to explain it to you, but as usual you weren't listening," he snapped. "Sam's in danger, and his daughter would be in even worse danger. Everyone wants a martyr. A dying old man would be good, his innocent young daughter would be even better. Do you think the American Congress would continue to sanction aid when an American citizen is murdered here?"

"But . . . I'm safe here."

"You're safe nowhere," he said harshly. "One of the people you had dinner with last night is here to kill Sam. And I have no way of being sure who it is." He ran a weary hand through the long brown hair, pushing it away from his darkly tanned face. "Until I am sure, no one is safe. Particularly not you, if the killer realizes you really are Sam's daughter. And he'll know very soon now."

"How?"

"Because Soledad will tell everyone she sees. I have no idea why she didn't say so at first—I have never understood her and never will. But once she decides to open her mouth there's no stopping her." Those dark hazel eyes swept over her, an unreadable expression in their depths. "You may as well see Sam. It won't do any good to put it off any longer."

She didn't move. "How long would you have put it off?"

"For as long as I could. I don't expect it could have gone on forever. Carlos has informed me that Ortega and his men are no more than twenty-five miles away. I expect we'll have some unwelcome visitors this afternoon."

"Apart from me?"

His eyes met hers. "I would have rather had a dozen Ortegas show up than you," he said in a frank voice. "But there's nothing that can be done about it now. Do you want to see your father or not?"

"He knows it's me?"

"He knows."

"And he didn't want to see me?"

Jake hesitated. "He decided to trust my judgment."

"Damn him then," she said in a small, cold voice. "And damn you too."

He stood very still watching her. "You can damn me all you want. And you can damn Sam, but you're going to see him, and you're going to put a good face on it."

"Or what?" she retorted, moving back toward the bed, determined to sit there and not move until she was good and ready.

She only got two feet. Jake's strong hands clamped down over her arms, jerking her against him. "I don't even need to go into the alternatives," he said with sinister softness. "You'll do as I say. This isn't a democracy here, lady. It's a dictatorship, and right now I'm boss. Do you understand?" He gave her a sharp, painful shake. "Do you?"

She considered kicking him, kneeing him, breaking free of his iron grip and raking her fingernails down that tanned, implacable face. She didn't believe his threats, any more than Soledad did. But some last trace of common sense stopped her.

"I understand," she said, determined to keep the sullen note out of her voice.

His hands didn't release her, his body didn't withdraw. He stood there, looking down at her, and for a fleeting moment she thought she could see that expression on his face that she'd glimpsed once before.

He was going to kiss her again, she thought. And she was going to struggle, and hit him, and yet there was nothing in the world she wanted more than to have him kiss her. She must be going crazy.

She stood there waiting, waiting for him to make the move she wanted and dreaded. And then he broke away without touching her, spinning away from her before she could see his face.

"I'll see if Sam's ready," he said over his shoulder, and was gone. Leaving her to stare after him, more lost and confused than ever.

CHAPTER TEN

For the first time in the last twenty-four hours all thoughts of Jake were effectively banished from her brain. She had spent the last half hour waiting for his return, and then followed him up the wide, littered flight of stairs to the third floor of the aging hacienda. And now she stood waiting outside the scarred, heavily guarded door of Sam Lambert's room, about to see her father for the first time in fourteen years.

She wasn't quite sure what she felt. A little numb, a little frightened, a little angry, and absurdly hopeful. Despite the fact that he'd repudiated her when she first arrived, despite the fact that he'd never answered her letters, she still had a small ounce of hope that he might be her father again, that tall, distant figure with the deep voice and the loving eyes. Her hands were shaking, and she stuffed them in the pockets of her dress.

Enrique was guarding the door, his battered, bruised face a combination of reluctant politeness and sheer rage. He stood to one side of the scarred, bolted door, his eyes straight forward. He had changed his grubby T-shirt from ET to cavorting gremlins. Maddy couldn't help but think the latter slightly more appropriate.

127

She could feel Jake behind her, his tall, lean body seemingly at ease, and she couldn't tell if the tension that permeated the area was only hers or his too. "What are we waiting for?" she asked in a subdued voice, just a decibel over a whisper.

"For Doc to say it's okay. He's not having one of his good days," Jake said in a grim voice.

"Who? Doc or my father?"

"Don't be cute—it doesn't become you," Jake said. "Do you even realize how sick your father is?"

"No."

"Well, you will soon enough." The heavy door creaked open, and Henry Milsom emerged, looking pale, hung over, and bad-tempered.

He looked Maddy up and down through red-rimmed eyes, then snorted unappreciatively. "You may as well go on in," he said abruptly in the gravelly voice that still held a trace of a southern accent.

Maddy made no move. Indeed, she couldn't with Jake's heavy hand clamped down on her shoulder.

"Is he any better?" Jake asked.

Milsom shrugged. "No. But at this point I don't think he's going to get any better. She may as well see him while he's still able to manage it. Besides, he wants her now."

Lines of dread and despair were shooting through Maddy's reed-slim body, and only the warm force of Jake's hand steadied her sudden descent into grief. How could she have finally found her father, only to lose him again?

"All right, we'll go in." Jake moved forward, but Milsom shook his head.

"No, Murphy. He wants to see her alone."

Maddy couldn't help it, she flashed a triumphant smile

128

over her shoulder at the impassive Jake. Her father finally wanted her; for once Jake Murphy took second place.

The hand released her shoulder, slowly, reluctantly, and he stepped back. "I'll wait for you here."

"You're not still afraid I'm going to run away?" she questioned cattily.

Jake's hazel eyes flickered for a moment to Enrique's bruised, sullen figure, and then back to hers. It was warning enough. Maddy swallowed, nodding slightly, and moved to the door that was still open a crack. And then she went through into the shadowy room beyond, closing the door behind her with a soft thud.

Her pulse was pounding, her heart beating rapidly, and her palms were sweaty as she slowly advanced on the hospital bed that took up only a corner of the huge, cavernous room. An abandoned wheelchair stood by the window. It must have been from there that he watched her in the garden yesterday. Watched her and decided not to see her, to lie to Carlos. Hadn't Jake told her it was for her own good? She had to remember that, block out the feelings of anger and betrayal that still simmered below the surface.

"Allison Madelyn?" He'd always called her by both names. She could recognize that voice from her childhood, even in its weakened condition, slightly patrician, slightly distant, but still her father. She could feel a sudden upsurge of joy rush through her, and she started quickly toward the bed and its shrouded figure, ready to fling herself in his arms in a reunion that was beyond anything she had dared hope.

"Are you alone?" His next words slowed her rapid pace a trifle.

"Yes."

"Good. Then come here, girl. We haven't much time, and I can't afford to waste a moment of it."

Maddy's footsteps slowed even more. For a moment she considered telling herself that it was their reunion he didn't want to squander, but already she knew otherwise. Slowly she came up to the bed, to look down into the pale, autocratic blue eyes and austere, pain-lined face of the father she hadn't seen in fourteen years. And she waited for some sign that he was glad to see her.

"You look the same," he said abruptly. "A little older, perhaps. It's a shame you don't take after your mother in looks."

Sudden rage filled Maddy. "Stephen did."

The sigh that echoed from the bed was shallow and weary. "Tell me what happened to your brother, Allison Madelyn. Your mother never would tell me all of it."

The grief was as fresh and raw as it had been that day so long ago when the word had come. "He died."

"Drugs, wasn't it?" Even in the weakened voice Maddy could hear the sneer.

"So they said." Her voice was flat and unemotional. "The autopsy said he had a combination of thirteen different drugs in his body. Enough to kill a horse. He left a note, but I never saw it. It was addressed to you."

Samuel Eddison Lambert didn't even flinch. "Stephen was a weakling," he stated.

Maddy's finely boned hands clenched into fists just out of his range of vision. "Stephen was only twenty-three years old. Don't you feel any responsibility, any guilt?"

"None," said the old man, and his blue eyes were clear and unclouded by any emotion other than fanaticism. "It was his choice, his life to squander. Everyone has a calling, and it's up to them whether they choose to heed it.

130

Are you going to let me down like he did, or are you going to prove to be stronger?"

Bastard, she thought. "How do you want me to prove it?" Her voice was cool and icily detached, and Sam Lambert, the Saint of San Pablo, nodded his approval.

"You'll do," he said. "You came here unwanted and unasked, putting everyone in even more danger. You can earn your keep."

"How?"

"There's something I want you to take back to the States with you. I want to make sure it gets into the right hands. And that means not your mother's hands. Did she put you up to coming?"

"She said you were dying."

Sam didn't even flinch. "She was right. Sooner than you think. What did she expect you to do about it?"

"Bring you back." In the face of it the idea was absurd. This sick, ascetic old man had no tie with her apart from an accident of birth. He wouldn't have gone with her if his life depended on it. As, indeed, it might.

Sam Lambert laughed, a martini-dry sound in the tropical stillness. "She still has no idea what kind of man I am. Why I'm here. Do you?" He eyed his daughter fiercely.

"Of course," she said. "You're El Patrón. The Saint of San Pablo." Her voice was cool and mocking, but Sam Lambert didn't even seem to notice.

"Exactly," he said, his pain-thinned voice filled with satisfaction. "And I need you to ensure my legacy to my children."

That did startle her out of her shell of reserve. "Your children?"

"The people of San Pablo," he clarified without a trace of shame. "I need you to take the box of candy over there

131

by the window, take it to someone important, someone who thinks as we do. We've been too long away from the States, I no longer know who the right people are. I'll have to trust you to decide."

"A box of candy?"

"Don't be obtuse, Allison Madelyn. You never were when you were younger. The candy box contains any number of important things, including a videotaped interview with me. My last interview before I die," he said dreamily. "In it I make clear just how thoroughly the government of San Pablo has violated human rights. All the proof we need is in that box. There's no way Congress will keep appropriating the money for Morosa once they find out the truth."

"You think it will all be that simple?"

Samuel looked up at his daughter's coolly distant face. "Life is never that simple," he declared. "This time I've made it simple. You'll take that box, give it to the right sort of person—a congressman, perhaps, or a news reporter—and things will fall in place just as I planned."

Maddy looked over at the box of Whitman's raspberry creams sitting beside the wheel chair, then back at her father's face. "I'll do it," she said with cold resignation. "When do I leave?"

"I knew you would. You take after me," he said with pleasure. "I was afraid you'd turn into a cowardly dreamer like your brother, but I should have known one of you would have some spark of determination in you. You'll have to be prepared to go at any time. Jake got the Mary Margarets out this morning. You and Soledad will be in the next shift. Sometime in the next couple of days, I imagine."

Maddy slowly crossed the room, retrieving the candy box. It still looked factory-sealed, and if it was slightly heavier than it should be, it wasn't such a great difference that anyone would notice. Besides, she had the feeling she wouldn't be traveling through San Pablo customs when she left.

From across the room she looked back at the small, shrunken figure of the man who had been her father. "Did you ever get my letters?" she said suddenly, cursing herself for needing to know.

"Your letters?" His voice was querulous, momentarily confused.

"I wrote you after you left. For the first year I wrote you. I never got an answer. I don't even know if you received them." She could feel the pain creeping into her voice, and carefully she snuffed it out. "I wondered whether Mother might have intercepted them."

Sam Lambert didn't even flinch. "I remember your letters now. Adolescent maunderings. You were an atrocious speller, my dear. I hope you've improved in the ensuing years."

"Did you answer them?"

He didn't hesitate. "Of course not. You and your brother were part of a life I left behind me. I had more important things to concentrate on. The emotions of two ordinary children don't mean much when weighed against the lives of thousands of San Pablans."

"No, to you I suppose they don't," she said softly, clutching the candy box in icy fingers.

"Jake agreed with me."

Maddy knew a sudden sinking in the pit of her stomach, just when she thought she was already hollow inside. "Jake?"

"You sent him a letter too."

"Did he show it to you?"

"He refused. I could well guess how it read though.

133

That pitiful passion you conceived for him was no secret, Allison Madelyn. I'm sure you were foolish enough to commit it to paper, equally misspelled."

"He must have had an amusing time at my expense."

"You haven't learned much about human nature in the last fourteen years, Allison Madelyn, if you think that. You were always Jake Murphy's tiny little island of innocence, his moment of sanity. The one part of his adult life that was untainted with guilt. At least, I presume he didn't taint you?" There was only the trace of distant curiosity in his voice.

"No, Father. It was up to other people to shatter my innocence."

He looked at her sharply. "I don't know if I'm convinced that it's gone. But I can't be bothered to find out." He closed his eyes, suddenly weary. "I think you'd better leave me now. If I feel up to it I may have you come back this afternoon. There's something else I want to tell you." He sighed, and a moment later the heavy breathing told her that he'd fallen asleep.

Maddy looked down at him for a long moment, clutching the candy box in nerveless fingers. "Tell me that you love me, old man," she whispered. "Tell me that for one moment in your miserable, holy crusade you felt a trace of human love for your daughter."

But Sam Lambert slept on, the lines of pain etched deep into his pale face.

Damn it, she was not going to cry, she told herself fiercely as she headed back toward the door. He wasn't worth it. She'd always known what he was like. This shouldn't have come as any surprise to her.

The sunlight in the upstairs hall blinded her for a moment when she stepped out of the shaded bedroom, and it took her a moment to reorient herself. Jake was leaning against the railing, smoking a thin brown cigarette, and his expression was hooded. And with a sudden, childish embarrassment Maddy remembered what Sam had said.

The eyes that missed nothing glanced down at the candy box in her hand, then away as if it were of no importance. Maddy wasn't fooled for a minute. He took her arm, though today it was slightly less of a manacle and more of a polite gesture. She knew it could change back the moment she struggled.

"How was he?" He was leading her away from Enrique, back down the stairs, and the feel of his hand on her arm was stupidly soothing.

She moved down the stairs, her sandaled feet scuffing slightly. "The same."

For a moment she thought his hand tightened on her arm, then she realized she must have imagined it. "I'm sorry," he said, and for a brief second she was transported back fourteen years before, and Jake Murphy was everything she ever wanted. And then she remembered how explicitly she'd told him just that in the letter she'd sent him. Adolescent maunderings, Sam had called it. Her pitiful passion that everyone had known about. It must have given Jake a good laugh, that first year of exile, to know just how enamored she'd been.

The subject of letters was a dangerous one, but she couldn't help herself. They were heading down his deserted hallway when she finally spoke.

"He never wrote to me."

"I know," he said gently.

"I used to think Mother destroyed his letters, rather than let me see them. I was sure he couldn't just ignore my letters." Her voice was weary and on the edge of tears. An edge she was determined not to cross.

"He didn't ignore them, Maddy. He just thought it was

135

better not to answer, not to encourage you. He knew there was no chance he was coming back, no way he could make a normal life for you." The rough warmth of his voice soothed her until she realized that he wasn't talking about Sam Lambert at all. He was talking about them.

He was perfectly right, of course. He'd chosen exile. There was no room for a girl nine years younger than he to go along. No room, and no rightness in it. So why did she still feel so bereft?

They were alone in the dimly lit hall, the heat of approaching midday beating through the thick plaster walls. "Sam said my letters were horribly misspelled."

He'd released her hand when they reached his door, and he was standing there, looking down at her, the faint glimmer of a smile breaking through his distant face. "True," he allowed. "I still didn't have any trouble recognizing what you were saying."

His voice was husky, almost caressing in the stillness. Maddy ran a nervous tongue over suddenly dry lips. "I'm a much better speller than I used to be," she said.

"I'm sure you are." He moved very slowly, almost carefully then, and the touch of his hands was magic on her parched skin, the touch of his mouth a tiny bit of paradise as he gently brushed her lips. She trembled, shutting her eyes, and leaned back against the wall as his mouth softly moved along the tender skin of her neck, kissing, biting, soothing. For a moment she felt lost, and gladly so, ready to dissolve in the long-imagined feel of his hands on her flesh. The box in her hand began to slip from nerveless fingers, and suddenly remembrance returned, and she jerked away from him.

He seemed unsurprised by her sudden withdrawal. Once more he shielded the expression in his eyes, and she wondered briefly if there'd ever been a moment when she'd known what he was thinking. "Stay in your room," he said, moving away. "You might begin packing. I have no idea when I'll be able to arrange transport, but it might be any time." His eyes dropped to the candy box, then moved back to her troubled face. "You'd better pack that on top."

"Why?"

"Because if you tried to hide it people might become too suspicious."

"Do you know what's in there?"

"I can imagine. It means a lot, you know, that Sam's willing to trust you."

"Something I can cherish in my declining years," she said in a sarcastic tone of voice, hoping to shore up her sagging defenses.

"It's better than nothing," he said in a weary voice, and it was all Maddy could do to keep from reaching up a soothing hand and pushing that extraordinary length of sun-streaked hair away from his face.

"Maybe," she said. "Maybe not."

The room that had felt like such a prison only hours earlier had suddenly taken on new dimensions. Bright sunlight was streaming in the window overlooking the courtyard, and the cheerful twittering of the birds, the rich scent of flowers, and the warm breeze were all curiously cheering. Maddy tossed the box of candy onto the bed, remembering for a moment the hours she'd spent last night, sleeping next to Jake. The ropes were still looped around the bedstead, and she tried to summon forth a righteous rage. All she could manage was an uncharacteristic smile.

Such games men played. The old man who had once

been her father was going to die for those games, and Maddy had no guarantee that Jake wouldn't also. His tiny island of innocence, Sam had called it. The very thought should have rankled. She had never felt less innocent in her entire life, and doubtless Jake recognized that fact. It hadn't seemed to dim the desire that flared between them at the most unexpected moments.

She'd repacked her suitcase when she'd gotten it that morning, hating the thought of alien hands pawing through her silky underclothing, her toiletries, her books. In the half hour she'd been with Sam someone had searched again, and Maddy accepted the fact with resignation, refolding the clothes neatly and placing the candy box on top. For a moment she wished they really were raspberry creams. She'd give five years of her life to satisfy her chocolate addiction, and raspberry creams were her favorite. She couldn't look at the box without her mouth watering. Damn Sam Lambert anyway. That was one more she owed him.

She sat back on her heels, staring down at the neat suitcase, at the box of candy lying innocently on top. How well did Sam Lambert know her, after all these years? Did he really expect her to meekly do his bidding, to smuggle the candy box back to the States without even looking inside? He'd never had such insight into her thought processes before; why should he have changed?

There was no way she was going to be his obedient little daughter, not anymore. Oh, she'd take the candy box back, deliver it to someone properly sympathetic. But she wasn't going to do it without checking what was inside first.

She reached out a tanned, slender hand to the box of candy and then hesitated. Maybe she didn't really want to find out what was inside. Maybe she was better off not knowing.

But she knew damned well that box could prove extremely hazardous to her health. If she was going to die for something she might as well find out why. Without further delay she grabbed the box, ripped off the cellophane, and looked inside.

No chocolates, of course. Beneath the empty tray that had once held raspberry creams lay an unmarked videotape. No papers, no photographs. Just the tape.

There was nothing she could do but put it back, close the box, and place it in her suitcase. Puente del Norte didn't even boast television, much less something as sophisticated as a video cassette recorder. If transporting the videotape proved her downfall, she'd have to die in ignorance. Damn Sam Lambert again. With a despairing sigh she turned back to the bed and her limited supply of reading material.

If the Faulkner novel had been uninspiring earlier on, by now it was deathly. The trials of the Snopes family paled beneath Maddy's current dilemma. She felt restless, bored, edgy, and nervous. And frustrated by a long-haired, half-savage soldier of fortune who should have been the last person in the world to get through her well-built defenses. It must only be the memories of the past, she told herself, ignoring the fact that there was a world of difference between the short-haired, dark-suited Secret Service man and the man who'd shared her bed last night. Just as there was a world of difference between the shy, adolescent passion she'd formed for him and the very real, very physical longing that she was having a hard time ignoring.

Jake knew exactly what he was doing, each time he looked at her, each time he kissed her, each time those strong, dangerous hands of his brushed against her. The very sense of imprisonment had been faintly, perversely erotic, but now that she was no longer captive she found herself wanting him even more. Damn him, and damn that elusive power he still held over her.

She closed Faulkner with a snap, turning to the pile of books beside the bed. Maybe Hemingway would be better. At least there'd be plenty of action and terse dialogue not unlike her present situation.

She was two chapters into *The Sun Also Rises* when a short rap on the door pulled her out of the first moments of forgetfulness she'd had in days. Before she could reply the door opened to reveal a grinning Carlos, ammunition belts swathed around a naked, sweating torso, jeans hanging low on his hips, a knife in his belt. Maddy sat there on the bed, holding herself very still, wondering whether she had time to scream.

CHAPTER ELEVEN

Carlos's grin broadened. "So the little *gringa* was everything she said she was." He moved further into the room, but Maddy noted with distant relief that he hadn't bothered to close the door behind him, and his hands were tucked in his belt, far away from the lethal-looking knife. "That must have come as quite a surprise to our friend Murphy."

Maddy said nothing, just watched him out of wary eyes, and Carlos's smirk took on a distinctly lascivious cast. "Or perhaps it was no surprise at all. Perhaps he knew just who you were from the moment he saw you. I would think you would be unforgettable, but who can say how Murphy's memory has held up over the years. He certainly hasn't been a monk, lighting candles to your sainted memory."

There was a malicious glint in his lizard eyes, a glint that Maddy refused to respond to. "What's the matter?" Carlos continued, moving closer, so that the strong reek of sweat and chili peppers permeated her nostrils. "Cat got your tongue? Are you still afraid of me, Sam's daughter?"

"Of course not," she lied, moving toward the edge of the bed. "Why should I be?"

Carlos grinned. "For a great many good reasons, *mi amiga.* Jake would be more than happy to tell you several dozen."

"And what would you tell me?"

Carlos moved closer, and one filthy hand reached out to grasp her chin in an ungentle grip. "I would tell you to beware of the jackal," he said softly, and not for one moment did Maddy doubt him.

He pulled away then, and it took all Maddy's reluctant willpower not to wipe the feel of his hard, sweaty hand from her face. "You're wanted, little chicken," he said then, moving away from her. "You have a visitor."

"Visitor?" Sudden uneasiness assailed her.

"In the front parlor, waiting for you like a suitor."

"Who?"

"Who else but the peaceful Minister of Agriculture?" he countered with heavy irony. "General Ortega, presenting his compliments to the daughter of El Patrón. You'd better hurry, *gringa,* before Jake cuts his throat with a table knife. There's no love lost between the two of them, and I left them staring at each other like dogs about to fight over a tasty bitch. Go on, *perrita.* See if you can ease trouble rather than cause it."

If anything, Carlos had understated the case. She found Jake and the suave general together in one of the dusty, disused rooms on the first floor of the hacienda, and if the general managed a certain elegance, seated on a sheet-covered divan with his spotless gray uniform already streaked with dust, Jake looked nothing more than murderous. Maddy could feel the waves of hatred billowing through the room, and she knew with sudden certainty that that hatred went two ways and had very little to do with her.

Jake straightened from that deceptively casual slouch when she entered the room, and she heard the whisper of a sigh as she moved past him. "Keep him busy." Then he was gone, and General Ortega had risen, kissing her hand and showering her with meaningless compliments, all the time his dark-brown, almost black eyes stared at her unwinkingly, very much like Carlos's lizard eyes.

She'd spent more pleasant hours in her life. With the charm and deftness of a cobra Ortega twisted his way into her brain, asking a question here, a question there, until she was completely flustered and totally livid. He was a master at this kind of interrogation, and she was a novice. All she had was a determination not to hurt her father by being too free with her tongue. And then she realized that her father could hang for all she cared. It was Jake she wanted to protect.

"So your father was looking well, Miss Lambert? I wonder if I might be permitted to visit with him for a few short minutes? I wish to present President Morosa's compliments and assure him that any aid he desires will be his."

"I'm sure you do," she said, and there was only a light tinge of sarcasm gilding her words. "But I'm afraid that's out of the question. My father is recovering from a serious illness, and his visitors are limited. I was only able to see him for the first time this morning, and then only for fifteen minutes."

"He is recovering, Miss Lambert? We have had the most disturbing word that El Patrón might be more seriously ill than even we supposed. President Morosa's personal physician can be flown by helicopter at a moment's notice, should you think it necessary."

For a fleeting moment Maddy remembered Henry Milsom of the bleary eyes and the incessant drinking, and almost succumbed. And then she remembered the look of her father, the look of death hovering just beyond reach, and she knew in her heart of hearts that no fancy doctor could help him any more.

She shook her head regretfully. "I thank you for the offer, General Ortega, but there is no need. He's gaining strength quite rapidly. Perhaps in a few weeks you might come back. . . ."

"I am pleased to hear he's getting better. Perhaps I might speak to him for just a minute, then, if his strength is improving. . . ."

And so it went, Ortega probing, Maddy lying, and never knowing when those lies were unnecessary, when they were idiotically clear, or when they did more harm than good. Various people appeared at the door, glanced in, and quickly disappeared. No one seemed eager to rescue her from the tenacious bull terrier of a general and one hour stretched to two.

No one came to offer them refreshments, and Maddy could well understand why. The provisions in the old villa were limited indeed; it seemed unlikely that the fastidious general would welcome an afternoon tea of bean paste and stale tortillas. Nor did he need to know their supplies were so low. It would have provided a welcome distraction, one that Maddy badly needed in the midst of all the feint and parry, and when Soledad finally slouched in she greeted her stepmother with a cry of real gratitude.

Her relieved greeting fell on preoccupied ears. It took her two seconds to remember her erstwhile stepmother already knew the general, in the biblical sense as well as the social one. For a moment Maddy wondered if there was any man the luscious Soledad had missed in her formative years. She could still remember the sound of that pleading, drunken voice outside Murphy's door. Well, tonight Maddy wouldn't be there, and he could let Soledad in, once more betraying the man he was supposed to worship.

"Madelyn, my sweet," Soledad cooed, "why don't you go on now? I'm sure the general will excuse you. He and I have a great many old times to talk about."

She could just bet they did, Maddy thought cynically. "Then I think I'll go up and spend some time with my father."

"No!" It was a tiny shriek, quickly covered by a nervous laugh. "I'm sorry, darling, but Samuel is busy right now with Jake and the others. Perhaps after dinner."

Ortega followed all this with great interest, and for a moment Maddy wondered whether Soledad could be trusted. Apparently, for all her extramarital activities, Jake did trust her, or he never would have let her near Ortega. As far as she could tell Jake didn't make mistakes, certainly not of that magnitude. She had no choice but to trust her also and be grateful that she could finally escape to the coolness of the second-floor bedroom. The tropic heat and the briefness of her sleep last night had left her uncharacteristically drowsy.

She could feel two pairs of dark, hispanic eyes following her as she left the room once all the polite words were said. There was no sign of anyone as she climbed the stairs to the second floor, and for a brief moment she considered climbing one more flight. Her father had said he had something to tell her. Maybe there was a vague, distant possibility that he would tell her he loved her. Hope sprang eternal, she thought in disgust, stopping on the second floor and heading down the hall toward Jake's room.

145

Someone had closed the shutters, someone had put her copy of Hemingway back on the pile of books, someone had once more searched her suitcase. The candy box lay on top, still untouched amid the tangle of clothes, and Maddy swore, a short, obscene word that gave her great satisfaction.

This time she didn't bother to repack. What was the use? The moment she left her room it would be torn apart again. With a sigh she dropped down on the narrow bed, closing her eyes. She should take out her contact lenses, but she was only going to rest for a moment. General Ortega had been exhausting, with his relentless questions and unending probing. In ten minutes she'd feel more like herself, and then she'd go up to the third floor and demand to see her father once more. After all, if they were about to spirit her away with that damned candy box, she deserved every moment she could snatch with her father. It had been more than clear that once she left the hacienda and Puente del Norte she would never see him again.

The scent of the flowers carried upward on the hot wind, wrapping around her tired body as she lay on the bed. Never would she smell the scent of wild gardenias and roses and not remember San Pablo, she thought wearily. The smell had penetrated her skin and melted into her bloodstream, weaving its hypnotic, erotic spell, leaving her powerless to fight it. Just ten minutes, she promised herself. . . .

Once more she was a prisoner. The room was dark, velvet black, and she was trapped on the bed, unable to move, unable to say a word, entirely at the mercy of the man who'd been part of her life, both consciously and unconsciously, for the last fourteen years.

And she had no desire to escape. There was something blissfully simple about being caught by him, held by him. She no longer had any choice. Whatever he forced her to do, whatever pleasure he inflicted on her would leave her guiltless and free. The threat he presented was more than implicit. It was deadly clear and the dreaming Maddy had no intention of running.

The bed sagged suddenly, and her eyes flew open. It was the night, the darkness surrounded her, and Jake sat beside her on the bed, staring down at her with fathomless eyes.

His arms were on either side of her, his hands pressing deep into the mattress, holding her there without touching her. The chambray shirt was unbuttoned, and she could see his chest in the dim light, the smooth, silken muscles, the faint trace of hair, the hint of scars recent and distant. His long hair was no longer held back by the bandanna, it fell around his face, and Maddy could tell it was wet. He must have just taken a shower, and she could smell the faint scent of shaving soap.

Say something, she ordered herself, not moving. Ask him if you can have a shower too. Tell him you want to see your father. Tell him to get the hell off your bed.

The silence lengthened, stretched and grew into a thick web of dazzling beauty. Those deep, unreadable eyes must have hypnotized her, she thought, as she carefully, deliberately moved her hand up inside the prison of his braced arms, moved up without touching him past the open shirt, the lean, strong shoulders, and gently touched his shadowed face.

His skin was smooth and hard and warm, and the wet hair was a silken swathe against her fingers. He shuddered, a small, almost delicate movement, and then suddenly she could read everything in his mind and for a moment she was terrified.

His hands left the bed to gently cup her shoulders beneath the crumpled shirt-dress. Slowly he moved her up, pulling her away from the bed, and the careful certainty of his movements gave her more than enough time to pull away. Her hand slid down from his face, trailing against the muscled column of his neck, and then her hands were clasping his shoulders as his were clasping hers. And bending his head further, he gently placed his lips against hers.

If his other kisses had swamped her with their erotic force, the tenderness of this swept across her emotions, leaving them shattered and wanting in its wake. He made no move to deepen the kiss. His lips seemed content to learn the contours of her mouth, her face, her willful chin and high cheekbones. Her eyelids fluttered closed beneath the gentleness of his mouth, and her fingers closed more tightly on his shoulders, pulling him closer, until her breasts were pressed up against that strong, smooth chest.

And then he was easing her back down on the bed, following her, his mouth traveling back to hers. And suddenly she was afraid of him, afraid of his power over her, and she kept her mouth tightly shut against the encroaching advance of his tongue.

He moved away, a bare fraction of an inch, and she could feel the soft breath of his laughter on her upturned face. "You aren't seventeen any more, Maddy," he whispered. "You should know by now how to kiss. Open your mouth for me."

She was startled enough to obey, and he took immediate advantage of it, dipping his tongue inside with a calculated wantonness that drew an immediate response

148

from her. Her hands slid down the front of his chest, inside the chambray shirt, and for the first time revelled in the warm sleek hide of him.

He trembled again, and the feel of his response against her swept the last misgivings from her mind. His hands were still on her shoulders, but this time he was pulling the dress away, down her arms, down to her waist, and she couldn't even remember when he'd unbuttoned it. He undid the front clasp of her lacy bra, his mouth never leaving hers, his lips and tongue a soothing litany, stealing away any doubts or fears. And the feel of his hard, calloused hands on her breasts was another wonder, a miracle that she'd never thought to experience. All she could think, as she arched against his strong, clever hands, was that she wanted more.

She could feel reality and common sense slipping away from her in a haze of desire unlike anything she'd ever felt before. He felt so good, smelled so good, tasted so good, that she didn't think she could ever get enough of him. Nothing had prepared her for the intensity of her response to him, the dazed wonder of her movements beneath his practiced touch. She hadn't known it could be like this, ever.

Then suddenly, like a snake in the garden of paradise, reality began to intrude, accompanied by its bastard kin, self-preservation. With every last ounce of effort she pulled herself back from the abyss into which she'd been sinking, and her hands slid away from his chest, back up to his shoulders, and she began to push.

She expected more of a fight. With only a lingering of regret his hands left her taut and tingling breasts, pulling the dress back up her arms and around her as he broke off the kiss. She stared up at him out of angry, passion-dark eyes, but once more his mask was in place.

"You changed your mind?" he asked quietly, his husky voice one more part of his seductive arsenal.

He'd moved far enough away, and he was no longer touching her, but she could still feel the heat emanating from his body, and her skin could still remember the touch of his hands. Carefully, so as not to touch him and start something anew that this time she couldn't stop, she pushed herself until she was sitting up, back against the bedstead.

"I learned long ago," she said, and her voice was rusty and a little raw, "never to sleep with men I despise. It's bad for my self-esteem."

He didn't even flinch. A small, doubting smile played at the corner of his mouth. "So you despise me, do you? What made that happen? A few hours ago I thought we were going to be friends."

"I'd forgotten about Soledad."

He sighed, the small smile diminishing somewhat. "I've told you before, Maddy, I'm not going to offer you any excuses about Soledad."

"And you feel no qualms about sleeping with Sam's daughter as well as his wife while he lays there dying?" She was pleased to see him wince then, a shadow of pain cross his face.

"I can't stop him from dying, Maddy. I can't stop from . . . wanting you." His voice was low, hypnotic, and she found herself slipping beneath its spell once more. "Life and death are cheap and quick here. I've been living that way for too long to start paying attention to a lot of half-formed ideals that have never been tested. Right now things are black and white. I want you. And you want me."

If he touched her again she'd be lost, and they both knew it. She couldn't refute his calm statement, not with

150

her breasts aroused and aching from his touch, not with her mouth swollen and tremulous and barely able to keep the words back that would call him to her.

"So why else do you despise me?" he asked gently. "There must be more to it than Soledad."

Everything she could say in response would only damn her more. Yet she knew him well enough, recognized the nuances in his distant expression, to know that she would get nowhere until she told him.

"You left me," she said on a bitter sigh. "You took my father and you left me without a word, without saying good-bye. You let my father abandon me and my brother without a backward glance, not caring what kind of person my mother was. You knew her as well as anyone, hated her. And yet you left me to her."

"Maddy, I had no choice—"

"You had every choice," she interrupted ruthlessly. "You've never let anyone else dictate your life, you can't blame that on anyone. You left, and you ignored the letter I wrote you. For God's sake, Jake, I was a poor, love-starved teenager! Couldn't you have written back, let me dream a little longer? Do you have any idea what kind of hell my life was for the next few years?"

He was very still. "I can imagine."

"But like my father, you thought the starving masses were more important than a stupid, lovesick child." She shook her head, trying to banish the clawing sense of desertion that had washed over her unbidden. She managed a shaky smile. "Well, I suppose you're right. I shouldn't hold grudges, or wallow in self-pity, or any of the weak, unpleasant things I've been doing."

He still didn't move, but she could see the flash of pain in his hazel-dark eyes.

"But I'm not going to get embroiled with you again. It

was bad enough when I was seventeen. Now I should be old enough to know better. Anything I feel for you is nothing more than nostalgia for a lost childhood," she said ruthlessly. "It has nothing to do with reality."

"Of course," he agreed, his voice distant and toneless. He moved from the bed then, and in the darkening room she couldn't see his expression. Not that it would have told her anything if she could. "Someone will bring you up something to eat. I assume you'd prefer it wasn't Soledad."

"Is she even here? I thought she might have gone off for a roll in the hay with General Ortega," she said cattily, her heart aching for the loss of him, for his sudden withdrawal, ignoring the fact that she'd driven him away.

A smile lit his dark, weary face. "She did. She's back already."

"Do you think that's safe?"

"Soledad has a good head on her shoulders, despite her particular weaknesses. Alcohol and passion have never made her politically indiscreet. Socially indiscreet, perhaps, but she's always been acutely aware of how tenuous life is." He hesitated for a moment. "You might try not to judge her too harshly. This has been a hard life for everyone, and Soledad gets lost and frightened sometimes."

"Is that the story she told you?" Maddy shot back. "I think she gets drunk and horny sometimes." It was an impossibly bitchy thing to say, and Maddy was ashamed of herself the moment it came out. She tried to tell herself it wasn't jealousy that made her hate Soledad, tried and failed.

Jake withdrew even more. "I'll have Ramon bring you something to eat."

"Why can't I come down?"

"I don't think it's a good idea."

152

"But—"

"It's not open for discussion, Maddy. You'll stay in your room."

"Why can't I eat with my father?"

"He's . . . asleep. You wouldn't want to disturb him."

"I wouldn't disturb him. I'd just sit quietly by his bed," she said, pushing.

He moved closer then, stopping on his way toward the door, and his face was bleak and cruel. "Do you really think Sam Lambert would care one way or the other?"

It was worse than a low blow, it was a glittering shaft of pain that left her breathless. "May all heaven and hell damn you," she whispered, stricken.

"Yes," he said wearily, "I expect they will. As a matter of fact, I think both heaven and hell already have." Without another word he was gone.

CHAPTER TWELVE

Bean paste again, this time without even the dubious saving grace of tortillas. The sight of the candy box was driving Maddy crazy, and even the knowledge that only an inedible videotape rested inside didn't soothe her chocolate cravings. She spent the hours after dinner planning just how many raspberry creams she was going to eat once she got back. There was a French confectionnaire in Manhattan Beach. She might even stop on her way home from the airport, assuming she was ever going to see LAX again. At this point even that seemed doubtful.

For a while she lay there in the dark. The dim light bulb wasn't much to read by, and it attracted the swarms of mosquitoes that Ramon still insisted were nothing compared to a real infestation. Every now and then she thought she heard the muffled sound of gunfire, and each rumbled blast shot through her body like lightning. She was beginning to understand something of what Jake had told her. The guns seemed to be getting closer. He had told her life and death were quick and cheap, and she wondered if she was going to die in her bed that night.

Not her bed. Jake's bed. Would he dare come back to

try to join her there? She remembered the bleak, cynical look in his eyes, and she knew he wouldn't. She had driven him away, forever, and he wouldn't come near her again, not unless she made the first move.

What a ridiculous thought! Why should she make any move toward him? For once in her life she'd been smart enough not to get involved with someone who was no good for her. Her luck up to then hadn't been spectacularly good. Tom McAndrews and Carl Aguilar hadn't been a noticeable improvement over Jake Murphy. And nothing, not even Carl's athletic and inventive sex, had moved her the way a simple kiss from Jake's hard, unsmiling mouth moved her.

Except there was nothing simple in Jake's kisses. They were all wrapped up with guilt and wanting and childhood dreams that had never quite died. There was no way she could view them objectively, no way she could view her feelings about him objectively, except to treasure her good sense in leaving him alone.

So why was she lying there in the dark, thinking about him, dreaming about him, being obsessed by him? For all her denying his power over her, it was unavoidable.

Sighing, she climbed off the bed, moving toward the light. Maybe Hemingway would distract her once more.

The night was dark and silent, and she paused at the short string for the light, then moved on without pulling it to stare out the window into the dark garden. The moon was behind the clouds, and not for the first time Maddy wished she knew what time it was. Probably after ten, judging by the utter stillness of the rambling old hacienda. She looked upward, to her father's bank of windows, and saw nothing but darkness. She wrinkled her forehead in sudden worry. With a man in her father's weakened condition she would have thought someone would be there at all times and at least a small light be kept burning. Uneasiness washed over her in waves, an uneasiness she pushed away. If there was one thing she could trust, it was that Jake would keep Sam Lambert safe.

Closing the shutters, she went back and pulled the light cord, flooding the small, barren room with dim yellow light. At some point during the afternoon her purse had been returned, and surprisingly enough, the money and passport were intact. The only thing missing was the stash of candy bars. At that point Maddy would have gladly forked over the five hundred dollars in travelers' checks for one Hershey bar.

It didn't take her long to wash up that night. She managed a fairly thorough sponge bath in the small, stained sink in the bathroom. Even if the water was rusty and only lukewarm she felt somewhat refreshed and definitely more human. She'd asked earlier, but apparently a shower was out of the question. The water supply, such as it was, was extremely limited. She had no choice but to make do.

There was no sign of a living soul in the darkened hallway as she made her way back from the bathroom, and no sound permeated the thick walls except for the distant, almost constant thud of gunfire.

Boy, it felt good to get the contact lenses out. She perched her thin, wire-rimmed glasses on her nose, pulled on a loose cotton nightgown, and climbed between the rough sheets.

Hemingway had lost his charm. She dropped *The Sun Also Rises* with a sigh, pushed the Faulkner away, and concentrated on the others. It wasn't a promising choice, probably culled from the deserted library of the old hacienda. There was Dickens, and she'd rather die than read

David Copperfield again. Joyce Carol Oates wasn't worth the effort. Only the last held promise. It was an aging volume of *The Oxford Book of English Verse,* dated 1901. With a sigh of pure pleasure she settled back against the lumpy pillow, ready to lose herself.

The book opened readily enough to Christina Rossetti. It was "A Birthday," one of the most beautiful love poems of all time. Maddy felt the pain slice through her heart at the simple, elegant lines.

"Damn." She slammed shut the aging volume, and a cloud of dust tickled her nose into a sneeze. What the hell would Murphy be doing, having that by his bed? With that section marked? Well, the book offered more than enough poetry for every taste—she'd find something dour and depressing and wipe Christina Rossetti's lush romanticism out of her soul.

She opened the book again, searching for something deathly, but the papers tucked into the middle of the book interfered, and she pulled them out, tossing them to the bed beside her before turning back to the book. Then she froze.

Slowly, carefully she shut the blue leather book once again. A trembling hand reached down to pick up the papers that had held his place.

It was the photograph Stephen had taken a lifetime ago. There she was, seventeen and anxious and terribly in love. She remembered well when that picture had been taken. Stephen had returned, reluctantly, when the scandal hit and Sam and Jake disappeared. He'd done his best to make Maddy smile, telling her long, fanciful stories of his trip out west, feeding her milkshakes until she was nauseous, keeping her out of range of her mother's intense rage. He'd taken that picture two days before he left to go back to college. She was wearing the flowery dress she'd worn for her birthday, and her long legs were bare, the thick mane of dark hair a curtain down her back. She looked lost and lovely, and when she'd had the pictures developed she'd sent that one on to her father, with the absurd hope that he cared enough about her to want it.

Jake must have taken it from him. The shiny photograph was creased and wrinkled, fingerprints and marks marring the finish. It had been held a lot, looked at a lot, and beside it were the crumpled sheets of her letter to him.

She hadn't been into elegant stationery at the time; yellow lined legal pads had seen the outpourings of her heart. The paper was crumpled and shredding, fourteen years old and soft as cotton with the passage of time. And all this time Jake had kept the letter, the picture, with him.

His tiny island of innocence, her father had called her with a trace of his aristocratic disdain. His moment of sanity, the one part of his adult life untainted by guilt. Well, it was untainted no more. She'd told him just how completely he'd destroyed her life, he and her father. After she left he'd probably come back and destroy the letter and she wouldn't blame him.

Slowly, carefully she unfolded the delicate sheets of paper, leaning back to read the embarrassing words of her childhood. And then she refolded it without reading a sentence, putting it back in the book, this time next to Christina Rossetti's own impassioned outpouring. She didn't need to read it. All she had to do was lean back and close her eyes and she could feel the emotions washing over her. Because they were still there, still as strong, tempered by time and distance and a reluctant maturity that couldn't talk her out of it. She still loved Jake Murphy, and she expected she always would.

The sudden flash of light was brilliant, blinding. The thunder that followed it shook the building, and Maddy could hear the crash of broken glass, the cracking, tumbling sound of part of the building collapsing. It took her a moment to realize that it wasn't a thunderstorm. Sam Lambert's fortress was being shelled.

The next one was even more frightening, now that she knew what it was. She was about to dive under the bed when common sense reared its ugly head, and she realized that the second floor might not be the wisest choice. The first thing she had to do was to get her father down into the basement, and to safety. She couldn't count on anyone there, with the exception of Jake, to see to that. And Jake would need help.

She didn't hesitate before she leaped from the bed. She considered changing for only a moment before the next shell hit even closer, and the bed shook on the rough wood floor. She grabbed her sandals and headed out into the hallway, just as the power flickered off.

The darkness closed around her like a tomb. She paused long enough to slip on the leather sandals, then moved off into the darkness, running a hand along the wall for a small measure of security. She could smell the acrid scent of gunpowder mixing with the dryness of plaster dust, and the floor beneath her feet crunched with the bits of the building that had rattled loose.

The next shell was the worst. Closed in the darkness, Maddy sank against the wall, whimpering in sudden panic, as the villa shook around her. At any moment she expected it to crumble into dust, at any moment she expected to be blown to kingdom come. Fast and cheap, Jake had said of life and death. She was learning the hard way.

She slipped on the stairs, scraping her hands and knees

159

against the plaster rubble. She had no thought in mind but to try to reach her father's room, not because it would do any good but because Jake would be there.

She heard him calling her from a distance, his voice harsh and curiously panicked. She never would have thought Jake would be frightened of anything. She turned back from her father's room without a moment of hesitation, making her way carefully back down the debris-strewn staircase in the darkness.

"I'm here, Jake." Her own voice sounded raw and frightened, and the next shell held her panicked, motionless, unable to move until the rattling, rumbling power of it passed by and the house was still standing.

"Where the hell are you?" His voice was desperately angry and blessedly close in the darkness. She vaulted off the steps in the direction of his voice, and a moment later felt her trembling body crushed in the fierce safety of his arms.

"Where were you?" he whispered, pressing her head against the solid warmth of his shoulder. He smelled of plaster and sweat and Jake, and the unexpected scent of crushed gardenias. Even chocolate paled next to his earthy scent, and she buried her face closer to him.

"I was looking for you," she murmured against his shirt. "I thought you'd be with Sam, so I was trying to get up there."

"Sam's okay—you needn't have worried," Jake said, his gentle voice at odd variance with the rough strength of his hands on her body.

"I wasn't worried about Sam. I was worried about you."

He hesitated, and she could feel the tension running through his body, a new tension, not caused by the shelling and the house falling down around them. "You shouldn't have bothered. Nothing gets to me."

"I know. But if I was going to die I wanted to be with you." It was very dark, but when she moved her head to look up at him she thought she could at last read his expression. It was a fierce, possessive joy.

"Why?"

What was the good of hiding? she thought wearily. They might be dead in another minute. "Because I love you. I always have, and I always will."

It took her a moment to realize that the sudden stillness was without as well as within. The shelling had stopped, and she was standing there in Jake's arms, having just bared her soul to him and wiped out any last defense.

Then he spoke. "You know I'm no good for you?"

"Yes."

"You know I can't go with you when you leave?"

"Yes."

"And you know that I love you?"

It had been years since anyone had said that to her—not since her brother had died, and not often before then. She closed her eyes with a sigh. "Yes."

His mouth gently brushed hers, a benediction, a promise made to be broken. He scooped her up in his arms, a fragile burden. "This has been a long time coming," he said, and his voice shook just slightly.

"Yes," she said, twining her arms around his neck through the long thick silk of his hair. "Yes."

He made his way unerringly to the bedroom they'd shared the night before, kicking the door shut behind them and tumbling her down on the bed with a glorious disregard for the papers and books she'd left strewn on

161

top of it. She knew a moment's regret as she heard the papers hit the floor, and then regret was the last thing on her mind, as she felt her nightgown being stripped away by clever hands.

Very gently he removed her thin, wire-framed glasses, his mouth caressing each eyelid in a touch feather-light and unbearably moving. Her hands weren't nearly so deft; she trembled as she tried to undress him, and finally he caught one struggling hand in the grip of his larger one, a soft laugh filling his voice. "I'll take care of it." He pulled away for a moment, and the loss of his hard, strong body against hers was an ache that was a sudden presage of times to come.

Then he was back, half beside her, half on top of her, his body naked against hers, hard where she was soft, muscled where she was lean, strong where she was weak. With a sudden desperation she clutched at him, trying to pull him over and onto her, and her mouth rained rapid kisses over his face, his mouth, his neck and shoulders.

"Slow down," he murmured against her skin. "We're in no hurry. We've waited fourteen years, we can wait a little longer."

"I don't know if I can," she whispered against the hard, silky flesh of his shoulder. "I want you now."

His hands were sliding down her trembling body, soothing and arousing feelings she'd never thought existed. When his hand reached the soft, damp mound of her femininity he groaned deep in his throat, a sound of pleasure and frustration. "I guess you do want me now," he said between tiny, stinging kisses that trailed across her fevered skin. "But you'll have to wait. I have every intention of doing this right."

His lips, his teeth, his tongue performed wonders on every inch of her body, bringing her to a fever pitch. In return she covered him with frantic, hungry kisses, delighting in the smell and taste of him, the sharp edge of frustration that his deliberate pace incited only carrying her further along on the tide of sensuality that threatened to drown her. Just when she thought she was about to explode, his mouth found her, wet and warm and seeking, and the thrust of his tongue sent her gasping and clutching, over the edge into oblivion.

Before she had time to catch her breath he had moved, up and over her, poised and waiting between her legs. She opened her eyes then, meeting his in the flood of moonlight that washed through the garden window, carrying with it the tropical night breezes and the scent of gardenias. Slowly he pressed against her, filling her with his massive strength that seemed almost more than she could accommodate. But there was no pain, only a tightness that quickly faded to something beyond ecstasy, and she closed around him, her arms, her legs, her body, and arched up to meet the last tiny bit of his thrust.

"I don't . . . want to hurt you," he murmured in her ear, his voice ragged, his body taut with his fierce control.

"No," she whispered. "You couldn't . . . ever. . . ." And if she thought she'd reached the pinnacle of release before, the slow, diabolically clever movement of his hips against her, his body against hers, proved that she had only begun.

It built slowly, steadily, until it reached a fever pitch, and she was clutching at his sweat-slick body, his long hair all around her, in her eyes, in her mouth, and she could hear her voice sobbing, whimpering, weeping against him in a helpless litany of a pleasure that was almost pain.

And then she was there, past the struggle, in a white-hot flashpoint that shattered and scorched and disintegrated everything around her. She felt his body stiffen against her, rigid in her clinging arms, and knew he'd joined her in the conflagration.

Slowly, slowly she tumbled back to reality, back to the narrow bed in the barren room in the besieged villa. She wept then, burying her face against his salt-damp skin, and he held her as she wept.

When the storm of tears finally abated he pushed the wet, tangled curls away from her face. "No Kleenex," he whispered with gentle understanding. "Do you want to use my shirt?"

She nodded, then realized he might not be able to see her, and opened her mouth to speak. But he'd already leaned over to retrieve the soft chambray shirt he'd been wearing, and she sat up to wipe the tears from her face.

"Are you that good in bed?" she said in a shaky voice. "Or did I just imagine it?"

She could feel his smile through the moon-shadowed darkness. "I'm not that good," he said, and his voice was rich with amusement. "Love is a powerful aphrodisiac."

She lay back down with a sigh, curling into his arms. "It certainly is. I didn't know I could feel that way."

He lay very still against her, and she could tell he was searching for the right words. "Haven't you . . . felt like that before?" His voice was very careful, but she knew that he wanted to ask what he felt he had no right to ask.

"Never," she murmured against his chest. "I waited for you as long as I could, Jake, but I couldn't wait forever."

"I didn't want you to."

"Didn't you?" She was faintly, happily skeptical. "I've had two lovers. One in college who was straightforward, unimaginative, and short-lived in more ways than one. It didn't seem worth the effort to get involved again, until I met Carl three years ago. He was the opposite of Tom, fiery, emotional, very inventive. I enjoyed being with him but something always seemed to be missing."

He said nothing, but his hands began to move down her arm, long, lingering strokes that couldn't disguise his tension. Then he spoke, and his voice was a deep rumble beneath her ear. "I don't think I've ever been jealous before in my life except for the time I found you necking with Eric Thompson."

Maddy laughed. "You don't need to be jealous. There was something I forgot to tell you. Both those men looked exactly like you." She reached out and ran her hand through his silky mane. "Without the hair, of course."

She could feel the tension leave his body, and his hand slid down her arm to lightly catch her hip. "You don't like my hair?"

"It's very erotic. It might not do too well in the States nowadays." The moment the words were out of her mouth she could have bitten her lip, and grief washed over her.

But Jake only smiled. "When I come back to get you I'll cut my hair."

Maddy said nothing. There were no guarantees. They could be killed in their sleep that very night, they could be separated by the fortunes of war and never see each other again. There was even the distinctly farfetched possibility that it might work, that he might come and find her in L.A.

But fate had never been their friend, and Maddy wasn't about to trust in it at this late date. She was going to take what was hers, in front of her, warm and strong and close at hand, and the devil take the future, be it five years or five hours away. She reached up her arms to him, and the sudden desperation that sparked their coming together was an overlying veil of sadness that made their union bittersweet, and all the more glorious. This time her release was expected and, impossibly enough, even more shattering, so that she buried her face against the side of Jake's neck to muffle her incoherent cries. And as he followed her in a tumult of hopeless love, she wept into the darkness of the San Pablo night.

CHAPTER THIRTEEN

Maddy was alone when she awoke. She was lying face down in the center of the narrow bed, her head buried in her arms, and the murky light that filtered in the single window was shrouded in early morning mist.

She lay there, unmoving, a thousand disparate emotions washing over her. Her body felt rich, warm, and full, blissfully sated and wondrously loved. But there was no sign of Jake, no evidence that he'd even shared that bed with her, apart from her physical well-being. There was tension in the air, as thick as the damp-laden fog, and the eerie sound of silence that permeated the villa brought her fully, completely awake, wiping out the last trace of lingering lassitude.

It took her only a few moments to dress. She pulled on jeans and a loose cotton shirt, slid her bare feet into her Nikes and headed for the door, determined to track down Jake. For all her vaunted common sense, she had no intention of leaving Puente del Norte without him. Too much time had been wasted already. If the dark hours of the night had made it all seem hopeless, even the filtered light of predawn made everything possible. Yanking the door open, she started into the hallway, only to be brought up short. Her door was guarded.

Richard Feldman, better known as El Nabo, or The Turnip, smiled apologetically, hefting the machine gun over one shoulder with a curious expression of distaste. "I'm glad you're awake. I heard you moving around in there."

It was an inane enough conversation. "Why are you guarding my door, Richard?" she asked carefully. "Are you keeping people out? Or keeping me in?"

The smile went beyond apologetic to downright miserable. "A little of both, I guess. Jake asked me to make sure you're ready to leave. Are you packed?"

"No."

"I'll help you, then." He herded her back into the bedroom with surprising efficiency, rather like a kindergarten teacher with a recalcitrant crew of toddlers. He pulled the rumpled bed together with a matter-of-fact air that wiped out any embarrassment Maddy might have felt and dumped her tumbled suitcase on top of it. She watched him fold her clothes for a moment, then motioned him out of the way, taking over the task for what seemed like the five hundredth time.

"Where's Jake?" she questioned, placing the candy box squarely on top.

"He's arranging for the jeep. Carlos and Ramon will be taking you and Soledad the northern route, up through Guatemala. You'll be able to catch a plane from Puerta Pelota and be back in the States in no time."

She thought she heard a plaintive note in his voice, and she turned to look at him, her hands still. He was about forty, with a head full of curly brown-gray hair and the saddest eyes she'd ever seen. His thin, dejected body didn't suit the modified combat gear he wore, and the narrow hands that had held the machine gun were shaking slightly. A thousand questions rushed into Maddy's mind, and for once she allowed them free reign.

"Why don't you come back with us?" she suggested suddenly. "Don't you miss the States?"

El Nabo smiled a wry, discouraged smile. "Didn't Jake tell you? I can't go back."

"Why not?"

"I'm wanted. AWOL, for one thing. There are other charges against me too." His voice was simple, resigned.

"I can't imagine you could have done anything hideous," Maddy said gently. "I'm sorry, I don't mean to impugn your machismo or anything, but I don't think you could hurt a flea. How long have you been on the run?"

Richard looked at her then, and the expression in his muddy brown eyes was that of someone who had looked into the jaws of hell and never been the same. "Since 1970. I was Jake's commander in Vietnam. At Den Phui. You know about Den Phui."

It wasn't a question. Indeed, Maddy knew far too well about Den Phui, about the civilian massacre and the subsequent army coverup. One day when she'd been feeling masochistic, a few months after Jake left, she had gone to the library and looked up the old newspaper accounts of the massacre, of the inept commander who'd let it happen. Of the soldiers who'd been unable to stop it. Of the massive smokescreen and eventual trials of those involved and Jake's reluctant part in bringing it all to light. And then she understood why Richard Feldman looked so haunted.

"Yes," she said. "I know about Den Phui. I'm sorry." Somehow it seemed inadequate. And why should she apologize to the man whose ineptness allowed it to happen? But still, pity welled up in her. Richard Feldman carried the weight of that day with him, and would for the rest of his life. It was a burden too agonizing to contemplate.

He seemed to shake himself, like a terrier who'd taken an unexpected bath. "Well," he said briskly, reaching past her and fastening the suitcase, "then you know why I can't go back."

A thousand objections came to mind. Surely after all this time the military tribunals would let the charges drop, or give him a token sentence and a dishonorable discharge. Looking at Richard, she knew that wasn't the problem. He wasn't afraid of too harsh a punishment. He was afraid of too lenient a one.

"Ready?"

"I want to see my father first." And after that she was going to find Jake, she thought with a fiery determination. She'd twine her arms around his neck, press her body close to his, and beg him to come with them. And if he loved her even a tiny bit he would.

El Nabo shook his head, and Maddy didn't even notice the furtive regret in his dark eyes. "You can't, I'm afraid. Doc says your father needs all the sleep he can get. He had a . . . disturbed night last night, and he's finally resting comfortably."

"But he said—"

"I know. He asked me to give this to you." Out of his pocket Richard pulled a dull gold chain. On the end was a medallion, a religious medal of some sort. It was obviously extremely old, extremely heavy, and extremely valuable. But what Samuel Lambert would be doing with an antique religious medal was beyond her comprehension.

She took it numbly, staring down at it. St. Paul, the

patron saint of San Pablo. Wouldn't you know it?" "Why?"

He reached out and closed her fingers around the heavy medallion. "He said I should tell you it's the most valuable thing he owns and he wanted you to have it."

Maddy stared down at the solid weight resting in her hand. The most valuable thing he owned, and it was for her. Perhaps he really did love her, and this was the only way he could tell her. The gold felt solid, warm, and tangible in her hand, and she closed her fingers around it tightly, managing a tremulous smile. If this medallion was Sam's love for her, she'd accept it.

There was the faint sheen of tears in her eyes as they met Richard's. "Tell him thank you," she whispered. "And tell him—"

The heavy pounding on the door drew them apart, and she slipped the medallion around her neck, inside the loose cotton shirt, moments before Carlos swaggered into the room.

He must have been wearing twenty pounds of weapons, Maddy thought critically, and that smile was a little too sharklike to set her mind at ease.

"Ready to go, *gringa?*" he inquired with his usual charm. "The jeep is loaded."

"Where's Jake?" He couldn't let her leave without saying good-bye, he couldn't.

"Jake is with your father. He is far too busy to waste time seeing you off. I'll give him your regards when I get back."

"Will you be coming back?"

"Of course. Carlos the Jackal never misses a good fight," he said simply.

"But if my father's awake—"

"*Gringa,*" Carlos said in an amiable tone of voice, "ei-

171

ther you come now, with no more foolish babble, or I will have my friend El Nabo tie you, gag you, and drag you downstairs by your hair. The choice is up to you." His smile was curiously endearing, but Maddy had no doubts that he would do just that. Even if El Nabo refused, Enrique would doubtless be more than happy to do the honors.

"But—"

"Now!" He nodded at Richard. "Bring her suitcase, *amigo. Vamanos!*"

She had no choice. Wordlessly she followed Carlos down the plaster-strewn staircase. The shells of last night had done even more damage than she'd thought, and she wondered dizzily if the tumbled-down old villa would survive another such shelling. The weight of the medallion hung heavy between her breasts, and she took what comfort she could from it as she picked her way over the rubble and out into the humid morning, with the dawn light just breaking above the tangled jungle. Richard tossed her suitcase on the back of the jeep that looked suspiciously like World War II vintage. Soledad eyed her without comment, her narrow, composed face offering no greeting.

Helplessly Maddy turned back to Richard. "Tell Jake—"

Richard put a hand across her mouth, gently, silencing her. "Jake knows," he said. "Believe me, he knows."

There was nothing more she could do. She looked up for a moment at the crumbling hacienda, wondering if Jake was up there, watching her. There was no way she could tell.

"Get in the jeep, *gringa,* or be left behind," Soledad said in a chilly voice.

"Don't give her that choice, *mi amor,*" Carlos said.

172

"She'd much prefer to die in the jungle than find her way safely back to California. Wouldn't you?"

Maddy didn't bother to answer him. She took Ramon's hand and climbed into the back of the ancient jeep. The last thing she saw as they drove away was El Nabo's sympathetic, apologetic smile beneath the haunted eyes of a murderer.

Sam Lambert's bedroom was dark and musty, the early-morning sunlight barely making an inroad in the murky stillness. Jake stood at the far window, looking down into the overgrown courtyard, at the jeep that was already packed to overflowing with Soledad's trunks.

Maddy came out, following Carlos with that spurious docility, and Jake knew a moment's wry amusement. With Ramon there to back her up, she wasn't about to take any crap from the Jackal. He would have liked to hear how she put Carlos in his place.

He would have liked to have been in Carlos's place. But that was out of the question. There was no way he could leave, no way he could abandon the people who'd depended on him for so long, not even when things were so close to the end. So he had to watch her leave, unable to stop her, not even daring to say good-bye. Because he knew damned well that if he'd stayed in bed that morning, if he'd told her himself that she was leaving, he wouldn't have been able to let her go. She'd been in his soul, his blood for fourteen years now and last night had only put the seal on it. He'd left her once, and now he was forcing her to leave him and there was nothing he could do about it.

He stared down the three flights at Maddy's proud, elegant carriage, at the long legs and the elegant tilt of her head, and he felt the customary tightening in his gut,

173

combined with something a little more spiritual. He'd betrayed her, of course. There was no way he was going to let Sam Lambert use her any more than he already had. He'd kept her away from Sam at the end, and he knew Maddy would never forgive him for that.

And she might never forgive him for sending her away. Last night had been a mistake, of course, but one that was predestined since the beginning of time. But God knew, it only made the parting worse.

The jeep started up, and he watched it rumble down the narrow track into the northern, denser part of the jungle. She looked up then, and for a moment he thought she was looking directly at him, and the clear brown eyes behind the thin glasses were shining with tears. Then he realized she was looking at her father's bedroom, not at him at all, and he swore, softly, fluently, feeling helpless for the first time in years.

Then they were gone, out of sight in the murky undergrowth. He watched for a moment longer and then turned on his heel, walking out of the room, past the empty hospital bed, down the shell-shattered staircase.

It seemed to Maddy as if they'd been traveling for days. The morning sun had seared through the mist, scorching down on them in the uncovered jeep, strong enough to give Maddy a blinding headache, not strong enough to evaporate the suffocating humidity that made every breath a torture.

No one had said a word about food, and despite the empty gnawing in her stomach, Maddy didn't bother to ask. Leaning back against the uncomfortable seat, she shut her eyes to the blinding glare, thinking back to the night before.

"Did Jake show you a good time?" Soledad asked suddenly from the front seat, swiveling around to bestow a sunny, malicious smile on her stepdaughter.

"Go to hell," Maddy said, not bothering to open her eyes.

"I'm only asking out of concern for you," Soledad persisted. "After all, coming on top of such a shock, I'm surprised you felt in the mood for Jake's brutish charms."

Jake's charms had been anything but brutish, Maddy thought with a familiar tightening in the pit of her stomach. Then the rest of Soledad's speech sank in, and Maddy's eyes flew open.

Carlos had a leering grin on his face as he maneuvered the jeep down the narrow trail that led them farther and farther away from Puente del Norte, and Ramon looked exceedingly uncomfortable as he avoided her gaze. She turned to Soledad, and her expression of spurious concern made her stepdaughter's strong hands clench into fists.

"What do you mean, such a shock?" she asked in a quiet tone of voice.

Soledad's mouth dropped in a disconsolate bow, as her black eyes glittered with cheerful mischief. "Why, the death of your father, of course. Not that it was unexpected, but still, these things are always painful."

Maddy said nothing, and Soledad continued in an airy voice. "Of course I don't blame you for drowning your pain in the arms of a handsome man. It is, in fact, exactly what I would have done." The flirting, sidelong glance at Carlos made it more than clear that it had been his task to comfort the grieving widow. "But I don't know if, in your case, I would have picked the man who kept me from my dying father's bedside when he was calling for

175

me. But then, we Latins have stronger feelings about family, do we not?"

Maddy sat forward, clutching the back of Soledad's seat, her clenched fingers only inches away from the silky black hair. She chose her words very carefully through the white-hot haze of fury that surrounded her. "If you don't explain yourself, clearly, and in detail, Soledad, I will rip out every hair on your head and stuff them down your throat. And that would only be a beginning."

The violence in her words and feelings shocked her even more than Soledad. Never before had Maddy wanted to hurt another human being like that. It had to be the pervasive effect of the San Pablo revolution, the cheapness of human life, that was destroying her last claims on civilized behavior.

Soledad had paled, pulling forward, but there was no way she could escape Maddy's reach. "Carlos wouldn't let you touch me," she spat back.

"You think not? Look at the grin on his face. I think nothing would entertain him more."

Soledad slid a sideways glance at the driver, and her self-assured expression faltered. "Surely you don't mean to tell me that you didn't know?" she stalled.

"I mean to tell you nothing. What happened? When did my father die?" The heavy gold medallion lay like a stone against her breasts.

"Your father died last night. Surely Jake—"

"When last night?" Maddy interrupted ruthlessly. "Did he die in the shelling?"

"He died a few hours before the shelling began. He was slipping fast all day. We were all there, of course. All except you. He kept calling for you all afternoon, begging Jake to bring you to him. He didn't care about the rest of us and our deathwatch," Soledad said with a bitter smile. "He only wanted you."

"But why wasn't I called?" Pain and bewilderment had taken the place of rage.

"Because Jake refused. No matter how much the old man begged, Jake wouldn't let you come to him. Dios, at the end even I was ready to fetch you. But he wouldn't hear of it."

"But . . . why?"

Soledad shrugged her thin shoulders. "Who can say? Jake Murphy is a very complicated man. Maybe he was jealous, or maybe he didn't trust you after all." With that Soledad turned back to face the front, pleased with her good deed for the day.

Maddy sat very still in the backseat. She could feel Ramon's moist, sympathetic eyes on her, but she didn't turn her gaze to meet them. She sat there, huddled in a cocoon of pain and betrayal, her father's medallion heavy on her chest, the feel of her lover's hands still imprinted on her flesh.

Grief combined with a raw fury threatened to tear her apart. Never, never would she forgive Jake for robbing her of her last moments with her father. He'd wanted to tell her he loved her, the medallion was proof of that, and Jake had kept her from him. Somehow, someday, she'd repay him for that.

They stopped an hour later, for cold tortillas and the doubtful amenity of the bushes, and then they were on their way again. Maddy spoke not one word, and Soledad seemed content to leave her in peace. In fifteen minutes they were back on the road again, with the full force of the midday sun beating down on them.

It seemed to get no cooler as the day wore on. The steamy heat and bumpy ride put a strain on the three other passengers, so that even Carlos lost his grin. The mosquitoes became worse, and the narrow track precluded the option of outrunning them. They bumped along the miserable track in silence, only the desultory swatting of bugs competing with the uneven *chug chug* of the jeep's engine.

"Hey, *gringa.*" Carlos's voice broke the silence, and Maddy pulled herself out of her shattered abstraction for a moment to look up. "Does this look any different?"

She gave a cursory glance around her. Some of the tangled undergrowth had thinned, and the narrow track had widened into something more like a road. There was a different smell in the air, fresher, less of decaying vegetation and more of something familiar that she couldn't quite place. "As a matter of fact, it does. Why?"

"We left San Pablo an hour ago."

He had her full attention now. "We did? I thought—"

"You thought we were going to have to run for the border, under a blaze of bullets, did you not, *gringa?*" Carlos looked pleased himself. "This road is not well known, not well traveled."

"Obviously," Maddy said.

"That is one reason why I was the one to bring you out."

"And Ramon?" She cast a look at her silent companion.

"He was Jake's idea. To make sure I brought you out safely. He's a very careful man, Jake Murphy."

"I'm indebted to him," Maddy said in a low voice, and Soledad chuckled happily.

"We'll be at the coast in another hour," Carlos continued. "I'll be meeting with a friend. He'll arrange transportation back to the States. There's a small airport in

Puerta Pelota. If you are lucky you may be back in California by tomorrow."

"It couldn't," she said icily, "be too soon."

"You will not mind me accompanying you, my little daughter?" Soledad purred. "The daughter of El Patrón will receive more attention than his widow. I was never well liked."

"I wonder why?" Maddy muttered.

"You don't mind?" Soledad ignored the crack.

"No, I don't mind," Maddy said with a sigh. "Just so long as you don't talk to me. If you do, I'll do my best to push you out of the airplane."

"And you always seemed like such a sweet, shy young giant," Soledad said.

"That one, she's a tigress," Carlos announced. "A worthy mate for Jake, whether you like it or not, Soledad."

Soledad's smile faded, and she sent a flashing glare in Carlos's direction. He drove on, unchastened, down the widening track to the ocean.

Puerta Pelota was a larger, and far more prosperous village than Puente del Norte, in a clearly more prosperous country. The clean fresh smell of the ocean, the cool breeze wafting over her face was sheer heaven to Maddy, enough to lift her tortured thoughts from the morass of pain and despair that Soledad's carefully chosen words had plummeted her into. When Carlos finally pulled up outside of a neat, large residence, she climbed out of the jeep with at least a modicum of determination. The airport that Carlos had promised lay in sight, beyond the building, and if the small, twin-engine airplanes had clearly seen better days, Maddy no longer cared. She would have jumped off the roof in a pair of wax wings if she thought it would take her home faster.

"Señorita," Ramon whispered next to her. "Don't lis-

179

ten to everything that one says. There were reasons. . . ."

Soledad and Carlos had already disappeared into the whitewashed building, and at that moment a loud scream split the late-afternoon air. A woman screamed no over and over again, until the sound of a slap, sharp like the crack of a gunshot, silenced her.

Maddy and Ramon raced into the building. Soledad was huddled on her knees in the middle of the floor, a hand to her cheek, her huge eyes brimming with tears. Carlos stood deep in conversation with a large, balding man, and they were both grim and pale as death.

"What's happened?" It was Maddy's voice, sounding strained and not her own, that asked the question.

Carlos looked up at her. There was no trace of a grin on his face, and his lizard eyes were cold and grieving. "Esteban has just had word. The villa was shelled an hour after we left. It took a direct hit. Everyone left inside was killed."

Maddy could hear Soledad weeping in the background. Ramon stumbled out of the house, away from them, and Maddy felt him leave with a moment of regret. "Are they certain?"

"Absolutely. They've identified El Nabo already." Was that sympathy on the Jackal's swarthy face? Surely a man with his past was incapable of such emotions. "Esteban has a pilot who'll be ready within the hour. The sooner you're gone the better. Both of you."

Maddy looked down at Soledad's weeping figure. She felt numb, blessedly removed from the pain and horror that surrounded them. "What about you? Are you coming with us?"

He did smile then. "Why, *gringa,* one would almost think you liked me after all. No, Ramon and I will go back to Puente del Norte." He reached out a rough hand and chucked Maddy under the chin. It was a painful gesture, and just what she needed. "We will bury our dead. I'll say a few words over Murphy for you, shall I?"

It was impossible, Maddy thought, but the sense of inevitability was washing over her, weighing her down. The whole thing had been impossible—the guns, the shelling, the threats. The most impossible of all had been the night she'd spent in Jake's arms.

The medallion was weighing down around her neck, and for a moment she considered handing it over to Carlos. It had been her father's most treasured possession and now was hers. But it wasn't the right thing. She'd held it for too short a time for it to matter.

Reaching down, she pulled the thin silver ring off her grubby hand and gave it to Carlos. Stephen had given it to her a week before he died, and it had never left her hand. It was the only thing she had that connected her to a love that died, and now it was going to another one. "Bury this with him," she said, her voice raw and quiet.

Carlos nodded. "I will. Go with God, *gringa*. And if you can help it, never come near my cursed country again."

Maddy met his gaze with achingly dry eyes. "I won't. I promise you, I won't."

CHAPTER FOURTEEN

Maddy Lambert ran down the last few steps, onto the heat-soaked pavement of Hollywood Boulevard, and moved swiftly up the street toward the parking lot. Her sandaled feet were light on the burning pavement, her sunglasses firmly in place on her small nose, her loose cotton shirt dress wilting under the pressure of the heat and humidity of Los Angeles in late October.

She climbed into her car, a 1966 Alfa Romeo whose eccentricities only made it more lovable, rolled down the windows, and pulled out into the traffic. For a moment she looked down at her slim, tanned hands lightly holding the steering wheel. She could never look at them without remembering Stephen's ring and where it lay. The weight of the gold medallion couldn't even begin to compensate.

It had taken six months, she thought, running a hand through her mop of hair. Six months to regain the semblance of a rational, level-headed woman, six months to get past the danger of tears at unexpected moments. The flashes of panic still assailed her, when she was sitting at her desk at the Greater Hollywood Help Network, struggling through the tangled mess of paperwork all grants seemed to require, or sometimes when she walked along the strand, the wide boardwalk running along the ocean, a few short blocks from her little house in Hermosa Beach. She'd feel a shadow behind her and be ready to run, a complete, unashamed coward.

But there had been no running from the fact that Jake Murphy was dead. The papers, the television networks, the news magazines, were full of it.

She'd been a fool to run to her mother. When had her mother ever provided her the solace she'd needed? But when she and Soledad finally arrived back in the U.S.—in Houston's Hobby Airport of all places—she hadn't been able to face the thought of her small, deserted house. Things had been difficult enough, with Soledad lacking anything as useful as a passport or money. It had taken Maxfield Henderson's considerable influence to ease their welcome into the United States and Maddy's tidy credit resources to get Soledad safely on her way. By the end of their ordeal Soledad had softened considerably, becoming positively warm toward her wary stepdaughter. Maddy had little doubt that the comfortable sum of money Max wired them helped mellow her father's widow, but she also knew that the trauma of the last twenty-four hours also accounted for the cessation of hostilities. Whatever was more influential, Maddy didn't care. She saw Soledad off on a plane to visit friends in Miami and then finally turned her weary attention to her own problems.

And problems there were, problems too immense to face.

Torn with grief, all Maddy could think was that she needed help. So she'd taken the next plane to Washington, a limousine to her mother's house in McLean, and walked the last few feet to collapse on her mother's chintz sofa while the latest in a succession of proper German maids went to find Helen.

"You look like hell," her mother had greeted her. "Couldn't you have stopped long enough for a shower and a change of clothes?"

Maddy had opened her tired eyes to look up at the owner of that querulous voice. Her mother looked perfect, as always, her slim, elegant figure encased in Moygashel linen, not a crease in evidence, her silvery hair a perfect coiffe for her remote face.

"Sam's dead," she said abruptly.

"I'm aware of that. It would be hard to miss. It's been all over the news for the last twelve hours. Did you see him?"

There wasn't the slightest trace of regret in her mother's cool tones. "For a short while. Don't you care that he's dead?"

"Not particularly." Helen moved into the room, seating herself daintily on a chair a little removed from Maddy's rumpled figure. "We severed all our ties years ago."

"Then why did you want me to go get him?"

Helen made a moue of disdain. "Because he was an embarrassment to me personally, to our government, to Max. He was a half-mad old troublemaker, and it finally looked as if he was sick enough to be brought home where he could do no more harm."

Maddy shook her head despairingly. "He'll do no more harm where he is now."

Helen smiled. "St. Sam. Sitting on the left hand of God, no doubt. I hope St. Peter doesn't mind being deposed. Did he send anything back with you?"

The question was idly phrased, and Maddy was almost tired enough to miss its significance and answer honestly. Almost.

184

"Like what?" she countered.

Helen brushed an imaginary speck off the spotless arm of her chair. "I'm sure Sam wasn't about to die in peace. He must have sent you back with exhortations to blacken the name of the San Pablo government, perhaps even gave you papers and documents." She smiled affably at her daughter. "You ought to give them to me if he did."

"Why?"

Helen's eyes narrowed. "Because the San Pablo government has suffered enough at the hands of that old man. "It's—"

"The San Pablo government is a corrupt nest of snakes, and President Morosa is the biggest snake of all," Maddy interrupted. "Give me one good reason why I should want to protect an evil bully whose family for generations has sucked the life blood out of San Pablo?"

"I'll go you one better. I'll give you two very good reasons. Number one is quite simple. You've seen enough of what's happened in Central America over the last twenty years. Morosa may be a pig, but he's as anticommunist and pro-capitalism as they come. As FDR said about Somoza, 'He may be an S.O.B. but at least he's our S.O.B.' The thought of another communist stronghold on our doorstep gives me shudders."

"I don't think you care one tiny bit about communist strongholds on your doorstep, Mother," Maddy said shrewdly. "What's your second reason?"

"It should be your reason too, Madelyn. After all, you're now my only heir."

"The thought touches me deeply," Maddy said in a dry tone of voice.

Helen ignored her. "I have substantial investments in San Pablo. Investments that date back to the time of your grandfather."

"Get rid of them."

"They've been very lucrative, Madelyn dear. I have no intention of dissolving them until absolutely necessary."

Maddy pulled herself up from the sofa, her muscles screaming with weariness. "If I were you, Mother, I would do something now. You forget, I was down there. Morosa and his bullies are not going to be in power for too much longer."

Helen didn't move, just looked up at her daughter with a serene smile on her face. "Perhaps. Perhaps not. Why don't you go on up and get some rest, darling? You look exhausted. And then maybe tomorrow we can call a news conference. I've told reporters that I won't talk to them yet, but that we'd have a statement soon enough. Max will help us work it out tonight when you're feeling better."

Maddy stood there, swaying slightly. "What sort of statement?"

"Oh, something tactful and reasonably supportive of our country's foreign policy, don't you think? Something to the effect that Sam was a wonderful old eccentric who'll be missed by all of us. President Morosa has been talking about a memorial in La Mensa. They'd want us down for the dedication. I promised him that we would present a united family front."

Maddy shook her head slightly, more to clear away the mists of disbelief than to argue with her mother.

"Now, now, don't make up your mind too quickly," Helen said, and the soothing tone was a mockery. "This wouldn't happen until sometime next year. They need to get the rebels under control first. But a monument to your father would be a wonderful healing gesture, and I think . . ."

Maddy walked out of the room.

The cook looked at her curiously when she walked into the kitchen, but made no comment when Maddy picked up the phone and called a taxi. For the ten minutes it took for the car to come Maddy sat waiting by the kitchen window, staring sightlessly out into the carefully manicured sidewalks, trying not to think about the rubble that once was a tumbled-down old villa.

After leaving her mother's house, her energy had carried her back into the District, up to Capitol Hill and through the miles and miles of hallways to Michael O'Malley, junior senator from New Hampshire and possessor of the most liberal record in all of Congress. He was also the most vocal opponent of military aid to San Pablo. They spoke briefly, she handed him the candy box, and an hour and a half later she was flying back to LAX.

Her mother hadn't spoken to her since the news hit the airwaves. The videotape included not only a last interview with Sam Lambert, looking wise and not at all fanatical, merely tired and grieving, but also atrocities committed by the Gray Shirts in their quest to wipe out the pockets of resistance that flourished around the mountainous country. Maddy had watched it once, on Dan Rather, but the sight of a tall, familiar figure in the background of one village scene had been too much. She'd switched off the television, sat back down on her sofa, and, for the first time since she'd left San Pablo, began to weep.

She'd cried from six in the evening till eleven the next morning. She'd wept and coughed and vomited and wept some more, and still the tears came. She screamed into her pillow, beat her fists against the bed, stuffed a towel into her mouth to stop the howls of anguish that threatened to overwhelm her. And nothing did any good. The only thing that finally stopped her was an exhaustion that was more passing out than falling asleep. When she awoke her eyes were dry and swollen, making the extended-wear contact lenses she'd bought when she came back to the States feel like pennies in her eyes, and her heart was like ice. The only thing that could warm it were her father's children.

The Greater Hollywood Help Network was a busy place, just three blocks down from the infamous corner of Hollywood and Vine. Maddy's job as administrator had little connection with their actual social service work. She saw to it that the money came but had little connection with how it flowed out.

They worked with street people, with the large inner-city population of Armenians, Asians, blacks, and with the vast influx of San Pablan refugees.

It must have started by accident. She heard a familiar accent and drifted out of her office, into the front room crowded with hungry, lost, frightened-looking people. Clearly to them she was one more of a vast array of officious *norteamericanos,* and they stared at her with a wariness at variance with the faint stirrings of hope. A small girl, not much more than four, wandered up to her, tugging at her skirt.

"Hey, *gringa,"* she said, "do you work here? I'm hungry, and they keep asking questions."

The entire room took in a deep breath of horror at the child's artless words. In the best of times *"gringa"* was a drawling insult, though clearly the child didn't know better.

A harassed-looking woman, clearly in the last stages of a monumental pregnancy, came up and pulled the child's hand away from Maddy's white skirt. The small imprint was clearly marked. "Please excuse the child, lady. Samuelita doesn't mean to give offense."

Two more blows to the memory. Jake had called her lady when he'd pretended not to recognize her. "Samuelita?" Maddy echoed.

The woman drew herself up proudly. "She is named after El Patrón, Sam Lambert. A *norteamericano* who—"

"I know very well who Sam Lambert was," Maddy said, the smile on her face only a little stiff. "He was my father."

You would have thought, she mused later, that she'd said she was the Virgin Mary herself. The cries of gladness, the crushing embraces, the tears were embarrassing and absurd and oddly moving.

The last grant hadn't come through yet, and the coffers of the Greater Hollywood Help Network were low. Twenty-seven San Pablans, Maddy, and three social workers closed the office, trailed down Hollywood Boulevard, and ended up in Burger King, with Maddy footing the bill. It was a few days later when she began hearing the phrase "La Patronita" when she walked by.

And the oddest thing of all, Maddy mused as she dodged and parried the twenty million cars that took to the L.A. freeways at rush hour, was her sudden friendship with Soledad Alicia Maria Mercedes Lambert de Ferrara y Morales. Her sleek, catlike stepmother.

Perhaps the days in San Pablo had made life in Hermosa Beach seem far too tame. Her friends, most of them married couples with meaningful jobs in advertising or insurance, no longer seemed to have anything in common with her. The rounds of barbecues, beach volleyball, and discos belonged to someone else, someone who lay buried in San Pablo with a childhood dream.

She ran into Soledad by accident one day, on Rodeo Drive of all places, and for a moment they'd circled each other like wary dogs, sniffing for danger. Then Soledad's

189

darkly beautiful face broke into a smile, and she'd held out her slender arms and cried, "Give your stepmama a kiss, little one." And to Maddy's amazement, she had.

Perhaps it was Soledad's undisguised venom toward all and sundry that was so refreshing. Or her passionate devotion to sloth, high living, and clothes that had little to do with pretensions and everything to do with being a wealthy widow. Or perhaps it was just the fact that they'd both loved the same men. For there was no question that Soledad had been in love with Jake Murphy in her own, lackadaisical way, and the terrifying, grief-benumbed trip they'd shared from Puerta Pelota back to the U.S. had cemented their odd relationship.

Soledad went through men at an amazing rate, yet there always seemed to be hordes waiting to take the last one's place. They were all very young, very handsome, and, to Maddy's amazement, very rich. Even in her hedonistic fervor Soledad had a head on her shoulders.

"Let me arrange a little something for you, Maddy," she'd suggested over cobb salad at the Rusty Pelican. "I know any number of handsome, inventive young men who would adore to make La Patronita forget her broken heart."

Maddy had shook her head, smiling. "Broken hearts take at least eight months to heal, *mi madrastra.* It's only been six."

Soledad had acquiesced. "As you say. But in two months' time expect a six-foot-tall, two-hundred-pound present awaiting you on your doorstep in Hermosa Beach."

And during the sunlight and shadows of those six months of mourning, only one thing had the ability to frighten both of them: word of Carlos the Jackal's reign of terror.

There was no doubt that Morosa's government would lie about the atrocities. No question but that they'd use propaganda, falsified photographs, lying witnesses, and altered documents to blacken the name of the man who was rapidly becoming one of the most well-known leaders of the Patronistas. But there was also no doubt that the hollow-eyed refugees who crowded through the offices of La Patronita would have no reason to lie. And Carlos the Jackal frightened them very much indeed.

Soledad had simply shrugged her shapely shoulders when Maddy had questioned her about it. "That Carlos, he was always a little mad, yes? Jake kept him under control most of the time, but he never trusted him. The danger with Carlos, daughter, is that he's a fanatic, just like your father. He doesn't care about himself, about human life, about anything more than his bloody cause. And that's the most dangerous man of all. Give me a bad, selfish man over a saint any day." She fanned herself vigorously.

"Well, he's no longer any concern of ours," Maddy had replied doubtfully.

Soledad smiled. "Perhaps not, as long as he stays in San Pablo."

"Why would he leave?"

"I have no idea. But then, I have never understood the working of Carlos's mind. Let us hope for both our sakes that he stays put. I wouldn't think he'd be pleased at our *norteamericano* lifestyle. He wasn't able to make use of your father's death. He might not be adverse to having one of us take his place."

Maddy shuddered. "Don't even mention such a thing, *mamacita*. I have enough on my mind." It had amused the two of them to call each other mother and daughter. Even though Soledad was actually two years younger

191

than her tall, slim stepdaughter, it entertained her to watch people's reactions when she introduced her. Maddy had no objections. She would have claimed anyone as her mother rather than Helen.

Her house was cool and dark as she let herself in that afternoon, and the sea breeze brought a freshening to the dead air of late summer. Tossing the stack of letters on her glass-topped coffee table, Maddy headed straight for the refrigerator, kicking off her sandals as she went. A few minutes later she sank down on the sofa, her bare feet on the table in front of her, a can of Tab in her hand, as she flicked on the remote-control switch for the TV and began to delve through the bills, advertising, charity appeals, and circulars that comprised her mail. Dan Rather was off that night, and she paid little attention to his replacement, sorting through her mail with half a mind trying to decide whether to go for a walk before or after dinner, when a name caught her attention.

"The latest delegation from San Pablo arrived in Washington today, headed by General Anastasio Ortega, to try to talk the U.S. Congress into reinstating military aid for that besieged country. This will be the fourth such mission . . ."

Maddy stared at the TV, at the smiling, handsome face of Ortega, clad in his natty gray uniform glittering with medals and orders and not a weapon in sight, and her hands clenched into fists. He'd been the one in charge of the shelling of civilians in that aging hacienda, and now he was in Washington to bleat about the peaceful efforts of the Morosa government.

He must have heard her thoughts. "I plan a great many things for this visit," he said smoothly. "I wish to set our case before your Congress, with all the true facts that have been ignored . . ."

192

True facts, Maddy sneered, taking a swig of her Tab.

". . . and pay my respects to the widow and daughter of our national hero, Sam Lambert," he continued smoothly.

Maddy grimaced. Soledad would be charmed to hear that.

But apparently Ortega had forgotten about Soledad. "I will be visiting with Senora Maxfield Henderson tomorrow afternoon, to present my government's condolences on the death of her late husband and to talk over plans for a suitable memorial to this great man."

This great man you wanted to kill, Maddy fumed. And with the suddenness of television news the story was over and gone, leaving Maddy feeling angry and just a little shaken.

She knew who would be on the phone when it rang shrilly in her ear a half an hour later. She hadn't heard her voice since she walked out of the house in McLean six months ago, but she knew the peremptory tone of the ring.

"Hello, Mother," she said politely.

"I assume you watched the news," Helen said without preamble.

"I did."

"Ortega wants to see you."

"Ortega can go to hell."

"Madelyn, do not be more difficult than you have been already. Now is your chance to do something positive for your beloved little Patronistas. I wouldn't have thought La Patronita would let them down for a matter of pride."

Maddy didn't even ask how her mother had heard that nickname. She knew with sudden weariness that as usual her mother was pulling the right strings. She'd have to

193

come, just on the off-chance that bloodthirsty, murdering Ortega might see reason. "When do you want me?"

She could almost hear Helen purring at the other end of the line. "Anastasio is coming tomorrow afternoon with his party. There'll be plenty of media around. I think you should be here to provide a united front. Come in the morning and I'll have your room made ready."

"I'll be there at three tomorrow afternoon," Maddy said. "And I'll stay at the Sheraton."

"But, darling, that's so far away."

"Sorry."

"You're being uncooperative," Helen said in a dangerous voice.

"I'm being far more cooperative than you have any right to expect. Tomorrow at three." And she hung up before her mother could say another word.

It was a vain hope that all the flights might be booked. It was a vain hope that her plane might crash over the Grand Canyon. And it was a vain hope that the taxi drivers would refuse to take her into Virginia, the limousine drivers would be on strike, and the rental agencies be out to lunch. At quarter of three Maddy pulled into her mother's spacious driveway, the clumsy American car ending a few feet beyond the front door with a screech of power brakes.

It was sheer luck that she hadn't rammed into one of the myriad television vans outside the house. Her hands were trembling slightly as she climbed out of the seat and headed toward the house, and she told herself it was the near miss with the unaccustomed vehicle that made her nervous. But she knew it wasn't.

It was going to take every bit of her self-control not to jump, screaming, on Ortega's compact little body and try to rip his eyes out. He would doubtless be surrounded by

194

brawny Gray Shirts imported for the purpose. Hadn't Helen mentioned his party? No doubt consisting of bodyguards and more bodyguards. He certainly didn't need a translator.

With a move that was now almost characteristic she reached down and touched the medallion through the light cotton shirt. The heavy warmth of it soothed her, reminded her to be patient as she walked through the door and definitely not to cry.

Her mother and Ortega were out on the terrace, the swimming pool shimmering in the background, a horde of reporters, cameras, microphones stuck in front of them. Her stepfather was off to one side, observing all this with a pleased expression, and for a moment Maddy watched them.

Suddenly it was all too much. Not for the sake of a thousand homeless refugees could she stand by and make polite conversation with that murderer. There had to be some other way, but right now she had no stomach for any way at all. Wheeling around, she headed back toward the front door.

The rapid buzz of San Pablan Spanish carried to her, and without hesitation she took a detour, moving toward the library and the french doors that led out into the curving driveway. It was bound to be deserted at this moment. Everyone was out drooling over Helen Henderson's carefully staged photo opportunity.

The room was not quite as empty as she could have hoped. Slamming the door shut behind her, she headed over to the french doors that were open to the early-autumn breeze. Out of the corner of her eyes she saw a gray-shirted figure rise from the chair behind the desk, and she almost broke into a run, instinctive panic taking over at the sight of that hated uniform. Then she stopped motionless by the door, before turning—to look directly into Jake Murphy's distant, unreadable eyes above the uniform of their enemy.

CHAPTER FIFTEEN

He caught up with her by the huge rental car. She had her hand on the door, ready to yank it open, dive inside, and lock him and everything that had ever betrayed her out, when his hand closed over hers, strong and hard and pitiless, yanking her around to confront a face she had thought never to see again and now wished to God she didn't have to.

He looked no different from when she had first seen him six months ago, a little older perhaps, a little colder, and those hazel eyes of his looked right through her without tenderness, mercy, or remembrance. That last night in the San Pablo highlands might never have happened. Or maybe she'd just been the spoils of war, she thought bitterly.

"Get your hands off me," she said in a low, controlled voice.

She should have known better than to have thought he'd take orders from her. His long fingers kept their tight grip, almost but not quite cutting off the circulation of blood. She'd have bruises there tomorrow. Bruises to remind her.

"Get in the car." His voice was low and rough, with

that gravelly texture she remembered all too well. The sound of it was another slice of pain, but she never flinched.

"That's exactly what I was planning to do," she said with great dignity. "If you'll just let go of me and step away, I'll be more than happy to leave."

"Get in the car, Maddy," he repeated, never loosening his grip, "and slide over to the passenger side."

"I'm not going anywhere with you."

"You don't have any choice in the matter, do you?" he countered, unmoved. "But no, you're not going anywhere with me. We're just going to have a little talk."

"I have nothing to say to you."

"I think you'll find that you do. Get in the car, Maddy. There's no one around, and I wouldn't think twice about forcing you." His tone of voice was deceptively polite.

"You already are forcing me."

"There's force and there's force," he observed pleasantly, and his fingers tightened a fraction on the slender bones of her wrist.

She had no choice. The metal of the car door felt warm beneath her cold, sweating fingers. She opened it and slid in, along the absurdly luxurious bench seat, with Jake following her, and when she reached the far edge of the bench seat he released her.

"Give me the keys."

"I thought you said we weren't going anywhere."

"We're not. But it's too hot to sit here with the windows closed, and I sure as hell don't want anyone overhearing us. I'm going to turn on the car and the air conditioning," he explained patiently.

"You've gotten pretty soft since you've joined Morosa's band of cutthroats," she scoffed. "I don't remember any air conditioning in Puente del Norte."

"No, there wasn't any," he said, starting the car and the air conditioner before turning to her. "I'm not about to make excuses to you, Maddy."

Why not? she felt her heart cry out, and quickly squashed it down. Why did he have to look so very wonderful to her, when she hated him? He'd cut some but not all of that glorious hair, so that it now trailed over the collar of his uniform. His uniform, she reminded herself, withdrawing even more. His face was tanned and austere, as withdrawn as her own, and his hazel eyes looked even more bleak. It took her a moment to realize that the last time she'd seen those hazel eyes she'd been lying beneath him, his eyes hooded and slightly glazed as he'd looked down at her. . . .

Now was hardly the time for erotic memories, she reminded herself. That Jake had died in San Pablo. The man beside her was nothing more than a . . . what? She didn't really know.

"What do you want from me, Jake?" she demanded wearily. "If you don't want to explain, why did you even want to see me? You must have known my mother sent for me."

"I asked her to."

"Why? I presume after six months that it wasn't a sudden upsurge of love?"

"No."

"Then what?" Her voice sounded admirably distant and collected. Her father would have been proud of her. But what would her father have thought of the turncoat sitting next to her?

Jake leaned back against the powder-blue upholstered seat, and the fluffy luxury of the big car looked absurd against his whipcord toughness and military bearing.

Damn, she hated that uniform. "Sam sent something back with you," he said.

"You know that he did. A candy box with a videotape that I delivered to Senator O'Malley. It was instrumental in getting almost all military aid to San Pablo cut." She couldn't keep a note of triumph out of her voice.

"He sent something else too. I want to know what and where it is, and I want you to give it to me." His voice and face were implacable.

"I wish I knew what you were talking about, just so I could tell you to go to hell," Maddy said. "But I don't."

"Sam sent more than the candy box home with you. He sent something that would incriminate the Patronistas. I have a pretty good idea what it is, but it won't do us any good until we find it."

"We? When did you and Morosa and Ortega suddenly become we? Doesn't it bother you that Ortega is responsible for the death of your friends?"

"What friends?"

"Richard Feldman, Dr. Milsom, Luis, Enrique, Jorge . . ."

"Only Richard died in the shelling," Jake corrected her. "And that was his choice."

"I'm sure it was. What did you do, give him the choice of betraying his principles once more and fighting for the Gray Shirts or dying? I'd imagine he'd choose dying quite happily. Since you betrayed him."

"You're so very sure of yourself and what you imagine happened," Jake said wearily. "And I don't have the time or the inclination right now to set you straight. You're having too good a time hating me as it is. I just want what Sam gave you. A book, another box, a letter."

Oh, Jake, I'm not having a good time hating you, she mourned. Not a good time at all. She could feel tears at

200

the back of her eyes, and quickly she blinked them away to glare at him fiercely. "I don't know what you're talking about, Jake. You should know as well as I do that I didn't see Sam after that morning visit. You didn't choose to let me, even though my father was on his deathbed, calling for me."

"No, I didn't choose to let you," he replied heavily. "For reasons I'm not about to go into. For Pete's sake, Maddy, give me a straight answer! Did someone bring you something? From Sam, perhaps?"

For a moment Maddy thought of the medallion that lay against her skin, then dismissed it. It was nothing more than a disk of solid metal, and it had nothing to do with this damnable tangle of politics. It had been a gift of love from a distant father, and there was no way she was going to give it up to Jake Murphy.

"Sam gave me nothing but the candy box," she said firmly, meeting his eyes then wished she hadn't. Jake's eyes had always been able to see everything, and they saw through her right now.

"You're lying, Maddy," he said. "I've known you long enough and well enough to know when you're lying to me. What is it?"

She managed an airy laugh. "I don't know what you're talking about."

"Of course you do. Maddy, you're no fool. You can't hold out against the entire forces of Morosa and the rebels combined. Carlos wants that information just as badly as I do, and Carlos has gotten a bit . . . overeager in the last few months."

"Why mince words? After all, you're on opposite sides now. Carlos has apparently become a murdering lunatic. I have no doubt he'd cut off my ears and nose just for pleasure, but I can't give you or him what I don't have.

My father gave me nothing but the box of candy, which I delivered unopened to Senator O'Malley. Talk with him if you don't believe me."

"We have." He stared at her for a long, frustrated moment. "When did you suddenly choose sides?"

"What?" It was an abrupt change of topic, and Maddy stared at him in confusion for a moment.

"I said, when did you choose sides? When you were down in San Pablo you seemed to think both sides were murdering cutthroats. When did you suddenly become so partisan to the rebels?"

She thought about it for a moment, uncertain whether to tell him the truth. Why not? she thought bitterly. What else did she have to lose? She met his gaze calmly. "When I thought you'd been murdered by the government." She shrugged her shoulders in unconscious imitation of Soledad's oft-used gesture. "My mistake, it seems."

He stared at her in absolute silence, and there was no way she could tell what he was thinking. Then he reached for the door, not for her, and she knew he was lost to her more than a bullet or an explosion could have made him. He was dead to her.

"You're going to have to give it up sooner or later, Maddy," he said finally. "If not to me, then to Carlos, and you won't like the way Carlos will get it."

"Carlos is in San Pablo. . . ."

"Carlos was seen in Los Angeles last week, Maddy. He'll find you. The only way to protect yourself is to give me what I want."

"I don't know what you're talking about," she said stubbornly. "Believe me, if I did I'd give it to you just to get you out of my life."

"And that's what it will take, Maddy. Because until

202

you hand it over I'm your shadow. You won't be able to enjoy your comfortable Southern California lifestyle, you won't be able to go anywhere without seeing me, remembering me . . ."

"Don't!" Her voice was ragged with unexpected pain, and swiftly she cleared it. "I don't know what you're talking about, Jake," she said urgently. "I really, truly don't. Go back to San Pablo and your beloved General Morosa and leave me alone. Please, Jake." She hated to beg, but she had no choice. It was going to take her a long time to get over this, perhaps the rest of her life. She couldn't even begin to recover until he was well and truly gone.

"I'll leave you alone when you give me what I want," he said, and there was no softness, no pity or caring in that gravelly voice. Then he was gone, the key buzzing angrily as he opened the door and hot air blasted into the car. Maddy lifted her head to watch him walk away, and she stared at his body hungrily, the tall, lean length of him in that damnable gray uniform that only meant death and oppression.

It was a good thing it was a Saturday afternoon and there wasn't much traffic between McLean and Dulles Airport. She pulled into the rental parking section in a state of shock that approached a mild drunk, and even her gait in the high-heeled shoes developed a slight weaving.

The flight between Washington and L.A. went by in a blur as Maddy stared sightlessly out the window, into the fluffy bank of clouds. L.A. traffic wasn't quite so merciful, but a small part of Maddy's brain was working by that time, and she made it back to Hermosa Beach safely enough, parking the Alfa at a haphazard angle on the street and stumbling into the dark interior of her apartment.

She dropped her purse and sat down on the sofa. It was past five, L.A. time, and dusk was approaching. Maddy sat there without moving, without turning on a light. She could feel the cool sea breeze from the ocean, but even that brought no solace. She sat there, numb, her hands folded neatly in her lap, staring into nothingness. It was there that Soledad found her.

"This is no good." She clucked, bustling in the open door and flicking on the overhead light. It was almost dark when she arrived, and Maddy hadn't moved more than a muscle or two in the hour since she came back. "You're made of tougher stuff than that, Maddy. No daughter of mine, even if she's a stepdaughter who's two years older, is going to give in so weakly. I'll fix you a good, stiff drink, some soup, and then you will tell me all about it."

Maddy turned her head, and the muscles were stiff and unyielding. "Jake's alive."

"I know, Maddy." For once in her life Soledad was kind.

"For how long?"

"He called me three days ago." Soledad told many lies when it suited her, but she also knew when the truth was needed, however painful it might be.

"You know he's working for General Ortega?"

"So he said." Soledad was busy in the kitchen, and her voice was distracted. A second later she reappeared, a dark amber drink in her hand. "Drink this."

Maddy took the glass, staring down at the lone ice cube and the withered slice of lemon that floated in the dark, pungent liquid. "What is it?" she roused herself to ask.

"Straight rum. Drink it." When Soledad used that tone of voice there was no denying her. Maddy drank, choking on the results.

Soledad sat down beside Maddy on the sofa, taking the empty glass from her and setting it on the table in front of them. "Do you have any idea what he wants?"

Maddy shook her head. "No idea at all," she said truthfully.

Soledad's dark, pretty face was troubled. "Well, we'd better try to find out. If Jake doesn't get it, Carlos will. And I—I am very much afraid of Carlos, my daughter."

A little frisson of fear ran across Maddy's backbone. "He won't hurt me," she said, not believing a word of it.

"Of course he will, and the only person capable of stopping him is Jake," Soledad said.

"Surely the police . . ."

"Carlos has been dodging one of the best-organized armies and terrorist squads in the world today. Do you seriously think the L.A.P.D. is any match for him?"

There was no answer Maddy could give to that irrefutable piece of logic. If the only person who could help her was Jake Murphy, then she would do without help. Besides, he was only likely to help her if she gave him what he wanted, and she truly had no idea what it was. Someone else must have whatever Carlos and Jake were seeking. Perhaps it had died with Richard Feldman in that steaming jungle.

"You really don't know, Maddy?"

She met Soledad's dark eyes. "I really don't know."

Her tiny stepmother nodded. "Then there's nothing we can do. I think you ought to go to bed, Maddy. You look dead on your feet."

"I'd rather not. I—I don't want to be alone."

Soledad nodded again. "Then lie down on the sofa. I'll

find you a blanket and pillow, and I will stay and keep you company."

"You don't have to do that," Maddy protested weakly.

"I know I don't. But I will."

The moon was shining in the darkened living room, and Maddy moved restlessly on the sofa. She could see the shadowed shape of her stepmother, keeping vigil in the darkness. "Soledad," Maddy whispered.

There was a moment of silence, and Maddy wondered if Soledad was asleep. "Yes, my daughter?"

"Do you still love Jake?"

The next pause was even longer, then she spoke. "Not anymore. Do you?"

Always and forever, Maddy had promised herself six months ago, fourteen years ago. "No," she lied, and Soledad's answering laugh was a cool lilt of disbelief.

The small house by the ocean was empty when Maddy awoke from her cramped night on the sofa. There was no sign of Soledad anywhere, only a note by the refrigerator.

"Gone away for a few days, daughter mine. If Carlos is in town I don't want to be here, and neither should you. Go to Jake if you need help. He is the most trustworthy man I know."

That wasn't saying much, Maddy thought as she made herself a pot of coffee. Soledad hadn't gone in much for trust in men, and if Jake was a prime example she'd done even worse than Maddy suspected. Soledad's spelling was atrocious, and for a brief, pain-swept moment Maddy remembered another ill-spelled letter that had been hoarded and reread until the yellow lined paper was soft with age. She slammed her hand down on the counter in a vain attempt to block out the memory.

She didn't leave her house until late afternoon that

206

Sunday, and then only to walk on the beach. Her brain had mercifully gone on automatic pilot, and she moved through the hours in a kind of beneficial fog.

But Monday dawned bright and clear, and the real world had to be faced. She could feel those eyes, watching her, as she drove through the early-morning traffic toward Hollywood, but she shrugged off the feeling. It had to be sheer paranoia.

She always arrived at the ancient, five-story building that housed the Greater Hollywood Help Network at a little past eight. At that hour she missed the very worst of the traffic, and it gave her a blessed few minutes of peace in which to drink her third cup of coffee, do the L.A. *Times* crossword puzzle, and generally gather her inner and outer resources before the stress of the day began. The social workers drifted in between eight thirty and nine, and their clients showed up any time after that, though early afternoon was usually the peak. Even though nominally Maddy had little to do with the clients, when a new group of San Pablan refugees arrived she always managed to be in the front room to greet them, particularly when there were children. There were times when only the innocent laughter of children could make her smile again.

It mattered little whether the refugees were legal or illegal aliens. The network was a private agency, not directly answerable to the federal government, and Maddy and the social workers made very sure not to ask too many questions.

The parking lot was almost empty when she stopped, and the attendant yawned extravagantly as he took the keys. The streets were deserted. Hollywood street people and bag ladies were nocturnal creatures. Maddy paused at the corner, staring around her, her feet resting on

Norma Shearer's gold star. She could feel the eyes on her, watching her, and a little shiver ran down her spine.

She wouldn't turn and look, she told herself. She wouldn't. There wouldn't be anyone there, and she'd feel like a fool. She wouldn't look.

But it was a losing battle. Slowly she pivoted on her high heels and there, five yards away on a deserted stretch of Hollywood Boulevard, stood Jake Murphy.

CHAPTER SIXTEEN

He was dressed differently, and Maddy didn't know whether to be relieved or more disturbed. He no longer wore the starched gray uniform that stood for everything she hated, or the khaki fatigues that reminded her of that jungle war, or the dark, three-piece suits of his days as a Secret Service man. He was wearing faded denims that hugged his narrow hips and swept the length of his long legs, an equally faded denim shirt, and boots that even from this distance looked like they were Frye's best. Fancy stuff for a simple soldier, Maddy told herself grimly. She could see a glint of silver around his neck in the early-morning sunlight, and a pair of dark glasses hid those merciless hazel eyes from her. She was just as glad.

The building was deserted as she headed swiftly into her office. For a moment she'd considered retrieving her car and driving away, as far and as fast as she could. But she couldn't spend the rest of her life in hiding from Jake Murphy. She'd faced him once, she'd face him again and prove to him just how unimportant he was.

She made the huge urn of coffee with practiced skill, having chosen that menial but undeniably crucial task for her own, then leaned back against Sally's desk to watch it perk. Sally Floody and her sister-in-law, Chris Morey, were the two best social workers on the staff, and every day Maddy thanked heaven for their sure, delicate touch and deep, human concern. Their only drawback was that they made lousy coffee.

It took forever to perk that morning, and Maddy badly needed that coffee. The sight of Jake had unnerved her, the silence that followed only made it worse. Any moment she expected him to pop out from behind a desk, to grab her and start demanding heaven knew what. If only she knew what he was talking about. She'd gladly give him anything Sam had passed on to her, just to get him out of her hair. But Sam had given her nothing but the gold medallion as a final, belated token of love, and she wouldn't part with that for the world.

The coffee urn finished its business with a *whoosh* and sigh, and Maddy poured herself a huge cup in the mug Soledad had given her. It read "I survived San Pablo," and suddenly Maddy was having her doubts.

Her office was in the corner on the cool northwest side of the building, and the narrow Roman blinds were still drawn from the previous weekend. The darkness was soothing. Setting the mug on her littered desk, she sank into her chair, a nervous hand playing with the medallion beneath her crisp cotton shirt.

This time she didn't jump. How he'd managed to slip past her in the dark, deserted building, how he'd managed to find her own private office was beyond her comprehension. But he was there, leaning back in the chair usually reserved for the social workers or San Pablan refugees. He might almost qualify as the latter, she thought with a trace of misplaced humor.

"Would you like some coffee?" Her voice was perfectly

modulated. Damn, she was cool, she thought with a shaft of real pleasure.

His small, careful smile acknowledged her control. "Not right now. Have you thought about what I asked you?"

"About some mysterious final mission from Sam? Yes, I've thought about it, and you're out of your mind."

"I've been told that before."

"I'm sure you have." She took a sip of her dark, scalding coffee, refusing to grimace as she burned her tongue.

"Carlos was seen crossing the Mexican border two days ago, Maddy. He should be in L.A. right now."

"Maybe he enjoys the climate," she snapped back.

"He won't take no for an answer."

"Neither, apparently, do you," she replied. "Listen, if you're here for some assistance I'll be glad to take your application. We do our best to aid all San Pablan refugees, no matter which side of the conflict they were on. If you don't need any aid, then why don't you kindly get the hell out of here?" She maintained her sweetest tone of voice.

Murphy only smiled. "I'll be back at the end of the day." He rose, and the silver at his neck glinted again in the morning sunlight.

"You don't even know when we close. We've got flexible hours. . . ."

"I'll know," he said, and she believed him. She rose, instinctive politeness momentarily overcoming her hostility, eyeing the silver with a curiosity she couldn't restrain. Jake had never struck her as the type to wear jewelry. But then, he had never struck her as the type to turn traitor. Then he moved, heading toward the door, and she recognized what he was wearing.

It was the silver ring she'd sent back with Carlos, sent

back to be buried with him. The ring Stephen had given her. Jake wore it on a silver chain around his neck, and suddenly Maddy went half crazy with rage.

Clearly he'd seen her reaction and guessed what caused it. "Don't even try it," he warned dryly.

She was past hearing him. Moving around the desk with the speed of a snake, she leaped at him, reaching to yank the ring from his neck.

His hands shot out and caught her wrists before she made it halfway there, and a moment later she was shoved up against the open office door, her arms held over her head by his manaclelike wrists, and the solid length of his body was pressed up against hers, holding her captive with only the solid wood supporting her.

The threat was there, physical, overwhelming, implicitly sexual. She could feel his belt buckle digging into her stomach, his hips hard against her, his chest pressing her breasts flat. She was terrified, furious, and for the first time in six months completely, gloriously alive.

"Give me that ring," she said, her voice low and dangerous.

Jake just looked down at her without saying a word. His face was only inches from hers, and she could feel the soft warmth of his uneven breath on her upturned, enraged face. Why would his breathing be uneven? It surely hadn't taken much physical effort on his part to subdue her. Or was it just possible that the proximity of their bodies had the same effect on him as it had on her?

There was a distant expression in his eyes, and slowly his head dipped down, his mouth reaching blindly for hers as his hands still held her captive against the office door. A distant part of her watched in horror as she tilted her head up for his kiss.

But before their mouths could touch the sound of

212

voices penetrated to the far reaches of her office, the noisy little tap of high-heeled shoes echoing through the building. She was released, Jake had withdrawn, just as Sally and Chris appeared in the outer office.

"There you are, Maddy," Sally greeted her with a cheerful wave. "Did you have a good time in Washington?"

Jake moved past her. "I'll be back," he said, his gravelly voice a threat and a promise. He walked out past the two curious women without a backward glance.

There was complete, absolute stillness in the room as the women watched him depart.

"Was that . . . ?" Sally whispered in a disbelieving voice.

Maddy nodded. "It was."

"But I thought he was dead."

"So did I."

Sally was doing her best to keep the confusion from her narrow, pretty face, and not doing a very good job of it. "But why aren't you happier?"

"Sally," Chris warned.

Maddy grimaced. "Sometimes I think it's a little better for people to die than for dreams to die," she said bitterly and vanished back into her office, closing the door behind her.

It was a blessedly busy day, too busy to allow Maddy time to brood. The fighting had gotten much much worse in San Pablo, spreading from the southern Mosquito coast up through the jungle highlands that held Puente del Norte. La Mensa was in a state of siege, and rumor had it that there wouldn't be much left for the victors to enjoy. The influx of refugees had increased tenfold, all needing assistance, in finding housing, in finding jobs, in simply getting enough to keep from starving on the mean streets of L.A.

Maddy was in and out of the main office all day. People had taken to seeking her out, as some sort of talisman or good luck charm. Any kin of Samuel Lambert appeared to be blessed, and La Patronita, El Patrón's daughter, was doubly so.

"You're going to be the patron saint of San Pablo at this rate," Sally muttered under her breath when one tearful old lady was particularly vocal, all in the heavily accented San Pablan Spanish that only Chris was adept in.

"If there's any San Pablo left," Maddy said. "Sally, I'm leaving early."

Sally had shrieked in protest. "We're jammed with people, Maddy. You can't do this to me, on one of our busiest days!"

"I have to."

"But Maddy . . ." Her voice trailed off, as she suddenly remembered Maddy's earlier visitor. "Do you think Jake will come back?"

"Jake assured me that he would come back. I want to make sure I'm gone. You can handle this, Sally. I have complete faith in the two of you."

"You can't run away from him forever, Maddy." Sally's voice was hesitant.

Maddy smiled wryly. "No, I can't. But I can run like hell right now."

But she couldn't run very far. It was only three thirty when she headed for the door, hours before she usually drove back to Hermosa Beach. It took her an additional fifteen minutes to get past the homesick San Pablans crowding the office, all eager to meet the daughter of El Patrón. She was at the door, gently disentangling herself from a loquacious butcher whose English was as small as his girth was large, when she felt his presence behind her. The eyes again, boring into her back. Different from the eyes that had been watching her last week, less vindictive.

"Are you ready?" Jake inquired politely, standing just outside the door.

She could have screamed in frustration. Instead she smiled sweetly, an instant, wicked idea sparking into her brain. He was proving to be more difficult to lose than she had imagined so this called for drastic measures.

She turned around, giving him a big smile that managed to startle him out of his dour determination. "Jake Murphy," she cried in a loud, carrying voice. "Friend of Sam Lambert! How good to see you." She stood there smirking as a wave of refugees swamped over him, chattering excitedly and with great joy.

She waved to him over the hordes of people surrounding him, entrapping him, and the expression on his face was one of acute frustration as she slipped past him, down the stairs, and out onto the street.

It would take him quite a while to escape from his admirers, Maddy thought, quite pleased with herself. Mrs. Mendoza was particularly long-winded, and the butcher from La Mensa had an admirable tenacity. She would be long gone before Jake made it out to the street.

Not that he couldn't be counted on to know where she lived. But she had locks on her doors, a responsive police force nearby, and even a haphazard neighborhood crime watch going. She could keep him at a distance once she got to Hermosa Beach. But that meant no walks on the beach for the next few days, until he finally gave up and went back to Ortega.

It was a strange thing, she mused, turning off Hollywood Boulevard and heading for the parking lot. She hadn't even had to clarify Jake's position in her father's life. The mere mention of his name had sent them hurtling toward Jake's tall figure, with nothing but excitement and pleasure on their faces. Surely they would know about his turncoat activities, know that he'd turned his back on everything her father had stood for. Yet they were furious and terrified at the name of Carlos the Jackal, and for Jake Murphy there was nothing but devotion.

Of course, they might all have been Morosa loyalists, Maddy mused doubtfully. But in that case why would they have left? And why would they be so fond of La Patronita? It simply didn't make sense. Jake Murphy should have been reviled as the lowest of the lows and instead he was treated like a conquering hero. She really ought to set a few people straight about . . .

The arm snaked out in front of her, the large dirty hand clamping down over her mouth, and before she had time to react she found herself being dragged into a narrow, cool alleyway. She could feel the sharp prick of a knife beneath her ribs as panic rushed through her, and it took all her strength of mind to force herself to be calm. In all her years of working in downtown Hollywood she had never been mugged. There was a first time for everything; if she was just calm and obedient she would make it through safely. Whoever had grabbed her was undoubtedly some frightened kid, just as scared as she was.

But she could feel the heartbeat of the figure behind her, and it was slow and steady. Ominously so. "I would suggest, *gringa,*" came the San Pablan voice, "that you think carefully before you struggle. This knife is very sharp, and I know how to use it. I promise you Jake wouldn't find you until you were very dead."

Carlos's high-pitched, almost girlish voice was unforgettable. Slowly he removed his grubby hand from her mouth, and she forced herself to take slow, steady breaths. The knife was still pointed sharply against her ribs, and she couldn't turn around to look at him. She didn't know whether seeing him would make her more or less frightened. The disembodied voice and the knife were enough to send a stronger woman into a gibbering panic.

"What do you want, Carlos?" Her voice was a little dry, rusty, but even enough.

"You know perfectly well what I want, *puta*. I want what Sam gave you."

"I don't know what you and Jake are talking about," she said wearily, and the knife pricked closer. "Sam didn't give me anything but what I gave Senator O'Malley. I swear—"

"I do not believe you. We know for a fact the old man sent something else back with you, and it's not something we can afford to be made public."

"What do you think I have, for God's sake? Jake wouldn't even tell me."

Carlos snorted. "What a fool the man is. I'll tell you what it is. It is a tiny map of the northwestern section of San Pablo."

"A map?"

"It shows the location of a small Indian village. There used to be three hundred Indians living up there, away from the strife of San Pablo."

"And now."

She could feel him shrug behind her. "And now they are all dead. An unfortunate mistake."

"On whose part?"

Carlos laughed. "I am no traitor like your lover. The Patronistas are not perfect saints, unlike your father and now yourself. They thought they were hiding some Gray Shirt informants and . . ."

"And?"

"And they burned the town. With everyone in it, I'm afraid. Men, women, and children." His voice was cool and unconcerned.

"And where were you when all this happened?"

She didn't want to hear the answer she knew was coming. "Why, right there, *gringa.* I gave the order."

Maddy broke out in a cold sweat, her battle against panic lost. "I don't have the map."

"But you know where it is."

"No, I swear—"

"I don't believe you, *gringa,*" Carlos said. "I will give you twenty-four hours exactly to come up with the map. Do not think to hide. I will know where to find you. And don't expect anyone to help you. If you give the map to Jake I will cut your liver out. It will be very easy," he said in a dreamy voice. "Just a little slice"—Maddy felt a cool, stinging against her side—"and it will be gone. And that will be for a beginning. Think about it, *gringa.*"

Then she was released, sent spinning against the brick wall. She heard his feet running down the alleyway, and she looked up in time to see his dark figure disappear around a corner and into the L.A. traffic.

She looked down. He'd sliced neatly through the cotton shirt, and the stinging in her side warned her that he'd connected with more than cotton. She should go to a hospital, she thought dazedly. She should go to the police, but the only place she wanted to be was home. Clamping an arm against her side to hide the rip, she moved back out of the alleyway, into the innocuous afternoon sunlight.

She was halfway to Hermosa Beach when she noticed

the car behind her. A Toyota, like all the rental cars in San Pablo. With Jake Murphy at the wheel.

She should have been frightened, she told herself. She should have been furious. Instead she was relieved, deeply, almost blindly grateful. The stinging in her side reassured her that she wasn't about to bleed to death before she made it back to her tiny house, but despite Carlos's assertion that she had twenty-four hours, she had no guarantee that he'd stick to it, particularly when he knew Jake was close by.

Her house was cool and dark and empty when she let herself in the front door. She didn't bother to close it behind her. Jake had parked the rented Toyota a few cars away from the Alfa and would doubtless be there in a moment. At that point she had no energy to run any more.

Moving in to the kitchen, she undid her shirt and gingerly pulled it from her jeans, away from her side. It clung for a moment, and Maddy bit her lip as it pulled away with a deeper shaft of pain. She tossed it to the counter, pulled the medallion over her head and dumped it on top, and then surveyed the damage.

There was a long, thin line directly below her bottom rib, razor thin, just barely breaking the skin, with beads of blood dotting the surface. It stung, feeling more like a bad scrape than anything else. She moved to the sink to splash cold water on it, not even lifting her head when Jake walked into the kitchen.

She could feel his eyes on her, but she was damned if she was going to cower because she was only wearing a blue lace bra. He'd seen her in a lot less, and she had more on her mind at the moment than Jake's unpredictable libido.

"Carlos found you," he said, moving forward and taking the damp paper towel from her hand. He pressed it gently against the line of blood, and she let out a little gasp at the cool, stinging sensation.

"He could have killed me."

"Of course he could have but he wasn't intending to. Carlos is very good with a knife—a craftsman, in fact. He cut you just as deeply as he intended, and no more."

"Well, hurray for craftsmen," Maddy shot back, her fear receding as anger took its place.

"Do you have any disinfectant? Hydrogen peroxide, alcohol?"

"I thought the great Carlos knew what he was doing," she snapped.

"I said he was good. I didn't say he was clean."

Maddy glared up at him. "I'll get it. In the meantime you can fix me a drink."

"You aren't going to order me out of your house?" he countered.

"Would it do any good?"

"No."

"Then I won't bother. I don't have the energy to waste at this point," she said in a weary voice, stumbling toward the hallway. The hand that reached out and caught her was gentle.

"Why don't you go into the living room? I'll find the disinfectant and make you a drink. Then we can decide what you're going to do."

"I can't give you what I don't have, Jake." Her voice sounded almost lost, damnably weak, but there was nothing she could do about it.

He gave her a gentle push on her bare shoulder. "Go sit down. We'll talk about it."

She went obediently enough, too weary to fight any further. She lay back against the sofa, not even opening her eyes as he began painting her rib with iodine. She should have tossed that out years ago, she thought, biting her lip rather than complain.

"I've figured out what you can do," he said, and the sound of his gravelly voice had its usual, unbidden effect on her.

She opened one eye and stared at him distrustfully. "And what's that?"

"Run away with me."

CHAPTER SEVENTEEN

Maddy just looked at him. "Now that sounds like an offer I can't refuse," she drawled finally. "But I'm afraid I have to decline. You of course could always run away all by yourself. I'd like that a lot."

"No, you wouldn't." He was unmoved by her sarcastic refusal. "Right now I'm the only thing between you and Carlos's knife. If you stopped to think about it for a moment you'd recognize that fact."

"We happen to have a very fine police force in Hermosa Beach," she said stiffly.

"And in L.A. And you know Carlos. You were down in San Pablo. Do you really think *norteamericano* cops are any match for him?"

Maddy hadn't been able to argue that point with Soledad and wasn't about to try with Jake. "I can take care of myself."

"Sure you can. I'll remember to send flowers to your funeral."

"You do that," she snapped. "Okay, Jake, now you can leave."

"I thought we already established that it wouldn't do any good to try to kick me out?"

"Hope springs eternal. At least the police could get rid of you, even if they're useless with Carlos."

"Don't be so sure, Maddy. I've had the same training as Carlos." He sat back on his heels, watching her out of those opaque eyes, and suddenly she felt very vulnerable, sitting there in her jeans and bra and nothing else.

"Let me make it perfectly clear, Jake. I'm not going anywhere with you." He could make her, of course. They both knew it. All he had to do was put those strong hands on her and drag her out, and she wouldn't be able to put up much of a fight.

Jake shook his head, and she wondered if he could read her mind. He rose, towering over her as she lay back against the sofa cushions. "Let me know when you change your mind."

"Sure." Her tone didn't hold out much hope.

"I mean it, Maddy."

"Sure," she said again. "Good-bye, Jake."

So why was she mad when he left? she demanded of herself with an anger of noble proportions. Why did she feel lonely and bereft when he walked out the door, why did the sound of the Toyota starting up and driving off feel like nails in her coffin? Had she lost her last claim to sanity?

The dark amber drink sat untouched on the coffee table. Leaning forward, she downed it in one gulp, then almost spat it out on the carpet. It was iced tea.

Well, for once maybe Jake was right. A drink wasn't a very good idea, especially when she was feeling so shaky. Her best bet would be a long walk on the beach. She'd been haunting the ocean for the last six months, when only the pounding of the surf, the freshness of the sea breeze, and the immovable elements of nature had been able to soothe the raw wound that Jake's death had left.

223

The ocean still had the power to soothe her, in the midst of the tumult her life had become.

She headed back to the kitchen, picking up her medallion and dropping it over her head. The striped cotton shirt had a nice, clean slice through it, dotted with blood, and she dropped it into the trash with a belated shudder. Of course Carlos had known what he was doing. He would know what he was doing when he came after her again.

She pulled on her loosest cotton sweater, wincing as it grazed her side, changed into her Nikes, and headed down toward the strand. There were only a few runners out at that hour, the usual assortment of dog-walkers, and even one or two handholding couples. Maddy averted her gaze, ignoring the shaft of pain that sliced through her, and started walking.

She lost track of time, her long legs eating up the distance with a hurried, nervous stride that had little chance of calming her. She turned her options over and over in her mind, but none of them seemed the right answer. She could run, of course. Stephen had left her a small, rustic cabin in the mountains. Carlos would have a hard time finding her there. She could go to the police and hope against hope they'd be able to protect her. But Jake was right. Carlos played by different rules.

Or she could turn to Jake. Jake who had lied to her, who had let her father die without her, who had let her spend six months mourning him while he was turning traitor to everything her father had believed in. Jake who only wanted the mythical map to a massacre.

And how did that square up with his actions at Den Phui? He'd put his military career on the line in testifying about that other civilian massacre. Was he going to do it again, betraying Sam Lambert and Richard Feldman and all the Patronistas? The rebels had depended on the goodwill of the international press. This report would make them little better than Morosa's murderers.

The growling in her stomach finally brought her up short, and she realized with a start of pleased surprise that she was hungry. She hadn't eaten anything much all day, and despite the fright and trauma her body was reasserting its need to be fed. The sun was sinking low over the Pacific, and it was time to be getting back to the tiny house and find something for dinner. She'd been out for almost two hours, and if that hadn't brought her any answers, another hour wouldn't either.

There was no sign of the tell-tale Toyota as she climbed up the street toward her house. She wouldn't have put it past him to reappear, but it seemed as if he'd taken her dismissal as definite. He'd told her to let him know when she'd changed her mind. How was she supposed to do that when she didn't even know where he was? she thought irritably. San Pablo couldn't afford a consulate in California, much as they needed one. Maybe he was over in West L.A. in the teeming neighborhood of San Pablo refugees. Much good he'd be to her over there, she thought with a grimace.

The lights should have warned her. Later on she would blame Jake once more. She'd been too absorbed in thinking about him to notice that the darkened house she'd left now had the glow of electric lights. Even the unlocked front door didn't tip her off. She assumed she'd been too disturbed to lock it properly. After all, Hermosa Beach had very little crime so security had never been an obsession with her.

She walked in and stopped dead. The neat, clean lines of her small living room were suddenly blurred, and she sank back against the wall, a small whimper of horror breaking the silence.

Carlos had been there. The place was totaled. Every sofa cushion slit, the books torn from the bookcases, the pictures smashed, dishes and glasses a pile of rubble on the floor. Even the spindly dining-room chairs had been splintered.

It took her a moment to move. When she did it was stiffly, in a state of shock, as she picked her way over the torn books, the shards of glass, the piles of stuffing.

The kitchen was worse. He'd emptied out the flour and sugar bins and hurled them around the tiny area. Every can was pulled out of the cupboards, the refrigerator was gutted, and the floor was swimming with spilled milk and wine and smashed Tab bottles.

There was a strange, painful little murmuring, and Maddy realized it came from her own throat as she moved through the hall to her bedroom and stood there, staring in horror.

Carlos had slashed through her clothes, emptied her dressers, smashed the mirrors, and trashed her closets. But worst of all was the bed.

He'd ripped through the center of the bed, a deep slash, and then crossed it, like a crucifix. And somewhere he'd found something red, probably catsup from the refrigerator, and poured it all over the deep incision. Feathers were still floating in the air from the pillows, sticking to the red stuff, and suddenly Maddy's stomach heaved.

It wouldn't have made any difference if she'd thrown up in the middle of her bedroom, she thought as she leaned over the toilet. Carlos had festooned the bathroom with her shampoo, but all and all it was the neatest room in the house. Unfortunately there wasn't much in her stomach, and she sat back amid the rubble, shaking with reaction, wishing there was enough glassless space to curl into the fetal position. As it was, all she could do was huddle back against the wall, wrapping her arms around her long legs, and bury her head against her knees.

She hadn't even closed the front door, much less locked it. She could hear the sound of the screen door opening and closing, hear the heavy footsteps crunching through the broken glass. She didn't move, didn't even breathe. If it was Carlos, come back to make sure she got the message, then there was little she could do. There was no back door to the tiny house. She was finally and truly trapped. She viewed that possibility with an equanimity born of desperation and she viewed the sudden appearance of Jake Murphy in her bathroom door with undisguised relief.

His eyes swept over her, meeting her face when he'd finally assured himself that she wasn't hurt. "So Carlos changed his mind about giving you twenty-four hours," he said.

Her first answer was a croak, and she quickly cleared her throat. "Apparently so," she managed.

He reached down and took her hand, pulling her to her feet. She swayed slightly, and he held out his other hand to steady her. Her knees were weak, but her determination and anger were strong enough to support her.

"Are you ready to come with me?" he asked quietly.

She had no choice. She couldn't stay there, and the idea of an anonymous hotel seemed even more threatening. And Soledad was already gone. There would be no sanctuary with her. Slowly she nodded. "Yes, I'm ready."

There was no triumph in Jake's face. It must have been a trick of the light, Maddy thought, or a trick of her own emotions, that he looked almost despairing at her decision. Whatever that expression was, it was soon gone.

"Then let's get out of here."

They went in her Alfa. She climbed into the passenger seat without a word, fastened the seat belt, tipped the seat back, and promptly fell asleep. She had no idea in the world where he was taking her, and she didn't care. As long as it was away from Hermosa Beach, away from Carlos, it really didn't matter where.

Jake had had to force her to take care of business enough to call Sally and tell her she'd be out of town for a while. Sally promised to send professional cleaners over to the house as soon as she could arrange it, and bless her soul, she asked no questions, other than "Is Jake with you?" And damn her, that seemed to satisfy her worries.

She woke up once when they stopped for gas, a few hours later when they stopped at an all-night diner. "You need to eat something," he said gruffly.

"I'm not hungry."

"I don't give a damn. I am, and I'm not leaving you in the car all alone."

He had her full attention by now. "Do you think Carlos has followed us?"

"No, but I don't want to take any chances. Besides, you need something in your stomach."

She climbed from the car with a slowness that was part defiance, part real body aches. "Where are we?" she questioned as she followed him into the diner.

"Budgewell, California."

"Budgewell? But that's . . ." She let it trail off in sudden suspicion.

He ushered her into a booth. "That's about seventeen miles from your brother's cabin," he finished for her, handing her a plastic-covered menu. "Yes, I know. That's where we're going."

She didn't even open it. "How did you know where the cabin was?"

"How else, Maddy? Your mother told me."

"Of course she did," Maddy said bitterly, remembering for the first time in hours that she was with the enemy. At least Carlos had the dubious advantage of being on the right side. If there was such a thing, which Maddy doubted.

"What's that look for?"

Maddy took a careful sip of the coffee placed in front of her by a discerning waitress. "I thought I should mention, just in case you forgot, how much I dislike accepting your help."

A twisted grin slashed his face. "I hadn't forgotten." He ordered a huge breakfast for both of them, then turned his attention back to Maddy.

"That's a lot of food for you to eat," she said, taking another sip of the surprisingly good coffee.

"I ordered for you too."

"Too bad. I don't like scrambled eggs."

Jake smiled sweetly. "I have no objections to shoving it down your throat."

He probably didn't, she thought grumpily. The caffeine was doing its job, bringing her fully, unpleasantly awake, and the more aware of her surroundings and her company she became, the more uncomfortable she got.

"Is it possible Carlos found what he was looking for?" Jake asked carefully. "Maybe we don't even have to worry about him any more."

She shook her head. "There was nothing to find. How many times do I have to tell you that, Jake? You may be

229

completely untrustworthy but I happen to put a fair amount of stock in the truth. I don't have the map."

Jake's eyes narrowed. "How did you know it was a map?"

She wasn't fooled by his gentle tone of voice. "Because Carlos told me as he was slicing through my shirt. Not because Sam gave me such a thing."

"So you still insist you know nothing about it? That Sam didn't give you anything besides that candy box?"

"I'm not even going to answer you any more," she snapped. "If you won't believe me anyway it's a waste of breath. Let me eat my eggs in peace."

"I thought you didn't like scrambled eggs?"

Maddy only glared in return as she applied herself to the eggs. Something was nagging in the back of her mind, some tiny little inconsistency that she couldn't quite place. There was something wrong, something that didn't ring true in all this, and she couldn't place what it was. She pushed her hash brown potatoes around on the thick melamine plate and drank more coffee, racking her brain for the answer.

Jake had given up trying. He ate his breakfast quickly, efficiently, and Maddy wondered if he even tasted it. By the time he'd tossed money down on the Formica and escorted her back out it was approaching dawn, and Maddy still couldn't figure out what was bothering her.

They were already well up into the mountains, and Maddy could recognize some of the landmarks. She'd spent a lot of time there in the past ten years. She knew the terrain like the back of her hand. She had the sudden, eerie thought that her knowledge of the area might be more than useful.

Sliding down in her seat, she once more leaned back and closed her eyes. What with all the coffee and her sudden, nagging feeling that something wasn't quite right, sleep was the farthest thing from her mind. But she wasn't about to continue her useless tête-à-tête with Jake. No matter what she said, he wouldn't believe her, and no matter what he said, she'd still feel betrayed.

Jake looked down at the dozing figure beside him and that damnably familiar tightening in his gut began again. She looked white beneath her tan, and shadows of exhaustion lurked below her eyes. Even the light spattering of freckles had faded across her high cheekbones, and her mouth looked pale and vulnerable.

If only he could trust her to tell him the truth. If only he didn't have to do this to her. But the situation had traveled so far along this path that there was no turning back. She'd be hurt, even more than she'd been hurt already, and there was nothing he could do about it but administer that hurt, doing his best to shield her from it at the same time.

You could say one thing about Maddy Lambert, he mused. She was tough. Beneath that fine-boned face, patrician bearing, beneath her warm, loving heart, she was tough and strong and brave, and not about to take crap from anyone. It would take a hell of a lot to demoralize her, to break through that icy toughness that was right now fueled by anger.

Unfortunately he knew what it would take, and he had no choice but to use it, ruthlessly, to his advantage, and to her advantage too, if she'd only believe him.

Damn Sam Lambert to hell. He'd done everything he could to keep the old man from entangling his daughter further in his crazy plans, but he'd been circumvented. Probably by Richard, thinking, as usual, that it was all

231

for the best. But it was too late to ask Richard, and Maddy wouldn't or couldn't answer.

He couldn't see any way out for the two of them. Too much had happened, too much would still happen, for them to find some sort of peace together. If they even made it through this whole mess in one piece, there'd be no way Maddy would ever forgive him, and no way he could ask for her forgiveness.

She sighed, and the soft sound made him clench his fists more tightly around the steering wheel. For a rash moment he considered turning the car around, heading up toward Canada, running off with her and forcing her to love him.

But you couldn't force someone to love you, and you couldn't turn your back on your responsibilities, your debts, your destiny. The game wasn't finished yet. He could only hope the two of them would at least be left standing when it was all over. But he had the feeling that it was nothing more than a vain hope.

The cabin was a rough-hewn log structure, set in a small clearing, surrounded by white pines and ancient old spruces. She'd worked hard on it over the years, fixing the windows, patching the lost chinks between the logs, even having Sally and Chris out for a wine-soaked roofing party that left the house waterproof but not much more than that. The summer's flowers were long since past, and the cabin looked dark and deserted in the early-morning sunlight.

Maddy roused herself from her self-induced torpor to look at the cabin. The last twenty minutes had done little to calm her state of mind, and even the sight of her usually welcome retreat couldn't ease her worry.

She was climbing out of the car, heading toward the

front door, when she noticed that the sturdy padlock was gone. And then something fell together in her tired brain, and she turned back to Jake, watching him as he followed her down the path.

"How did you know it was twenty-four hours?"

"I beg your pardon?"

"I said, how did you know it was twenty-four hours?" she demanded, her voice shaking. "When you got to my house tonight you said that Carlos must have decided not to give me twenty-four hours. I didn't tell you that he said I'd have that long. How did you know?" Her voice was getting shrill, and there was no way she could control it.

And Jake, damn his soul, said nothing. Maddy heard a noise behind her, and she turned back to see Carlos standing there in her doorway, a grin on his face, his lizard eyes squinting in unholy amusement, his knife in his hand.

"Welcome, *gringa*," he said smoothly. "I've been expecting you. Come in and make yourself at home."

She whirled around, prepared to run. But Jake was right behind her, and the gun in his hand was trained on her, not on his supposed enemy.

"Go in, Maddy," he said, his voice flat and emotionless. There was nothing she could do but go.

CHAPTER EIGHTEEN

Shock and betrayal left her motionless, numb, physically and emotionally depleted. Even the gun in Jake's hand had no power to move her. She just stared at him.

"Gringa, if you think Jake wouldn't shoot you, you are even more foolish than I have already thought. And you should know by now that I would have no hesitation about carving you up a bit. Move." Carlos's final word had the power to waken her out of her stupor. She turned then, moving down the path, keeping her back stiff and straight and turned away from the man who had betrayed her on every possible level.

She walked into the cabin, holding herself away from Carlos's body, but he made no move to touch her. It was cold and damp and eerie in the pale light of afterdawn, and her small cabin was no longer a welcoming friend. It was the enemy.

"She didn't tell you anything, *amigo?"* Carlos addressed Jake as he followed her into the cabin.

"Nothing." Jake's voice was a distant rumble.

"And I thought you were the great lover," Carlos scoffed. "You told me it would be easier to charm it out of her than to cut it out." He made a slashing gesture with the knife, and Maddy watched him stonily, willing the panic to keep from rising and erupting into a scream. "But then, your charm is a highly overrated commodity, is it not?"

She could feel Jake's eyes on her, those fathomless hazel depths that could look right through her, through the cotton sweater and the skin and the bones, straight into the heart of her. She held herself very still, unwilling, unable to meet that merciless gaze.

"Apparently so," he said finally. "Ortega had her house trashed."

"Did he really?" Carlos sounded distantly entertained. "You don't suppose he found it?"

"His man was still watching when we left. I lost him on the freeway. If he'd found it he wouldn't have bothered trying to tail us."

"Who was it?"

"Chimichanga."

Carlos grinned suddenly, and his basilisk eyes were tiny slits of amusement. "You realize what that means, my friend? Ortega no longer trusts you. It would seem that your usefulness as Ortega's lieutenant is at an end."

"We always knew it would be."

"And you can come back and join us."

"No."

That caught Maddy's attention. She lifted her head, but the two of them were caught in a silent battle of wills, and for the moment their hostage was forgotten.

"Don't be a fool, Jake. We need you."

"Enough is enough. I told you when I started this, that getting the map would be my last job," Jake said in a rough voice. "I want Ortega stopped as badly as you do. But after that, I'm through. I meant it six months ago and I mean it now."

235

"So you can live happily ever after with La Patronita?" Carlos scoffed.

Jake's eyes met hers suddenly, before she had a chance to turn away. They were blank, opaque, completely unreadable. "No," he said. "I don't think that's an option."

Carlos snorted then, a sound of raw amusement. "You're not free yet, *amigo*. Go search the car while I take care of her."

"No."

"What do you mean, no? I thought the little Lambert was of no importance to you."

"I didn't say that, Carlos. I said living happily ever after wasn't an option." Jake smiled a cool, pleasant smile that should have stopped Carlos in his tracks, Maddy thought. Carlos was definitely made of tougher stuff than she was. "But if you put one finger on her, touch her with your knife again, the women of San Pablo will find you essentially useless from now on. Do I make myself clear?"

Carlos laughed, unmoved by the threat. "Completely, *amigo*. And I know you could do it. Get rid of your sweetheart, Murphy, and we'll search her car together. The closet would be as good a place as any. You told me she doesn't like being closed up."

To Maddy's horror Jake nodded, and he gestured with the gun. "Into the bedroom, Maddy."

It was the only closet in the place, and it boasted strong hinges and a sturdy padlock. Whenever she closed the cabin up for the winter she locked anything of value in its small, dark depths. She moved ahead of Jake, her feet stumbling slightly, her hands trembling in the panic that seemed to have taken permanent hold of her from the moment she looked into Carlos's eyes.

The shallow slash in her side was stinging her, and the

sight of the black, cold gun in Jake's hand terrified her more than anything had in her entire life. Anything, that is, but the dark confinement of the closet. All her life she'd hated being closed up. Even in the midst of winter she had to sleep with a window open, or wake up convinced she was suffocating in the darkness.

"Don't, Jake." Damn, how could she plead with such a man? But she had to. "Please, don't."

He'd opened the closet door. It was shallow and narrow, more like a coffin than a closet, and the panic bubbled up inside her. "Get in, Maddy." His voice was completely emotionless, as still and distant as his face.

"Jake," she whispered, her voice raw. "I'm scared."

How could he look like that? Grieved, and kind, and loving. "I know," he said gently. "Get in."

She wouldn't ask him again. Squaring her shoulders, she stepped into the closet, standing there in the tiny section of space as the door closed after her. She heard him fasten the padlock, and it took every last ounce of her strength to keep from screaming, to keep from pounding at the door and begging him.

Without a word she sank down to the rough wood floor. They'd emptied out the closet, probably with this purpose in mind, and there was just enough space for her to huddle there, forcing herself to take deep, steady breaths. She was trembling all over, covered with a cold sweat that ran down between her breasts and made the medallion cling clammily to her skin.

Think of something, she ordered herself. Don't think of the damned darkness, or that they'll drive away and never let you out, and you'll die here in the darkness, screaming. Think of mountains. Of clouds and sunshine and flowers. . . .

And unbidden the scent and color of wild gardenias

came to mind. And Jake's mouth on hers, his hands hard and loving on her skin, with the smell of gardenias all around them in the tropic night. Leaning her head against the cold, hard wall of the closet, she wept, small, noiseless tears, until she fell asleep.

She opened her eyes slowly, blinking them suddenly in the shadowy afternoon light. She was lying on the bed, a thin blanket over her, and the door to the main room of the cabin was open. She could hear the quiet murmur of voices, and as she gradually grew more alert she could see Carlos's smaller, burly form sprawled in the rocking chair. Jake was standing by the door, looking out, and she could only make out Carlos's part of the conversation.

Who had taken her out of the closet, and when? And did it really matter? Whoever had taken her out was also the one who'd put her in, and the reprieve didn't cancel out the crime.

What mattered was that suddenly her earlier, uncustomary panic had vanished. Sleep had done wonders, and as she lay there on the bed listening to them, her mind was busy with plans for escape.

"It has to be done, *amigo,*" Carlos was saying. "You and I both know it."

Jake turned then, and Maddy could make out his words. "Cold-blooded murder has never been my style, Carlos. Unlike you."

Carlos didn't even flinch. "Which only proves my point. Leave it up to me. Experience counts, you know. It will be painless, if that will make you feel better."

"Go to hell."

Carlos laughed. "What bothers you the most, Jake? The idea of what you call cold-blooded murder, or the

238

fact that you'll be involved in covering up what happened in the Indian village? To a man of your principles that must rankle most of all." His voice was sneering. "You're a good man to have been with El Patrón. Always so righteous, so sure of your decisions. Did you never have any second thoughts about turning against your friends, your comrades, when you testified about that village in Vietnam? Or do you still feel righteous and holy?"

"Why would it matter to you?" Jake took a drink of the coffee he held in one large hand, and Maddy's mouth watered.

"Because I want to know how you'll feel this time. This time you won't be able to turn me in, turn in the men you've lived and eaten and slept with for the last ten years. This time you'll have to watch them go free, praised by the international press, and no one will ever know that three hundred innocent Indians were slaughtered for no very good reason. And I want to know how you'll feel."

Jake set the mug down with a thud, and the sturdy pottery broke with the force. "I'll feel like hell, Carlos. I'll feel like I've betrayed honor, humanity, and any shred of decency. I imagine I'll feel exactly as I felt after I testified about Den Phui."

There was a moment of silence. "So you are well and truly caught between a rock and a hard place, my friend," Carlos said softly.

"Yes," said Jake. "And you can enjoy yourself, watching me squirm."

"You and the *gringa* are already providing me with much amusement. Cheer up, *amigo*. Most of the men involved in the Indian village are already dead in the fighting around La Mensa. I don't expect the rest of us to make it more than another couple of years. You won't have to worry about taking care of any more lost souls like El Nabo." Carlos sighed. "You always had an overwhelming sense of responsibility. It wasn't your fault that your company went a little crazy in Vietnam. That happens sometimes—I know only too well. And it wasn't your fault that Ortega is in such a position of power."

"Isn't it? You forget, I knew his connections. . . ."

"We all could have guessed his connections. He rose to power too quickly, arms and ammunition were far too available, for him to have been doing it without help. And now he's the real head of San Pablo, and Morosa's only a weak old fool who thinks he's important. It is in the past, *amigo*. And soon Ortega will also be in the past. Among others." With that cryptic statement he rose and came to the bedroom door. Maddy quickly shut her eyes again, but it wasn't fast enough.

"Speaking of which," Carlos said, "our little captive is awake. Do you suppose you could try some other tactics to persuade her to tell us where the map is?"

"What do you have in mind?" Jake drawled. "I forgot to bring my torture rack and iron maiden."

"You *norteamericanos.*" Carlos sighed with mock disgust. "Always so dependent on technology. Believe me, a great deal can be discovered with something as simple as a box of matches and an ice cube."

"I'll take care of it."

"You've decided not to be so squeamish after all, *amigo?*" Carlos questioned. "Good. Then I will leave it up to you. I'm going into town. I expect that everything will be taken care of by the time I get back."

"And when will that be?"

"Oh, I'll give you plenty of time. I won't be back before tomorrow morning. That should give you enough leeway to find out what you need to find out and then finish things up." He had moved away from the bedroom door, and Maddy opened her eyes a tiny bit. "If you finish sooner you can always meet me down in Budgewell. Otherwise I'll be back after dawn."

Jake said nothing, and Maddy couldn't see him from her position on the bed. She considered moving around, then decided against it. They didn't know for certain she was awake, and she needed all the time she could manage to decide what she was going to do.

"Unless, of course, you'd rather I—"

"No," Jake snapped. "Get out."

"I'm going, *amigo*. I'm going. Give my best to the little *gringa*."

Maddy lay there unmoving in the center of the bed, listening to the sound of a car starting up. It had a deep, throaty rumble, definitely not her Alfa. Maybe there was as little left to her Alfa as there was to her house. She couldn't count on it to get her out of here especially without the keys. Years ago Stephen had taught her how to hotwire her VW, but that particular talent had vanished from lack of use.

But there was no question in her mind, she had to get out of there, and fast. The conversation between Carlos and Jake had been anything but clear, but one fact had stood out with crystal certainty: Jake was going to kill her.

After all, they didn't really have any choice, did they? He had said there was no hope for the two of them, and that would have been the only way he could be guaranteed her silence if he seduced her into it. Kidnapping was a federal offense, and only one of many the two of them had doubtless committed, and she knew too much about the Indian massacre to keep her mouth shut. No, Carlos and Jake had been arguing about who was going to kill her, and Jake had won the toss. Would he make it as painless as Carlos had promised?

She wasn't about to lie here waiting to find out. Even if the Alfa was out of commission, she knew this area far better than they did. They might think they were eighteen miles from the nearest town, Maddy knew otherwise. There was a path that started from the back of the cabin and wound its way down the side of the mountain, some two and a half miles to the highway. She knew it like the back of her hand, but someone unaccustomed to it would become hopelessly lost. If she could just get ten minutes' start she'd make it.

"Are you hungry?" Jake's raspy voice came from the doorway. She considered keeping her eyes closed and feigning sleep, but he knew her too well to be fooled by it.

She opened her eyes and sat up, willing herself to be icily calm. "Bean paste and tortillas?" she questioned in a cool voice.

His face didn't register a change in expression, but she knew she'd gotten a reaction of approval, even of respect. But he just shook his head. "Not much better, I'm afraid. Carlos did the shopping, and he's a junk food junkie. You've got your choice of Twinkies, Yodels, potato chips, or Mallomars. To drink there's warm beer, warm Tab, warm Coke, or lukewarm instant coffee."

"That might almost be more effective than a pack of matches and an ice cube," she said, swinging her long legs off the bed. "Couldn't you figure out how to turn on the refrigerator?"

"There's no electricity up here."

"I know that. That's why it's a gas refrigerator," she said patiently, walking past him into the living room. Maybe she could hit him over the head with something heavy. He was no longer holding the gun, but she could see it tucked in the back of his jeans. Maybe she could lunge for it. . . .

As soon as the idea entered her head she dismissed it. Jake's reflexes were much more professional than hers. If she went for his gun she'd find herself dead a lot faster than she expected. With a completely spurious show of calm she went into the kitchen, picked a warm can of Tab from the counter, and grabbed the Mallomars. Warm Tab was better than no Tab at all.

"Which of you is on a diet?" she questioned, dropping into the chair Carlos had vacated and opening the can. Even at room temperature it tasted wonderful, and Maddy's returning strength increased.

"I told Carlos to get you some," Jake said, watching her from his position by the doorway.

"Did you?" She opened the package of Mallomars. "The last meal for the condemned prisoner?" She bit into the cookie, and chocolate bliss swept over her body. Things had come to a pretty pass, she thought ruefully, when Tab and Mallomars stiffened her backbone.

"What the hell are you talking about?"

She met his gaze fearlessly. "You're going to kill me."

If his face had been remote before, it became positively glacial. "I am?"

"Don't lie to me, Jake. I heard you and Carlos talking. You have no choice in the matter. Even if I knew where the map was and gave it to you, even if I promised never to say anything, you can't take that risk. I know as well as you do that Carlos went off so you could finish me off. I expect you're supposed to bury me before he gets back. I could suggest several places. The dirt's pretty loose up by the big rock."

Jake was standing very still. Then he spoke. "Thanks for being so helpful," he said in an ironic tone that had

243

Maddy suddenly wondering whether she was imagining the whole thing. "Do you happen to have a shovel, while we're at it?"

"I had one, but I don't remember where I put it. I think I took it back to L.A. with me. You may have to dig my grave with your hands." She was on her fifth Mallomar by now, and getting reckless.

Jake shrugged. "It'll have to be a shallow one, then. I hope you don't have a problem with coyotes up here."

Maddy found she could shrug too. "We may. I don't think I'll be in any condition to notice." She drained the warm Tab and started on her sixth Mallomar.

He merely looked at her. "No, I suppose not." He went into the kitchen, returning a moment later with another can of Tab and a can of warm beer for himself.

It had grown hot during the day, and his denim shirt was open halfway down his chest. The silver ring glinted around his neck, and Maddy's eyes clung to it with a sudden surge of emotion that was almost impossible to control.

"You might bury the ring with me," she suggested calmly. "It would be a nicely ironic touch, don't you think?"

"Still trying to get the ring back from me, Maddy?" he queried, tilting his head back and pouring the warm beer down his throat. "Forget it. This ring is my good-luck charm."

She shouldn't have succumbed to her curiosity, but she was feeling braver and angrier by the minute. "Is it? Why?"

Jake's long fingers touched the silver at his neck, and unbidden the memory of those long fingers on her skin came soaring back. "There was a time when holding on

244

to this ring was the only thing that kept me alive. I've become very fond of it."

She wasn't going to ask him any more, she thought. If he wanted to be cryptic, that was his choice. She wouldn't believe anything he told her, anyway.

Once more she shrugged, diving into the Mallomar package again. They were making her sick, but what the hell. She'd need the sugared energy if she was going to make it down that trail in the dark that was beginning to close around them. She had no idea how long she'd spent in that tomb of a closet.

"How long did you leave me in the closet?" she asked.

"Half an hour."

It had seemed an eternity before she fell asleep. "Who got me out, you or Carlos?"

"If it had been Carlos you wouldn't have been placed so neatly and carefully on the bed, *mi amor.*"

"Don't call me that!" she snapped.

Jake smiled, a sinister smile that didn't reach his eyes. "I don't think you are in any position to give orders, *mi amor.*"

Maddy set the almost-empty cookie package on the floor beside her. "You don't even need the matches and ice, do you?"

Jake's mouth tightened, almost imperceptibly, but it was the first sign of emotion she'd been able to elicit from him, and it was a small triumph. Her triumph was short-lived however, when Jake leaned back against the sofa opposite her and fixed that too-bright gaze on her. "How would you like me to do it, Maddy?" he asked in a conversational tone of voice. "Since you've decided I'm going to kill you, you may as well pick how I do it. Would you like me to strangle you with my bare hands? Or I could always use a scarf or a rope."

"Charming," she said, ignoring the icy fingers of fear that ran down her spine.

"I suppose I could use a knife," he mused, taking another swig of his beer. "But I'm not nearly as good as Carlos. I'm afraid it might . . . take some time. And hurt quite a bit.

"I think the gun will be the best bet," he continued idly. "It would be fast. A bit noisy, perhaps, but you won't mind that. And it would be much neater. They taught me quite well, years ago, when I was in basic training. I know how to kill very quickly and efficiently and you wouldn't bleed much. If someone came up to the cabin they'd probably never find any trace of what went on. That is, if we can count on the coyotes to leave you alone."

The Mallomars were rising swiftly, but Maddy was damned if she was going to throw up twice in twenty-four hours. Bravely she swallowed, fixing a cold, furious gaze on Jake's bland expression. "You can do it any damned way you please," she said. "Just spare me the details."

"But, Maddy," he protested in a gentle voice, "that's half of the fun."

The Mallomars would no longer listen to reason. Maddy lurched to her feet. "Excuse me," she mumbled, and ran for the door.

Not that the outhouse was the most appetizing place to vomit. The wave of nausea had passed, but she still made convincing noises in her throat as she headed toward the back of the cabin. If she made a run for it now, when it was almost dark, it might take him a moment or two to realize . . .

An iron hand clamped down on her shoulder. "Not that I think there's any danger of your getting away, *mi amor,*" Jake said, "but I've had a long twenty-four hours, and I don't fancy hunting you down like a frightened doe. Come back inside."

"But I—I have to . . ."

"For mercy sake, Maddy, don't be so damned coy!" Finally he was angry. "If you have to use the outhouse, tell me."

"I have to use the outhouse!" Now that she thought of it she did, and quite badly. The Tab had washed right through her.

"Well, go ahead," he snapped.

"I'll be back inside in a minute." It was worth a try.

"No, you won't. I'll wait right here for you just in case you get lost in the dark. We both know there's nothing around here for almost twenty miles, but I'm not into taking chances."

That little piece of information was enough to cheer her. "All right," she said pertly. "But you'll have a long wait." She slammed the wooden door of the homemade convenience as loudly as she could.

At least he didn't know about the highway that ran so close to the cabin. And there was a half moon, bright in the sky that night. It would give her more than enough light to find her way down there. If she could just immobilize him long enough . . .

"Come out, Maddy." Jake's voice filtered through the door. "Or I'll come in and get you."

She stomped out, slamming the door behind her. "Someday, Jake Murphy, I will pay you back for this," she said fiercely.

Jake only smiled. "How will you do that if I'm going to murder you, *mi amor?*"

She was momentarily nonplussed. "I'll haunt you," she said finally.

247

Jake's smile grew, and there was an unexpected flash of tenderness in it. "You already do," he said. "Inside, Maddy."

Still trying to decipher that sudden softening, she went.

CHAPTER NINETEEN

Damn her, he thought savagely. How could she believe such a thing? How could she have loved him, as she swore she had, for fourteen long years, how could she have lain in his arms and looked up at him as if he were the best thing that had ever happened to her in her entire life, and then believe it? She was a miserable, self-centered, cold-hearted bitch without an ounce of trust, love, or loyalty in her tall, skinny, unbearably gorgeous body.

Of course, she had reason to be scared, he added with an effort at fairness. She was sitting across the room from him right now, trying not to watch as he downed glass after glass of whiskey, trying to look interested in the three-year-old copy of *Time* magazine that was scarcely readable in the dim kerosene lamp light, trying not to let her panic show. She was tough, with more heart in her than anyone he'd ever met, but she'd been through too damned much.

She had reason enough not to trust him. He'd never been honest with her; scratch that, he thought, taking another drink. He'd never been straightforward or frank with her. He'd always been honest.

But he'd brought her up there, with her believing it

was refuge from Carlos, and instead delivered her into Carlos's hands. How was she to know that Carlos was the least of her worries? And he'd let her go on thinking he was working for Ortega, and she knew almost as well as he did how ruthless the leader of the Gray Shirts really was.

But still. Despite all the logic in the world telling her otherwise, she should have trusted him. That she could even begin to think he would ever hurt her, much less kill her, was a breach of faith far more devastating than anything he'd ever done to her. He still couldn't quite believe she'd think he was capable of doing such a thing. But that furtive, defiant look in her wide brown eyes told him she thought just that.

He drained the whiskey glass, rising on perfectly steady feet and heading for a refill. The damned stuff must be watered down. He hadn't yet begun to feel the numbness he was seeking. He wanted to drink himself into a stupor, be so blind drunk that she no longer had the ability to twist his gut into a knot, to turn him almost crazy with wanting. He didn't care if she ran out when he was too drunk to do anything about it. He almost hoped she would. Then at least she might not hate him quite so much, if she were able to salvage some of her self-respect from this whole wretched mess.

She looked up then, her face perfectly composed, and if he didn't know her so well he would have thought she hadn't a care in the world. But the doomed anger played around the corners of her mouth, and her hands were restless on the ancient magazine.

"Having another drink?" she inquired in a deceptively pleasant tone of voice.

Jake responded with a savage grin. "Of course. Any objections?"

250

"I wouldn't want your aim to be off because of too much liquor," she said tranquilly. "I would prefer a fast, clean death."

He almost threw the glass at her. His long fingers tightened around the glass, and it took all his self-control to meet that calmness with a cool distance of his own. "I never miss," he said.

Maddy nodded, bending down to peruse the magazine again, and he could see her tender, fragile nape beneath the tousled dark-brown curls. Her nape had always done strange things to him. He remembered when she was seventeen and he'd done everything he could to keep his hands off her, from telling himself he was a dirty old man to having her mother arrange a date with the boy of her dreams. But her nape when she wore her hair in braids had always had the power to unman him or just the opposite.

He wanted to set the drink down, cross the room, and press his mouth against that vulnerable skin. He wanted to shake her until she cried, until she told him she knew he could never hurt her. He wanted to hold her in his arms and lose the nightmare of revenge and justice that was destroying everything he'd ever wanted. He didn't move, just stood there, watching her with a hunger that she couldn't even recognize.

She looked up again, her eyes blandly curious. "Did you ever sleep with my mother?"

Hell, where had that come from? He did set the drink down, keeping his face carefully neutral. "No. Why do you ask?"

"Because you slept with my stepmother. I knew that loyalty to Sam wouldn't stop you, and I remember my mother was particularly passionate in her dislike of you. It seemed a logical assumption."

251

"And you're very logical." It was a statement, not a question. Logic had told her that he was going to kill her, and emotion, love, and other euphemisms wouldn't sway that belief.

Maddy smiled, a remote smile. "When all else fails logic has its uses. You're sure you didn't sleep with Helen?"

"I'm sure."

"Did you try?" She probed further. How did she know he was holding something back? He thought he'd learned how to school his features and voice to betray nothing.

"No."

"You hesitated before you answered," she observed. "That means you aren't telling me the whole truth."

"I'm telling you the truth."

"But there's something else, isn't there, Jake? You may as well tell me. We both know it won't have a chance of getting any farther than this room."

"I did not try to sleep with your mother, Maddy," he said.

Her smile broadened. "But she tried to sleep with you?" she guessed.

There was no way out of it. "Yes."

"And you turned her down?"

"Yes."

Maddy leaned back with a triumphant smile. "That explains a very great deal. No wonder she hated you so much. How very noble of you, Jake. My mother was a very attractive woman fourteen years ago. She's still an attractive woman, for that matter, and you turned down her importunate advances. I'm glad you had that much loyalty to my father." Her voice was cool and biting, and suddenly Jake wanted to wipe that distant smile from her face.

252

"I didn't have that much loyalty to your father. He wouldn't have given a damn if I'd slept with Helen. I told her no because of you."

If he'd hoped to jar her he failed. That smile stayed firmly in place as she nodded knowingly. "That explains why she slapped me the night of my birthday. Outflanked by her own daughter. It's little wonder she resented me."

"She slapped you the night of your birthday?" Why would a tiny incident of fourteen years ago suddenly send him into a rage? he wondered absently. Maybe it was easier to think of the past than this hideous coil of the present.

She was looking at him curiously now, and for a moment he wondered whether common sense had gotten past that damnable logic of hers. But then she clearly dismissed the possibility. "It doesn't matter anymore, Jake," she said. "Nothing does."

Jake stomped out to the kitchen. One of the many bones of contention between Carlos and himself had been Carlos's penchant for beating up his women. For the first time in his life Jake could understand the temptation. The last thing in the world he was going to do was kill Maddy Lambert, but he'd sure as hell like to crack her across the chops one time.

Maddy watched him go. He'd only be out in the kitchen for a moment, hardly long enough for her to make it to the pathway. She looked down at the magazine in her lap, at the angry face of the Ayatollah Khomeini glaring at the western world, and contemplated her cowardice.

She wasn't going to give him what he wanted. She wasn't going to beg, or plead, or cry, or cower. She was going to look him squarely in the eyes when he shot her, and she wasn't going to flinch. Pray God she wasn't going to flinch.

But she wasn't going to run away either. She didn't want him hunting her down in the moonlight like a fox chasing a rabbit. She didn't want to end up rolling down a hillside with a bullet in her back, and she didn't even want to escape. A world where Jake Murphy could calmly, cold-bloodedly kill the woman who loved him was no place she wanted to be. It was all that simple.

She could tell him, of course. Tell him she loved him, even though he was going to kill her. It might make it a little harder for him. Then again, it might make it easier. He seemed to have spent his life pushing love away. Killing her might make some strange sort of sense to him in the end.

He had been very cool and distant as he sat across from her all evening, drinking a really astounding amount of whiskey without showing it. She could feel his eyes on her, assessing her, and she told herself he was checking out a suitable target. Whenever she'd meet his gaze his eyes would suddenly go blank. But not before she'd surprised a hungry sort of expression that she couldn't, or wouldn't, understand.

She'd lost count of the drinks, and so, probably, had he. "Is that going to be your last one?" she questioned sharply when he reappeared, determined to goad him.

"Why?" He didn't take his seat again, he moved closer to her chair, and his tall, lean body towered over her.

She looked up at him objectively for a moment. It was beyond her comprehension how she could still find him attractive, but she obviously could. That old masochistic streak acting up again, she told herself with an attempt at wryness. Those faded jeans hugged his long legs, hanging low on his hips in a way that any other time would have had her foaming at the mouth. The pearl snaps on the denim shirt were open partway down, exposing his San Pablo–tanned chest, and the silver ring gleamed in contrast against the dark skin. He'd somehow found time to shave that day, but his face was lean and shadowed with exhaustion, his mouth grim, his forehead and cheeks creased with lines. The eyes that looked down at her were opaque and unreadable. The eyes of a murderer? Or an executioner? She still hadn't told him what he needed to know. If he believed she held something back he'd keep her alive. If he started to believe she was telling the truth there'd be no reason not to kill her and get it done with.

His hair was darker, not as sun-streaked, and it curled around his collar. "I'm sorry you cut your hair," she found herself saying. It amazed her almost as much as it amazed him, and he ran a hand through it almost absently.

"The Gray Shirts have rules," he said.

"I'm sure they do. Are you going back to them?"

"I would think my cover's been blown."

She put the magazine down, for the first time giving him her full attention. "Why did you do it, Jake? Why did you turn to the Gray Shirts, betray my father? Why . . . ?"

"What makes you think I betrayed your father? At the time I had little choice. The only way I could salvage any hope of peace for the people of San Pablo was to find out what I could from Ortega. And the only way I could do that was to pretend to take their offer of amnesty when I woke up in that hospital bed."

"A likely story." She snorted. "You've got an excuse for everything, don't you? An excuse for leaving me, an excuse for betraying your friends, probably an excuse for the massacre at Den Phui. What's your excuse going to be when you kill me? It's a dirty job but someone's got to do it?"

"If you don't watch your mouth it's going to be something I'll greatly enjoy," he grated.

She didn't doubt him for a moment. "Then where will you go when you're finished here? Once you've found the map?"

"I'm not sure." He took another drink of the whiskey. "Carlos will take it back to San Pablo."

"Why doesn't he simply destroy it? Surely it's too dangerous a thing to be kept around."

Jake shrugged. "He's not alone in this. There are others concerned who aren't necessarily going to take his word for it that it's been destroyed. They're going to want to see for themselves."

"But you won't be going back to San Pablo."

"No."

"Never?"

"Never." He finished the drink in one gulp, then set the glass down with a sharp snap on the bookcase beside her.

"But what, dear Jake, if they find my body?" she inquired sweetly. "Wouldn't it be better for you to be out of the country? Sally knows I went off with you; if I don't return she might start to suspect something. And Soledad is no fool. If I just disappear she'd make a fuss."

"Are you suggesting I shouldn't kill you?" he inquired pleasantly.

"Oh, heavens, no," Maddy said. "I wouldn't waste my breath. I just thought you might consider the consequences. You might try Canada."

"If I didn't go to Canada during Vietnam I'm not going now."

"Would you have gone? I assumed you'd enlisted." For a moment she was distracted from the problem at hand.

"I enlisted when I had no choice. I had just finished college and there was nothing to stop them from taking me." He was still watching her out of those unfathomable eyes.

She sat very still. She wasn't going to let him frighten her, she told herself. She'd deny him that pleasure, or that pain, whichever it was. She'd die like Sam Lambert's daughter, boldly, bravely.

"Are you going to kill me now, Jake?" she questioned softly.

There was sudden light in his eyes, a flash of emotion that looked like raw fury. He looked like he was about to hit her, and in sudden panic Maddy reminded herself that Jake would never hit her. But how could she think that? Of course he'd hit her. He was about to kill her.

Jake's mouth twisted in a bitter smile that didn't reach the anger in his eyes. "Sounds like a good idea," he said pleasantly, taking the gun from the back of his jeans. "Get up."

There was no avoiding the command in his gruff voice. Slowly Maddy rose. She wouldn't be afraid, she wouldn't be afraid.

Jake was smiling lazily now, the same smile that had always melted Maddy's resolve. "But we don't have to be in any hurry, now, do we? Carlos won't be back till tomorrow morning. It won't take me long to bury you. In the meantime we may as well enjoy ourselves."

"Wh-what do you mean?" Damn that sudden stammer!

"Into the bedroom." He gestured with the gun.

"No."

"Yes. Of course, we could do it right here, but it

257

wouldn't be very comfortable. Get in the bedroom." His voice was a sexy, pleasant drawl, the gun was pointed directly between her breasts, and she had no choice. It didn't seem as if he'd cocked the gun, but what did she know? Not enough to chance her life on it. She moved, slowly, steadily, back toward the one bedroom the tiny cabin had to offer.

He shut the door behind them, set the kerosene lamp on the rickety table and turned, the gun still trained on her. "Now take off your clothes."

"Jake, no." Damn, she was pleading.

Jake only smiled. "Better to die with a bang than a whimper, Maddy. The sweater first."

With trembling hands she pulled the cotton sweater over her head, leaving the medallion in place against her cold skin. He didn't even glance at it, just gestured with the gun again. "The bra, Maddy. And the necklace."

Her hand fumbled with the clasp, and the medallion slipped from her neck. The bra followed, and she let them fall on the floor. Jake's angry smile stayed in place as his eyes flickered over the rapid rise and fall of her small, soft breasts.

"Now the jeans."

"No, Jake."

"The jeans." His voice was inexorable, and it took her three tries to undo the snap. She slid them down over her hips, and then she was standing in front of him, wearing nothing but a pair of aqua silk panties.

Jake shook his head. "Everything, Maddy. I'm getting impatient."

She considered refusing. She considered running, right then and there, and taking a bullet in the back. But she met his gaze fearlessly, sliding her hands beneath the waistband of the panties and drawing them down over her legs, kicking out of them disdainfully and shaking her head back.

He moved closer to her then, and she could feel his body heat against her naked skin, through the denim clothes. He lifted the gun, and she closed her eyes for a moment in sudden panic, then shot them open again.

"Such a pretty idiot," he said softly. "So very gullible, and so completely untrusting." He ran the cold steel barrel of the gun down her cheek, an icy caress that should have broken the last barrier of her panic.

She looked up into his eyes then, unmoving as the gun traveled down her face. Sudden grief suffused her, as she finally saw past his remote expression, and she moved her arms up, pushing the gun away as if it were a flyswatter, and slid her naked arms around his neck.

"Oh, God, Jake," she whispered brokenly. "I'm so sorry."

He held himself very still as she pressed her body against his, the gun held in one loose hand. "Sorry?" he echoed warily.

Tears were pouring down her face. "You'd never hurt me. I'm such a fool. You'd never, ever hurt me." She pressed her mouth against his.

CHAPTER TWENTY

Finally Jake moved, his arms encircling her, pulling her into the strength of his warm body, and she felt him trembling against her. Her face was wet with tears, and as she reached her hands up to cradle his head she found his skin was wet too. From her tears? Or from his own?

She didn't even know what he did with the gun. It was no longer in his hands as they caught her naked body, pulling her closer, and she didn't bother to ask. She tried to move her mouth away from his to apologize, to question, but he wouldn't let her. His mouth followed hers, stealing her words with quick, hungry kisses that left her past the point of regret or curiosity. All she knew was the incredible wanting that had been building up in the last six months. No, the last fourteen years—that night six months ago had only made her hungrier.

The kerosene lamp lit the sparse room with a fitful glow, and the bright light of the half moon silvered the bed behind them. Never taking his mouth from hers, Jake scooped her up in his arms and carried her over to that bed, laying her down and covering her with his clothed body.

Her eager hands reached up to pull apart the remaining snaps on his shirt, and the warm tough skin of him was there for her to touch. She pushed him over on his side, and he went willingly enough, his eyes bright and warm with desire. Pulling the shirt from his jeans, she started to push it off him when she saw the scar.

Even in the dim light of the bedroom it was terrifying to look at. Added to the various nicks and scratches that had marred his body was a new line of red, keloidal tissue, traveling from his shoulder blade around his side to disappear beneath the waistband of his jeans. It looked raw and angry, and Maddy's haze of wanting was suddenly overshadowed.

She pulled away, sitting back beside him as his eyes watched her, knowing her so well. "It's all right, you know," he said softly, his husky voice a rasp in the darkness. "They put everything back where they found it and sewed it up again." She could see his grin in the darkness. "I promise you, nothing's missing."

"Oh, Jake," she said with a shaky laugh, "do you think I'd care?"

"I know damned well you would." He took her willing hand and placed it on his hip, where the scar disappeared into the heavy denim of his jeans. Her touch was gentle, exploratory, watching him for any sign of pain.

"How did it happen?"

"In the shelling." Her hand had begun to move closer to the snap at his waist, her fingers exquisitely arousing as they slid beneath the jeans.

"How?" she persisted.

"Everyone had left. Everyone but Richard. He'd gone back for . . . I don't even know what he went back for. And I went back for him." His hand covered hers as it lingered on the fastening of his jeans. "It was two months before I was well enough or sane enough to get in touch with you, Maddy, and by then it was too late."

"Shhh," she hushed him, leaning over to silence his mouth with hers. "We don't need to make excuses. Not now. Later, maybe." And she gently kissed the scar, pushing the shirt off him, following the angry line down as her hand unfastened his jeans with sudden deftness.

He reached down to help her then, sliding out of his jeans, and then they were skin to skin on the sagging old bed she'd never bothered to replace. And time and space seemed to disappear, it was only the two of them, together in the dimly lit eternity. He let her experiment, stroke, and caress the wonder of his body until both of them were shivering with reaction and arousal. Then he deliberately slowed the pace, pulling her into his arms and setting his mouth on hers, his tongue exploring the soft, seeking contours as his hands held her head still for him. She lay quiescent for a moment, content to receive him, and then she responded, her tongue meeting his, sliding along it, and her fingers dug into his shoulders, kneading the smooth, warm skin that felt like molten gold against her.

He moved his mouth away, to kiss her neck, and his tongue was wet and warm against her skin. "Please, Jake," she whispered. "Please, please. . . ."

He reached up, soothing the tousled curls away from her flushed, feverish face. "You're always in such a hurry, Maddy," he chided, a tender smile playing around his mouth a moment before he blocked out the light as he kissed her again.

"Please, Jake," she whispered against his mouth. "I need you. Now."

She could feel his smile against her lips. "Come and take me," he murmured. "Now." He rolled over on his back, pulling her with him, and for a moment she knew an agonizing shyness. But her need for him far overshadowed any second thoughts, and she moved as his hands placed her above him.

She wanted to watch his face as she controlled the movements that slowly brought them together. Her eyes met his as she sank down, his hands a reassuring support on her hips, but after a moment she had to shut them, collapsing against him, overwhelmed by the unspeakable glory of him within her. For a moment she couldn't move, could only lay there against him and absorb the sensations that threatened to split her apart.

His hands were warm and tender, soothing on her narrow back as she lay on top of him. "Perhaps this wasn't a good idea right now," he whispered in her ear, his voice just slightly strained. "Maybe later." He started to move, and she panicked.

"No," she cried, clinging to him. "Don't leave me!"

Before she'd even realized what was happening he'd turned her over, onto her back, and he was above her, the link never broken. He settled her back against the pillow, and there was a shaky laugh in his voice. "I didn't mean the whole thing wasn't a good idea. We'll just be more creative later."

Maddy breathed a sigh of mingled relief and anticipation, wrapping her arms around him and holding tight. "I can't help it if you overwhelm me."

"You think you're overwhelmed now? Just wait." He began to move then, thrusting into the welcoming warmth of her body, and she tightened her long legs around him, arching up to meet him.

An absent, benevolent section of her consciousness noticed the fine tremors that began to shake her body almost immediately, building in intensity with a rapidity she was unable to control. And Jake, Jake was lost too, unable to slow their headlong ascent into a whirlwind of love and completion that was astonishing in its magnitude. She shattered around him, crying out in sudden love and fright, and he was there with her, keeping her safe, as he flooded her with love and life.

Their breathing had almost returned to normal when he very carefully moved away from her, pulling away just for a moment before cradling her damp, exhausted body against his. "Are you still there?" he whispered, his breath blowing the wisps of hair away from her ear.

"I'm still here, Jake." Her face was pressed up against his shoulder, and her answer was muffled, serene, and garbled. And Jake understood completely.

"Good." His arms tightened around her for a moment, then relaxed a tiny bit, still keeping her safely held against him. "Go to sleep. Carlos won't be back till tomorrow morning," he drawled. "I still have plenty of time to murder you and bury the body."

She jerked her head away and stared up at him with a mixture of guilt and an anger that was too difficult to maintain. "I don't know why I thought you would," she said. "I should have known. . . ."

"Yes, you should have known. I was so mad I could have quite cheerfully strangled you when you came up with that one. Don't you know me, and know your own judgment, better than that?"

She leaned back against him with a sigh. "I knew you. But too many things have happened. I won't ask for explanations. I don't think they really matter in the long run. What matters is that I love you, and everything else is just a bunch of minor details."

"Minor details like why I brought you up here? Minor

details like why I wouldn't let Sam see you when he was dying?"

"You can tell me," she said without moving. "You can tell me if you want to. Right now I don't need to know."

"You know it wasn't Carlos who wrecked your house. Not that Carlos isn't a threat when he's not properly controlled. I happen to be one of the few people he'll sometimes listen to. But Ortega has always been much more of a danger to you. He'd have your throat slit on a whim. The man he sent after you, Chimichanga, is one of the deadliest men in the Gray Shirts. You wouldn't have stood a chance against him."

"But why would he want to hurt me?"

"To even an old score with your father. To wipe out any trace of La Patronita. Word has reached San Pablo of Lambert's daughter and her acts of kindness to the refugees. But most of all, he knows you have the map."

"I do not have the map!" she cried. "Why can't I convince you of that?" As she tried to sit up, the hands that had been cradling her so gently suddenly became strong on her shoulders, holding her down.

"You can't," he said, and the mouth that grazed her damp forehead with a kiss was soothing. "That's why I wouldn't let you go to Sam."

The kiss had only begun to placate her, the hands holding her captive both enraged and aroused her. "Why not?"

"Because I didn't trust him. He'd already given you the videotape to smuggle out. Any number of people would have gladly killed you to stop you, and he'd put you in that danger within minutes of seeing you for the first time in fourteen years. I didn't trust him not to make it worse, by sending the map out with you too. We all knew he had it. For the last month and a half I'd been

265

trying to keep Carlos from cutting his throat in order to get it. I made sure Sam still had it after he gave you the candy box, but apparently that wasn't enough. He must have gotten it to you. If the Patronistas or Carlos had known you had the map you never would have made it to the border alive."

"Sam didn't want to see me to give me the map," she protested, thinking of the medallion lying in a pile of clothes on the floor. "He just wanted to tell me he loved me."

"Maddy, Sam was incapable of loving anyone but his noble causes. I'd spent the last fourteen years with him. I knew him better than anyone. He didn't love you, Maddy. He couldn't. I'm sorry."

She didn't believe him. She had the proof lying close at hand, proof she'd discarded without a second thought when she'd stripped off her clothes for him. But she wasn't about to try to explain it to him. Later, perhaps. When they'd gotten past all this.

"Why won't you believe me, Jake?" she murmured, settling back against him, her fingers toying with the silver ring that still hung around his neck. "I don't have the map."

"You have it, Maddy," he said wearily. "I'll accept the fact that you may not know that you have it, but you do."

"What makes you so certain?"

"Richard Feldman told me."

"Richard?" She had been so sure, so very certain, and now that sureness was slipping away. Desolation yawned in its wake, and desperately Maddy pushed it away.

"He wouldn't have lied to me, Maddy. He knew he was dying. He told me he gave someone the map, and the way I figure it, it could only have been you."

There was no way she could make him call back the words. No way she could return to the last moment of innocence that was now forever shattered. It was gone, slipping away from her like a technicolor dream fading into the harsh monochrome of reality, and there was nothing she could do about it.

He must have felt her sudden stillness, the rigidity that lay in his arms. "What is it, Maddy? Do you know what he was talking about?"

Would she lie to him? Could she lie to him? It wasn't even an option. "The medallion," she said in a dead voice. "Richard gave me the medallion just before I left the villa. He said it was a present from Sam."

She was immediately released, the warmth and comfort of his body withdrawn as he leaped out of bed. The moon no longer shone in the window, and the kerosene lamp had burned down low. Maddy didn't even watch as he scrambled through her discarded clothes, searching for the necklace. She heard the chink of the chain, felt the shifting shadows as he blocked out the dim light.

"Of course," he said, his voice abstracted. "And I didn't even notice the damned thing." He tossed the medallion onto the bed, and it landed in front of her. She stared at it without moving. The heavy gold disk was actually two disks, hollowed out and hinged at the top. Jake had already removed the map.

She roused herself enough to look at him. He was studying the scrap of brownish paper with a mixture of disgust and acceptance. Then he was suddenly all energy and determination, moving back to the bed and picking up the medallion that she'd left, untouched, on the rumpled sheets.

Very deftly he replaced the map inside the medallion,

very deftly he slipped it back around her neck. She was too numb to protest.

"Don't take it off," he ordered, climbing back off the bed and throwing on his clothes. "I'm going to find Carlos."

He paused long enough to press a hurried kiss against her mouth, and then he was gone, without a second thought. She listened to the purr of the Alfa as he drove off down the mountain, not moving, the medallion cold and heavy around her neck. The sound of the car faded into the distance, and she was alone in the darkness.

There was a strange, whimpering noise in the darkened room, like a wounded animal seeking shelter. It took Maddy a moment to realize those sounds were coming from her own throat.

It had been a lie, it had all been a lie. Sam's last, uncharacteristic gesture of love had not been that at all. It was a last move in an international game of chess, with his daughter as a willing pawn, ready to be sacrificed for either side. She had been such a complete, abysmal fool to believe in him, even for a moment. Thirty years of neglect should have taught her something. Something she hadn't wanted to learn.

And Jake, Jake was cast from the same mold. Not for a moment had he considered her reaction, facing once more her father's betrayal. He'd been so excited over finding the map that he'd ran off and left her without a backward glance. Even if he never returned to San Pablo, even if they somehow managed to carve a life out together, he'd always be running off and leaving her when one of his damned noble causes called him. She wouldn't live out the rest of her life like that, and she wouldn't subject her children to it.

One thing was clear in all this, she thought as she

pulled herself out of the rumpled bed. Her father hadn't wanted the map and the information it contained to fall into the wrong hands. Without a moment's hesitation Maddy knew what she was going to do.

She was going to make her way down that steep trail to the highway, hitch a ride to the nearest airport, fly to Washington, and present liberal Senator O'Malley with the medallion. He'd make sure it got to the papers, just as he'd passed the information about Morosa's corrupt regime. The international press, Congress, and the American people needed to know that there were no heroes in that dirty little revolution, no good or bad side. Just a history of betrayal, on every level from personal to national.

She was dry-eyed and enraged, and quite desperate for a small measure of revenge against Samuel Eddison Lambert. Her hands shook as she pulled her clothes back on, and she refused to think back to what had happened when she'd taken them off. This time she wouldn't blame Jake if he wanted to kill her. But she wasn't going to change her mind.

It was rough going. It was darker than she'd imagined, and the undergrowth was thick around her long legs, night creatures were calling, and the medallion felt like a stone around her neck. The rough pebbles beneath her Nikes skidded, sending her tumbling part way down, and she ended up against a piñon pine, her face scratched, her knee skinned, her wrist wrenched, and still the tears didn't come. Sam Lambert wasn't worth one tiny moment of grief.

It was slower after that. Maddy had no idea how far Carlos had traveled, whether Jake knew exactly where he was or would have to spend time searching for him. But sooner or later, and with her luck it would probably be sooner, they would return to the cabin, find her gone, and start hunting. But there was no way she could rush down the treacherous steepness of the hilly path.

Dawn was breaking by the time she made it down to the highway, and there wasn't a car in sight. She was limping by then, her wrist throbbing, and more determined than ever. All she had with her was the medallion and her wallet containing every credit card known to man and a decent amount of cash. Once she found someone willing to stop her troubles, at least the transportation part of them, would be over.

It ended up being an eighteen-wheel semi carrying a load of cabbages to the East Coast. The driver was a thirty-nine-year-old grandmother named Rose, who cheerfully shared her coffee, her Dunkin' Donuts, and even offered her Nodoz to the exhausted Maddy. Almost delirious with thanks, Maddy took her up on the proferred bed in the back of the cab and slept till Utah.

Breakfast in a Utah truckstop put some heart back into her, and by the Colorado border Maddy had decided to accompany Rose all the way to the East Coast. There was no rush. The map had kept this long, it would keep longer still. If she was going to be intercepted it would be at an airport. She had no idea how pervasive Ortega's men were, or the Patronistas, for that matter. But she still couldn't walk into a McDonald's as they traveled cross-country without looking over her shoulder.

But no one would suspect Allison Madelyn Lambert Henderson of traveling from coast to coast in a cabbage truck. She was safe, blissfully safe, and free from the burden that was weighing down around her neck. Once they made it to the East Coast she would have to face up to it. For now she'd put her brain and her emotions on automatic pilot and was set to cruise, chatting to Rose of her grandchildren and her three ex-husbands and the ever-changing panorama of the American landscape.

It ended far too soon. Three and a half days later the fully loaded semi had reached the eastern seaboard, and Maddy climbed down just outside of Baltimore, clad in an oversized flannel shirt, a pair of jeans that was two sizes too big in the waist and two inches too short in the legs, and headed for the nearest train station.

CHAPTER TWENTY-ONE

She'd looked rumpled and disreputable the first time she bearded Michael O'Malley in his den. Just off the plane from San Pablo, she probably hadn't had more than a few hours' sleep, and she'd just found out the man she loved was dead.

This time she was at least clean, well rested, and secure in the knowledge that somewhere in the world Jake Murphy was alive and well and mad as hell at her. Despite Rose's outsized clothes and the unmistakable signs of grief and despair that marked her face, she felt a degree more human than she had on her last visit. In her current unprepossessing wardrobe she was expecting a lot more trouble getting in to see the senator than she experienced.

There were no delays. The first receptionist, a stranger to Maddy, took one look at her and picked up the phone. A moment later a preppy-looking aide appeared to usher her through the first section of rooms, where he handed her to an elegant young yuppie in Ralph Lauren suit and a coolly professional smile. O'Malley was at the end of this procession, shirt-sleeved, attractive—The perfect candidate, Maddy thought. It was lucky she trusted him;

otherwise she would have turned around and walked out, the medallion still safely around her neck.

He said all the right things, expressed all the right emotions. Shock and dismay and outrage and anger. Concern for her and all she had been through, grave doubts about the rebellion in San Pablo. And Maddy couldn't rid herself of the feeling that it didn't quite ring true.

"I promise you, Madelyn," he said with smoothly eloquent outrage, "that this will be dealt with, immediately. I can't tell you how much your trust means to me."

Maddy said nothing.

"I'll have someone drive you to your mother's house," he continued. "Or a hotel, if you'd rather."

"The airport."

"Surely you can't be planning to fly back to California right away? I may need to get in touch with you about this. I'm not quite sure what's the best way to handle it. The situation in San Pablo is very precarious indeed. Word has it that La Mensa is about to fall to the revolutionary front."

"Is it?" she replied glumly. If that were so, Carlos would miss it in his quest for the map.

"Let me put you up at the Hilton for a few days," O'Malley suggested smoothly. "That way I'll be able to call on you if I have any questions. . . ."

"I'm going to my mother's house in McLean for exactly fifteen minutes," Maddy said. "And then I'm going home. You can call me there."

"But—"

"Call me. But not for several days. I won't be answering the phone." She walked out without a backward glance, unable to rid herself of the notion that she'd made a very grave mistake.

273

The Pakistani taxi driver looked at her askance when she climbed into his cab. She sat back for the long drive into Virginia and went over her plan.

It was time to sever the ties. For too long she'd held on to the notion that parents were supposed to be loving, supportive, caring about their children. Somewhere along the way her parents had gotten sidetracked, if they'd ever felt that way at all. Stephen had paid for it, and still Maddy had clung to the illusion that beneath her mother's chilly exterior, beneath her father's causes, some distant strain of feeling remained. It had been a foolish illusion, causing nothing but pain, and it was time to break the last sticky threads of parental attachment.

It was a hot fall day. The windows of the cab were open as they careened across the Potomac and headed toward Virginia, and Maddy leaned back against the frayed seat, letting the wind blow through her hair. She'd have the cab driver wait when they got to her mother's house. He hadn't liked the looks of her, but a large-denomination bill would keep him in place while she took care of a little emotional housekeeping. Then she'd have him drive her to Dulles and wait for the next flight. Somehow she'd begin to make some sort of sense out of her life.

The house seemed quiet and deserted when the cab pulled up. Balwinder Singh, her cab driver, seemed content enough to wait once he grasped the fifty, and Maddy's steps were firm and purposeful as she strode to the front door.

No German maids today, no press conferences, no military hit squads roaming around, and no locked door. She wondered for a moment if she was expected, then dismissed the idea. After all, who could have told Helen she was coming?

Her mother's voice echoed through the spacious interior of the elegant old house. "I don't believe you for one moment," she was saying. "You're making it all up."

The response was low, rumbly, but Maddy could recognize those tones, even from a distance. For half a moment she wanted to turn and run, back to the doubtful protection of Balwinder Singh. But she squared her shoulders beneath the oversized flannel shirt and headed in the direction of the voices.

"I don't know why you'd think she'd bother to show up here, Jake," Helen was saying in her cool, controlled voice. "You know as well as anyone that we've never been close. She's much more likely to have gone straight back to—" Her sharp brown eyes widened as the rumpled figure of her daughter appeared in the doorway. "Apparently you were right, Jake," she said. "The prodigal daughter has returned. Where have you been?'

Jake whirled around. He was standing by the french doors that overlooked the pool, and his face was pale and shadowed with exhaustion. "Maddy" was all he said, his voice full of relief and anger and something else she didn't even want to decipher.

"Yes, Maddy." Helen was closer to her daughter, and she crossed the distance with a few graceful strides, the long legs that her daughter inherited speeding her along. "What have you done with the map?"

Maddy grimaced, looking from one to the other. "You'll be pleased, Helen. I've given it to Senator O'Malley. I expect it will be on the news by six o'clock tonight."

She didn't get the reactions she expected. Jake's shoulders sagged in sudden relief, and Helen reached out and slapped her across the face. "You fool," she said, her cold voice at variance with the sudden violence of her slap.

"Did you really think that O'Malley wouldn't cover up something like that? He's a politician, and politicians never lose face. I would have thought you'd have gained at least an elemental bit of sophistication. You weakminded, stupid—" She raised her hand to hit Maddy again, but Jake was there ahead of her, catching her wrist in one iron fist. Maddy watched her mother's face whiten with pain, and she slowly backed away from the two of them.

Helen tore out of his grasp, her face livid with fury and suddenly looking very old. "You are no daughter of mine," she said in a fierce, dead little voice. "Get the hell out of my house. Both of you."

For an exit it was quite striking. Maddy wanted to applaud her with just the right amount of mockery, but the energy needed failed her. If only it were true. But Maddy knew Helen too well. In another six months she'd be calling on the phone, cool and distant and wanting something, as usual. But this time Maddy wouldn't give in.

She looked up into Jake's hazel eyes. "So which side are you on, Jake?" she inquired in her coolest voice. "Ortega's or Carlos's?"

"Neither."

"And what would you have done with the map?"

"Destroyed it. Which is what will happen. O'Malley will hand it over to Carlos, and it will be gone."

"But people know. . . ."

"Rumors," he interrupted. "And there have been enough rumors in this nasty little war that no one is going to be believed without hard evidence. It was all for nothing, Maddy."

She met his gaze calmly. "I suppose it was."

"Why did you run?" He made no effort to move any

closer, and she could feel the distance between the two of them like a palpable thing.

"I had to," she said. "I couldn't let my father do that to me. I had to at least try."

"Couldn't you have left me a note?" There was a hint of pain beneath the careful control in his voice. "When we got back I was convinced that Chimichanga had found you. I thought we'd find your body out back, your throat slit—"

"I'm sorry." It was a useless thing to say.

His face was once more remote and distant, the stranger-lover she could never quite read. He shook his head then, a gesture of dismissal. "I have to go," he said.

"Where?" But she knew the answer to that as well as he did.

"To San Pablo."

"I thought you were never going back?" Don't leave me, she begged silently. Don't go back there; they'll kill you.

He shrugged. "I didn't want to. But the game isn't finished yet. I have to see it through to the end this time. I have to watch out for Carlos."

"Carlos?"

"If the revolution is to succeed, if any progress is going to be made, someone has to keep Carlos under control. It could go either way—a bloodbath or a relatively peaceful passage of power. Carlos needs to remember that a bloodbath would only hurt the cause."

"And you think you can remind him?"

"I'm the only one who can," Jake said simply, and Maddy believed him. "Go back to L.A., Maddy. Soledad has been worried about you."

He still hadn't touched her. Doubts flew through her mind like phantom butterflies, and she dismissed each one in turn. Logic had told her it would never work, self-preservation had warned her to keep away, not to let him break her heart the way her father had. But logic and self-preservation were cold and lonely company, and even a heart-breaking life with Jake was better than any kind of life without him. "When are you coming back to me?" Her voice was soft, low, and very certain.

He did touch her then, his hands reaching out and cradling her tired face, tilting it up to his. "As soon as I can, *mi amor*," he whispered. "You'll wait?"

"I'll wait," she said, the last doubt vanishing. Then he was gone.

It had been a long night, Maddy thought, pulling her weary body out of the bed. She couldn't even remember if she'd slept at all. Her head ached, her eyes were heavy with sleep and unshed tears, and her thoughts drifted and tumbled through her brain like drunken acrobats.

Christmas was coming. It was the first week in December, Jake had been gone for six weeks, lost in the war-torn confusion that was San Pablo, and Maddy was seven weeks' pregnant.

"I do not know whether I shall enjoy being a grand-mother," Soledad had said with a pout last night, clutching a glass of rum in one slender, jewel-encrusted hand. "A mother to someone as ridiculously tall and pretty as you is one thing, my pet, but not necessarily a grand-mother."

"Cheer up, Soledad," Maddy replied. "Just think, this might have happened to you." She patted her still-flat stomach.

Soledad shuddered delicately. "Never. I have better things to do with my life. Do you know what the worst problem with this *niño* of yours? You can't get drunk with me."

"Do you think we should be getting drunk?"

"I do indeed. In memory of Carlos," Soledad raised her glass. "And in memory of Anastasio Ortega. He was a worthy enemy. And here's to the fall of La Mensa!"

Maddy sipped at her mineral water. "And to a new democracy."

"Democracy, schmocracy," Soledad muttered obscurely. "To the triumph of the oppressed."

"Now you sound like my father."

"Not a bad way to sound. In many ways your father was a good man. I heard that they're talking about renaming La Mensa after him. Cuidad Lambert. What do you think of that?"

"Absurd," Maddy said, no longer moved by pain at the memory of her father's betrayal. Let him belong to San Pablo.

"And here's to the speedy rebuilding of the capital." Soledad drank deeply.

"What there is left of it," Maddy said.

"And here's to the return of the *niño*'s father," she added, draining the glass.

"Amen," Maddy said softly. "Here's to Jake's return." And she finished her mineral water.

Soledad passed out on Maddy's sofa. The fall of San Pablo to the rebels was an occasion worthy of note, even if that occasion brought the news of Carlos's death. Maddy accepted it as inevitable, squashing down the sudden feeling of fright. If Carlos could die, so could Jake.

The long night passed. She could hear Soledad snoring gently on the comfortable sofa, and more than once Maddy wished she could have partaken of the soporific effects of the strong Jamaican rum her stepmother favored.

It was just after five when Maddy gave up, pulling on loose-fitting white pants, a heavy cotton sweater, and a jacket and heading out into the early-morning sunlight. There was a brisk wind from the ocean, strong enough to clear away the cobwebs and the headache of a sleepless night. Maddy headed down toward the beach, wrapping her arms around her slender body and taking deep breaths of the fresh salt air.

She walked swiftly, covering a great deal of ground with her long legs, trying to drive out the worry that kept creeping up on her as more and more time passed without word from him. Fate had been unkind enough, it wouldn't have given her Jake just to take him away again.

The beach was quiet and deserted at that hour. It was too early for joggers and runners and dog-walkers to clog the strand. Maddy sank into the sand, her arms wrapped around her long legs, and stared at the ocean, remembering against her will the months when she thought Jake was dead, when the relentless strength of the ocean had brought her the only comfort she could find.

It was slowly getting lighter. As Maddy stared out into the blue-green waves she could feel the tight band around her heart ease and lift. She didn't even turn her head when she heard him, felt him moving behind her.

"I thought I might find you here." His voice was that well-remembered, rusty sound that played across her senses like a silver flute. He sank down in the sand beside her, and she allowed herself a brief, tentative peek at him. He was in one piece, weary, looking older than his forty years, and infinitely dear. His hair was growing again, trailing beyond the collar of the heavy sweater he wore. "Why was Soledad passed out on your sofa?"

"Too much celebrating," she said.

"Celebrating the fall of San Pablo?"

"Soledad would call it the rise of San Pablo."

"You heard about Carlos?"

"And Ortega. And Morosa escapes to Miami with most of the country's treasury." Maddy lifted her head, still not trusting herself to look at him fully, for fear he'd vanish in the early morning sea mist. "They're going to have a hard time rebuilding the economy with all the money gone."

"They can do it," Jake said. "If anyone could do it, the people of San Pablo can. Your father had reason to love them."

So it did still have the power to hurt her. She viewed that fact abstractly, poking at it a bit, like prodding a sore tooth. But the pain wasn't searing, just the remembered ache of an old war wound. She breathed a small sigh of relief. "Reason to love them more than me, apparently," she said, and saying it only hurt a tiny bit.

Jake was suddenly intense, the distant guise of politeness vanishing. "Maddy, listen to me. Just because your father was incapable of caring about anything more than an abstraction, just because your mother is a cold-hearted bitch, doesn't mean that you aren't worth loving," he said in a rough voice. "God knows, you have every reason in the world to be bitter. You're entitled to be screwed up, angry, incapable of love or trust. You're entitled to a cold, miserable life. You have every reason in the world. And you're entitled to hate me. I wouldn't blame you for a moment. I lied to you, I left you, again and again and again."

"Yes," she said. "You did."

"But I always loved you. You're worth loving, Maddy. You're worth far more than I can ever give you. I haven't got the faintest idea what I'm going to be doing a year from now, I have no idea how I'll live, where I'll live, what kind of person I'll be. I only know that I don't want to be without you. I should be noble and leave you alone, let you find someone who can cherish you, someone who can take care of you—"

"I don't need someone to take care of me," she broke in ruthlessly, turning to look at him for the first time. It took all her resolve not to throw herself in his arms. "And I think I've had enough of nobility to last me a lifetime."

"Then what do you want?"

She smiled then, a sure, joyous smile. "I want you, Jake Murphy. I always have, and I always will. And even though you left me, again and again and again, you came back. And damn it, next time you go, I'm going with you." She reached out then, touching his weary face with gentle fingers. "Agreed?"

"Agreed." He looked down at her, his eyes dark and clear and full of love.

"In the meantime I've got something for you," she added. "Something you need very badly, whether you realize it or not."

"What?" The wariness was second nature, Maddy thought. She'd teach him not to be wary; together they'd learn how to trust.

She took his hand and placed it gently on her stomach, feeling quite pleased with herself. "You may not know what you'll be doing a year from now, but I do. You'll be changing diapers."

His hand tensed beneath hers. His voice was hoarser than usual when he spoke. "You promise?"

She rose to her knees, cradling his face in her hands. "Oh, Jake, I promise," she said fervently. "And you damned well better make an honest woman of me, and soon."

He sat very still, suspicion an old companion. "Is that the only reason you want to marry me?"

Maddy laughed, and the sound of her amusement was liquid sunshine in the cool morning air. "Of course. Normally I can't stand you, but I'm so conventional I'll make that sacrifice for the baby's sake," she said blithely. She kissed him then, and her mouth trembled against his. "Soledad can give me away."

He smiled at her slowly, and for the first time the smile reached the weary depths of his eyes. "It might be more accurate if she gave me away."

"Don't remind me! Maybe we'll elope."

"I haven't asked you yet," he pointed out politely.

"Well, hurry up. We only have seven and a half months."

"That's more than enough time," he said, leaning back against the tufts of grass that poked through the fine white sand. "Let me think about it."

"Jake!" Maddy shrieked, and suddenly found herself sprawled on top of him, held firmly in the warm, strong circle of his arms.

"I've thought about it," he said with a grin. "Will you marry me, *mi amor?*"

She smiled down at him, at peace for the first time in her life. "With pleasure, Murphy. With pleasure."

And as the first streaks of sunlight touched the stormy Pacific and the cool sea breeze blew around them, the war was over. And life had just begun.

CANDLELIGHT Ecstasy Supreme

All-new
Candlelight Newsletter

An exceptional, _free_ offer awaits readers of Dell's incomparable Candlelight Ecstasy and Supreme Romances.

Subscribe to our all-new CANDLELIGHT NEWSLETTER and you will receive—at absolutely no cost to you—exciting, exclusive information about today's finest romance novels and novelists. You'll be part of a select group to receive sneak previews of upcoming Candlelight Romances, well in advance of publication.

You'll also go behind the scenes to "meet" our Ecstasy and Supreme authors, learning firsthand where they get their ideas and how they made it to the top. News of author appearances and events will be detailed, as well. And contributions from the Candlelight editor will give you the inside scoop on how she makes her decisions about what to publish—and how _you_ can try your hand at writing an Ecstasy or Supreme.

You'll find all this and more in Dell's CANDLELIGHT NEWSLETTER. And best of all, _it costs you nothing._ That's right! It's Dell's way of thanking our loyal Candlelight readers and of adding another dimension to your reading enjoyment.

Just fill out the coupon below, return it to us, and look forward to receiving the first of many CANDLELIGHT NEWSLETTERS—overflowing with the kind of excitement that only enhances our romances!

Dell **DELL READERS SERVICE—DEPT. B712E**
P.O. BOX 1000. PINE BROOK, N.J. 07058

Name_____

Address_____

City_____

State_____ Zip_____